Romance

Discovering Emily

by

Billie Houston
and
Carlene Havel

Dedication and Acknowledgment

For all those fortunate souls who find happiness the second time around.

Table of Contents

Chapter One

Emily Franklin closed her household ledger. "That takes care of my accounts for this month."

"Couldn't you have done it tomorrow?" Her husband Robert laid his book aside.

"I do volunteer work at the library tomorrow, and I have to take Boo to the vet." Emily used her fingers to enumerate. "There's Bible study, and I promised your mother I'd go by the nursing home to visit Aunt Beth. Then the Historical Society has a meeting tomorrow evening." She leaned back in her chair, and sighed. "So, I really needed to finish this tonight."

Robert's voice held a note of weariness. "I run a distant last behind a volunteer job, Bible study, a dog, an old maid aunt, and your civic obligations?"

"That's tomorrow. Tonight, you have my undivided attention."

"Really?" Robert lifted one dark eyebrow.

"After Larry's graduation I will have more free time."

"I am sure you will find new projects to take up the slack." At forty-seven Robert Franklin was still a handsome man--tall, with a well-proportioned body and aquiline, almost patrician features. His hair, once black as ebony, was now feathered with silver and beginning to recede. "Maybe I should have called earlier for an appointment."

"That's not necessary." Emily held back a sigh. "Neither is your sarcasm."

She paused, hoping for an apology. When she realized none was forthcoming, she picked up the conversation, hoping to turn it in a more positive direction. "Debra and I have been making plans for your parents' fiftieth wedding anniversary." Robert had said more than once he wanted this to be an elaborate celebration.

"I'm sure you and my sister have the situation well in hand." Robert was on his feet and prowling across the room.

1

"We are thinking of renting the hall at the Civic Center, and hiring a band. Then--"

"I thought I had your undivided attention." Robert stood with his back to her, and his hands behind him, staring out the window at a pale winter sunset.

Emily's felt an explained uneasiness take hold of her. "Have I done something to displease you?"

Robert's shoulders slumped. "I'm a little edgy tonight." Turning, he faced her. "It's nothing."

"It must be something if you think it's more important than plans for your parents' golden wedding anniversary celebration."

"What do *you* think is important, Emily?" Robert asked with a grimace. "Where are your priorities?"

"You seem terribly unstrung tonight." She shifted in her chair. "Is this about one of the boys?"

"Our sons are eighteen and twenty-three years old," Robert's eyes clouded with something Emily thought might be akin to sorrow. "We no longer have any 'boys'."

"It was merely a figure of speech." Emily's words came out sharper than she intended. Making an effort to be gentler, she asked, "Are there problems at the office?"

"I don't want to talk about work."

There was a time she knew her husband so well. Over the past few years he had become more and more a stranger, someone she couldn't seem to reach no matter how hard she tried. "What do you want to talk about?"

"I've reserved a room for us at the Rustic Inn in Cedar Creek. I thought we might go there for the weekend. That is, if you can spare the time."

Emily caught her breath. They went to the Rustic Inn often during the early years of their marriage. Recalling those bygone days evoked sweet, romantic memories. Her uneasiness gave way to enthusiasm. "I'd love to. I'm surprised you can spare the time."

"I'll make time." Robert sat down.

"Do you know how long it's been since we went away together for a weekend?"

"Not really," Robert picked up his paper. "I need some time with you and we have absolutely no privacy here."

Emily looked around the elegantly appointed living room. "We're alone now, except for Boo." She nodded toward the sleek black Labrador retriever lying stretched out, sound asleep in front of the fireplace.

"For how long?" Robert asked. "Until Larry comes charging through the door with half a dozen friends? Or Kevin calls to tell you about his new apartment or his new job, or an odd assortment of relatives or friends decides to drop by unannounced, or you get yet another urgent telephone call from one of your many charities or projects?"

Emily loved having a welcoming home where her boys and their friends liked to gather. "We have children and friends, you have family, and I'm involved in church and school activities. It goes with the territory."

"I'm not complaining, exactly." Robert straightened his shoulders. "At least I don't mean to be."

"You've been working too hard." Emily narrowed her eyes in her husband's direction. He looked tired, almost haggard. "A weekend away will do you good. I'll call Berta tomorrow. I can explain to Mrs. Perez on Thursday at the executive meeting--"

"Spare me the details and get it done," Robert interrupted.

The annoyance in his tone irritated her, but she spoke softly. "When would you like to leave?"

He stood and put his hands in his pockets. "Would Friday evening around seven be all right?"

"Friday at seven would be fine." Emily stretched and yawned. "Let's go to bed. I can begin to tie up all these loose ends tomorrow."

She was almost to the door when Robert said, "I have to go back to the office."

"Tonight?" Emily asked Her husband of twenty-five years had asked her to go away with him for a romantic weekend. She reminded herself to make allowances if he had to work late in order to keep that date. She couldn't help asking, "Can't it wait until tomorrow?"

"I'm sorry, but I have to go."

"Over the past six months you've spent more and more time at that office." Something told her to stop talking, but she couldn't. "Sometimes I wonder what the attraction there is."

"What is that supposed to mean?" Robert bristled.

"It means that I never see you anymore. You work late three or four nights each week. When you are home, you're too tired to do anything but fall into bed and sleep." Emily tried to smile. "I miss you when you're not here at night."

Robert reached for his jacket. "We'll talk over the weekend."

Chapter Two

It took some doing, but by Friday afternoon Emily completed arrangements for her weekend trip. She was standing on the porch with her suitcase beside her when Robert pulled into the driveway, a half hour late.

He stopped the car, leaned across, and opened the door. "Sorry I wasn't on time. I see you're ready to go."

"I've been ready for thirty minutes." Emily put her suitcase in the back seat. "I wish you would have called. I was beginning to think you'd had an accident." She got into the front seat and closed the door.

"Something came up at the last minute." Robert pulled the car into the street.

They passed the city limits and Robert pulled onto a highway access road before Emily spoke again. "Do you know how long it's been since we had a weekend alone?"

Robert turned to glance at her before looking back at the road. "Since before Larry was born."

He did remember. "We left Kevin with your mother and dad and drove up to Cedar Creek for a three-day weekend. You didn't know I was pregnant with Larry. I still remember the surprise on your face when I told you."

Robert maneuvered the car into the flow of freeway traffic. "We'd agreed not to have another child. I didn't think you'd get pregnant without asking me first."

Even now Robert didn't believe her second pregnancy was an accident. "I didn't plan for Larry. He just happened." Remembering made Emily smile. "I was so sure he would be a girl. When he got here, it didn't matter that he was Larry instead of Lorrie." She sighed. "Those were happy days."

"After I got over the initial shock, I was glad, too." Robert added sadly, "Where did those happy days go?"

His words had a chilling effect. "Does that mean you're not happy now?"

"That's not what I said." Robert's tone warned her against pursuing the subject.

Emily ignored the warning. "You implied as much. Is that how you feel?"

Robert pulled around a slow-moving eighteen-wheeler. "Since when have you cared how I feel?"

Much more of this and they would be quarreling. Emily didn't want anything to spoil this weekend. "I've always cared, and that was a heartless thing to say."

Robert reached for the stereo. "Would you like to listen to music?"

She suspected he preferred music to conversation. "Sure."

The soothing voice of George Strait drifted out into the car.

Emily leaned her head against the seat and feigned sleep until pretense became reality.

It was past nine o'clock when they pulled into the drive of the Rustic Inn. By the time they settled in their suite, it was almost ten. Emily frowned as she looked at the two double beds that stood against one wall of the room. "Couldn't you get a room with a king-sized bed?"

"We will have to make do with this." Robert tossed his hat on one of the beds. "I'll order dinner." He reached for the telephone. "What would you like?"

"Something light. It's too late for a heavy meal." Emily opened her suitcase and hung garments on a rack. "I brought you a pair of sneakers and a warm jacket. I thought we could walk down the scenic path behind the inn tomorrow. Even in the middle of winter the view should be beautiful."

Robert put his hand over the telephone receiver. "Will chicken salad be all right?"

"Chicken salad is fine." Emily hung up the last garment, grabbed her overnight case, and hurried to the bathroom. She showered before putting on a new satin gown and robe and slipping her feet into matching slippers. The ensemble cost a mint. She glanced at her reflection in the mirror on the bathroom door, and decided it was worth every penny. The robe fit snugly over her firm breasts and small waist, and clung delicately to her slim hips and long, well-shaped legs. It was the perfect shade of green to complement her auburn hair and hazel eyes. She leaned forward, studied her heart shaped face and slender figure. She liked what she saw. *Not bad for an old married woman.* She smiled, and her mirror image responded in like manner.

Dinner was delicious. Emily devoured her chicken salad and even ate a portion of her homemade apple pie. Robert hardly touched his food. "You're missing a good meal."

He didn't answer. She wondered if he'd heard her. "How do you like my new robe?" She was reluctant to fish for compliments, but it seemed to be the only way she could get one.

Again, there was no response. "Robert, I'm talking to you."

His head snapped back. "What did you say?"

"I asked you how you liked my new robe."

His eyes scanned her. "It's very nice."

"Very nice? Is that the best you can do?" She grimaced in good humor. "I was hoping for glamorous or maybe even sexy."

Robert pushed his chair back and stood. "I think I'll have my shower."

Emily pushed the dinner cart out into the hall, locked the door, and secured the chain. *Was Robert ill? Had he been stricken with some life-threatening disease?* Those thoughts were too horrible to contemplate. She closed her mind to such frightening possibilities.

Emily was sitting on the side of the double bed she'd turned down when Robert came out of the bathroom.

He sat on the bed across from her, and took her hand in his. "I'm sorry to drag you up here, but I have something important to say to you. I need absolute privacy to say it."

A shiver tingled down Emily's spine. It had been a long time since Robert made a special effort to be alone with her. The thought that he might want to rekindle the embers of passion that had once burned white-hot between them sent a warm glow flowing through her. "I was happy to come. I've always loved it here. Is there something you want to tell me?"

"This is very--" a sigh punctuated his words, "difficult."

Emily's heart pounded against her ribs. What she saw in the deep blue of his eyes was not a glow of desire, but a look of pain. "Are you all right?"

He snapped, "Don't fuss over me."

"I wasn't fussing." Fear, like a coiled spring, unwound in her stomach. "I'm concerned. I know you well enough to know something is wrong."

"I don't think you know me at all." He stared past her toward the wall.

The pain in Emily's chest brought her to her feet. She paced across the small room before pausing by the door. "Maybe I don't."

Robert ran nervous fingers through his hair. "Will you come back and sit down?" He added a painful, "Please."

Emily retraced her footsteps and sat on the side of the bed.

Robert cleared his throat. "I care about you, Emily."

"Well, I should hope so," she said, trying to lighten the moment. "I'm your wife."

"Don't make this," he looked away, "any more difficult than it is."

Whatever it was he wanted to say, the sooner he said it, the better. "Tell me what's so hard to say."

"I want." Robert took a deep breath before blurting out, "I want a divorce."

In the charged silence of the room, his words erupted like an explosion. Emily whispered, "I don't understand."

"I'm asking you for my freedom." His face was grim. "I can't go on this way."

Talk about being blindsided. In the space of a heartbeat, the foundation of Emily's world cracked and shifted, shattering her universe in one incendiary explosion. Even before she asked, she knew. "Is there someone else?"

Robert ignored her question. "I've leased an apartment near my office. That doesn't mean I will stop paying your bills or caring for you. You can have the house and one of the cars. I'll take care of Larry's college expenses and see that you have enough to live on."

Even in her agitated state, one fact became crystal clear. This was not a sudden impulse. "You want to move out of the home we've shared for almost twenty-five years?" Panic battled disbelief. "Why?"

Distress deepened the furrows in his brow. "Our marriage has been over for a long time."

A churning stirred in the pit of Emily's stomach. "I don't think of our marriage as over. I love you. I don't want you to go." Tears trickled from her eyes, ran down her face, and fell onto her new robe. "Tell me," she whispered in a voice that quivered with emotion, "what I'm doing wrong and I'll change."

In his granite stare she read an inflexible determination. "People don't change, Emily."

"Are you," she choked on the words, "involved with someone else?"

He hung his head. "Yes."

A dozen questions converged in her brain as she sat stunned and speechless, staring and not seeing.

"Don't tell me you weren't expecting this." After an anxious pause Robert ground out, "Say something."

She grew up with this man. Their parents were life-long friends. She could never remember a time when Robert Franklin was not the center of her universe. Jagged lines forked across Emily's vision as incredible pain shot through her head. She squeezed her eyes shut, and asked in a voice splintered by anguish, "What's her name? Do I know her?"

"Her name is Susan Barrett. She bought old Sam Snyder's share of the realty company when he retired last year." His voice was calm, yet oddly disconcerting. "I never meant for this to happen."

Emily was disjointed, separated from her physical body. "Are you sleeping with her?" Why hadn't she seen this coming? The signs had been there for months.

Irrelevantly, she added, "I don't know if I can live without you."

"That's utter nonsense." Robert's chest expanded and deflated slowly. "You have a full life without me."

The paralysis of shock froze her. "I have no life without you." This was too much for her brain to assimilate and more than her heart could bear. "I've been your wife for twenty-five years. I'm the mother of your children. We made a vow before God. How can you do this?"

"I never intended to hurt you." He bowed his head. "Please believe that."

His contrite words ignited a spark that singed through her frozen anger. She had a sudden urge to slap him as hard as she could. Rather than give in to the impulse, she attacked him verbally. "You sneaking cheat," she screamed.

He caught her by the wrists and held on. "Stop yelling. They'll hear you in the next cabin." Emily was past hearing anything he had to say.

He held her wrists in a vice-like grip. "Calm down, Emily. Get ahold of yourself."

A pall of utter futility swept over her. She fell back on the bed and cried, great gulping sobs she knew were wretched to watch and painful to hear.

Robert came to sit beside her, took her in his arms, and soothed her with soft words and gentle pats. "Please don't do this. You will make yourself ill."

She pulled away and leaned back to look at him. "You've made up your mind, haven't you?"

Grimly, he answered, "Yes."

"Nothing I can do or say will change it?"

"That's true."

Why had he brought her to the Rustic Inn, of all places, to ask for his freedom? "This last cruelty, this final betrayal, bringing me here to tell me. What was that for?"

"I want to make this as painless as possible." Robert catapulted to his feet. "Do you think this is easy for me? It isn't. I care about you, but I'm not in love with you anymore." He was visibly angry, but there was pain in his reply and an alienating distance she couldn't measure.

"But why did you choose this place to ask me for a divorce? You invited me to go away with you for what I thought would be a romantic weekend at our old hideaway. Now you calmly announce that you want your freedom. How can you hurt me like this?"

Chapter Three

Robert struck his forehead with the heel of his hand. "I thought it would be easier for you here, away from the boys and the family. Please don't construe this as unkind." He added, "There's no privacy at our house."

"How would you know?" she retorted. "You're never there anymore."

"I don't want to quarrel with you. I don't want to trade insults." *How many times had he rehearsed this speech?* "I would like us to part friends. It would be better for everyone concerned, the boys, my family, you, and me, if we could do that."

Emily's cold fingers brushed her flushed cheeks. "What will we tell them? Or am I the last to know?"

"We'll just tell them the truth." Robert's voice faded and then rallied. "That we've decided to divorce."

"We? You mean *you.*" Emily grasped one of her hands in the other, to stop them from shaking. "I don't know how the boys will take this."

"They are both adults. They will understand."

"What about your mom and dad? And Mike and Debra?"

For the first time since her parents were killed in an automobile accident five years ago, Emily was glad they were not here. They thought she and Robert had the perfect marriage. But then, until tonight so did she.

"It's really none of their business." Robert regained his composure. "Our divorce concerns only the two of us."

"You can't possibly believe that. Divorces have a ripple effect throughout the whole circle of family and friends. " Emily picked up her clothes and moved toward the bathroom. "I'll get dressed. We can go home now."

"I'm too tired to make that long drive tonight."

"I'll drive." She was dying inside. "I don't intend to spend the night here with you."

For the first time, he looked her full in the face. "Oh, please, Emily. You're behaving like a child."

Tears spilled from her eyes. "I feel like a child, like a foolish, betrayed, neglected little girl who wants to go home." She wiped her eyes on the sleeve of her new robe. "I don't want to be in the same room with you."

"You're in no condition to drive and neither am I." Robert dropped his head and stared at the floor.

"What about your mistress?" Emily taunted. "Don't you want to get back to her?"

"Don't call Susan my mistress." The hand he brushed through his hair was trembling.

"What would I call her?" Emily's voice rose. "Your mistress is what she is."

"Let's leave Susan out of this. Our divorce is between you and me."

"There is no way to leave her out." Somewhere in the back of her confused mind, Emily knew she was teetering on the brink of hysteria. "She's the third member of a dirty little triangle." She was appalled that she could feel such intense hatred for a woman she had never seen. She wanted to say more, but she didn't have the strength.

Robert's voice quivered. "This is not easy for me either. Go to bed. You will feel better in the morning."

By sheer force of will, Emily regained a measure of self-control. He was right about one thing. She was in no condition to drive. She could hardly think. What did it matter where she laid her head? Without bothering to remove her robe, Emily lay on the far side of the turned down bed and pulled the covers up under her chin. "How can I ever forgive you for what you've done to me tonight?"

Quite calmly, he asked, "Shall I turn off the lights?"

"I don't care, but I suppose darkness suits you."

After Robert flicked the light switch, Emily heard him moving about the room, preparing to retire. After a while the sound of squeaking springs told her he had settled down on the other bed.

Robert was leaving her for another woman. A fist of pain closed around Emily's throat, making breathing difficult. *Oh, God, what am I going to do?* She sat up, gulped, and gasped for breath.

"Emily?" Robert's voice sounded in the darkness. "Are you all right?"

"Quit pretending you care how I feel," she said between sobs.

He got into bed with her and took her in his arms. "I had no idea you would react so emotionally."

How long had it been since he held Susan in his arm? Emily pushed away from him. "Don't touch me. Not now. Not ever again."

Robert released her and sat on the side of the bed. "You can dispense with the drama, Emily."

What had she done that was so wrong? Emily sat up and scooted to the side of the bed. "Don't you have any shame? How dare you come from the arms of your mistress and try to make love to me?"

"Emily, please." His pleading words bled out into the charged atmosphere. "I'm so sorry, so very, very sorry. Say you forgive me."

"For betraying me? Or for trying to use me as a substitute?" Bitterly, she croaked, "You have stripped me of my pride and broken my heart. All I can promise is that I'll pray for you."

Robert turned on a lamp and narrowed his eyes against the light. "You don't understand."

He was right. She didn't understand. "How can you say our marriage is over and then try to make love to me?"

He lay down on the other bed, crossed his legs, and put his hands behind his head. "I was trying to comfort you. You seemed so distraught."

Never before had she felt so used. "You really are a scum-bag."

"If it makes you feel better to call me names, go ahead. You have every right." He reached to turn off the lamp. "Get some rest."

Emily tossed and turned most of the night. Several times, she tried to pray, but the words would not form. She finally fell asleep around dawn. When she opened her eyes the next morning, the sun streamed through the window. Robert sat fully clothed on the end of his bed. "I sent for breakfast and packed your bag."

Emily sat up and ran her hands through her hair, as the events of the night before rushed into her mind. "I'll be ready in fifteen minutes."

"There are a few details that have to be ironed out." Robert said. "We should do that here instead of waiting until we get home."

She looked up in startled surprise. "I thought you had everything mapped out. Say what you have to say."

"There are some practical matters that must be attended to." A knock on the door brought him to his feet. "That will be breakfast."

While Robert was dealing with breakfast, Emily escaped to the bathroom and dressed. When she returned, Robert was pouring coffee into cups. "I ordered bacon and eggs. I hope that's all right."

"I'm not hungry," Emily said with a belligerent lift of her chin.

"Emily, please." Robert slammed the coffeepot down on the serving cart. "Don't do this."

She was telling the truth. She couldn't force food down her throat. She took the coffee he offered, being careful not to let her fingers touch his hand. "This is all I want."

He stopped pressuring her. He took his time eating, cutting the bacon into small pieces and pushing the eggs around on his plate.

Emily perched on the end of the bed, drinking her coffee and trying to get her thoughts in order.

After a while, Robert pushed his plate back and sighed. "Do you want to get the divorce, or shall I?"

"If you want your freedom, you will have to divorce me."

"I thought as much." He took a quick sip of coffee. "I'll file the first of the week."

Emily stared into her coffee cup. "Then it's all settled."

"Not quite. I want you to have the house, your car, and half of our savings." Robert seemed to have difficulty keeping his voice steady. "I'll still own the business, but you will be comfortably well off..."

Emily slammed her cup down on the table beside the bed. "Shut up." She shot to her feet and grabbed her handbag. "We can settle our differences in a court of law." She stopped at the door opening. "Get moving."

Slowly and with deliberate actions, Robert picked up their suitcase and followed her outside.

The ride home was endless. At first, Robert tried making small talk. When Emily refused to respond, he asked, "Do you want to listen to music?"

"What does it matter to you what I want?" She was dangerously near tears, and the last thing she wanted to do was cry in front of him again.

"It matters to me. You matter to me." His grip on the steering wheel tightened. "I care for you, very much."

Sheer desperation drove Emily to plead, "Then don't throw our marriage away. We may have lost some of the magic somewhere along the way, but we can find it again."

"Just don't start crying. This is not worth your tears."

She turned toward him, tears spilling from her eyes. "I happen to think the death of my marriage merits mourning." She fought to control the blistering anger that seared through her incredible pain. "Are you sure this is what you want?"

His answer rang loud and clear. "I'm positive."

She did have some pride. When she could control her voice, she said. "I'll pack your things. You can pick them up the first of the week."

On the end of a distressed sigh, he breathed, "All right."

Chapter Four

Emily kept her word. Saturday evening, after Larry went out with friends, she packed Robert's personal belongings in boxes and stacked them in the garage.

She called Kevin and invited him to Sunday dinner. She had to tell her sons about the divorce. What had she done that drove Robert into another woman's arms? She admitted, not denying the pain it brought, that she had often taken him for granted. He had always been a part of her life. She assumed he always would be.

The thought of Robert with another woman was more than she could bear. Even now was he holding Susan, whispering to her, making love to her? Excruciating pain made her open her eyes and cry out. "No!" Numb with shock and grief, she sat on the end of the couch and stared into space.

Boo's barking brought Emily back to now just as Robert's sister Debra came through the front door. She and Emily had been best friends since first grade. "Hey, Em? I thought you were away."

Emily shrugged, "Obviously, I'm not."

"I rang the bell and got no answer. Then I heard Boo barking. The door was unlocked, so I came in." Debra stared down at her sister-in-law. "Are you sick?"

"I... No." Emily asked again, "What are you doing here?"

"I was passing and I saw your light. I knew you and Robert were out of town for the weekend. I figured Larry went out and left the lights on..." Debra's words faded before gaining momentum again. "You look terrible. What's wrong?"

Emily nodded toward a chair. "Sit down, Debra."

"I only have a few minutes. Mike and I are babysitting the grandchildren tonight." Debra perched on the edge of a low footstool and looked around. "Where's Robert?"

Emily swallowed over the lump in her throat. "He's gone." The finality of those words rang in her ears like a death knell.

Debra frowned. "I thought the two of you went to Cedar Creek."

"We came back this morning." Had it been only this morning that Robert deposited her on the doorstep and drove away without looking back? It seemed at least a decade had passed since then.

"Did Robert have to come back because of business?"

Shame and humiliation swamped Emily causing her to weep like a helpless child. "Robert wants a divorce."

Debra's mouth fell open. "My brother wants a divorce? Why?"

Emily cried so hard she couldn't answer. Debra stepped across the small space between them, and sat beside her. "Robert loves you. He would never leave you and the boys."

Between sobs, Emily explained. "He's in love with someone else."

Debra's eyes rounded in disbelief. "Robert could never love anyone else. He's hopelessly devoted to you. He always has been." Her teeth worried her bottom lip. "There has to be some mistake."

There was a mistake, and Emily made it. She believed her husband's love would last forever, and it didn't. "Robert is suing me for a divorce. Does that sound like hopeless devotion?"

"I don't know what to say." Debra reached into her sweater pocket and offered Emily a slightly crumpled tissue. "Tell me what happened."

Slowly, Emily gained some composure. "He says he's in love with her."

"A younger woman no doubt." Debra's full mouth pulled into a thin line.

"I don't know." Emily daubed at her eyes. "I never thought to ask."

"A divorce in our family would kill Mama and Daddy."

"What do you think it's doing to me?" Emily lifted tear-drenched eyes.

"Oh, Emily, I didn't intend to sound unfeeling." Debra's hands rose and fell in a hopeless gesture. "Do Kevin and Larry know?"

"Not yet. I'm going to tell them tomorrow." Emily sniffed and blew her nose. "You're the first to know."

"You can't stay here tonight. Come home with me." Debra stood and grasped Emily's hand, pulling her to a standing position.

"I can't leave." Emily pulled her hand away. "Larry will be home soon."

"Larry won't be home until the wee hours of the morning."

Emily's bones hummed with fatigue. "I'm too tired to go anywhere. I have Boo here with me."

"Boo is a dog," Debra argued. "You need to be with your family. I'm going to have a long talk with my brother.

"No." Emily caught her arm. "You mustn't."

"Somebody has to bring him to his senses."

"I've thought about this most of the day." Emily sat back down. "This wasn't an easy decision for Robert."

A puzzled frown pleated Debra's brow. "How can you defend him if he's been cheating on you?"

"I'm not defending him. I am trying to be honest with myself." Emily wiped at a wayward tear. "No one can force him to come back if he doesn't want to be here."

"If you won't go home with me," Debra declared, "I'll stay here with you."

In spite of herself, Emily smiled. "And leave Mike to manage two toddlers alone?"

"That's probably grounds for divorce." Debra scowled. "I'm sorry. I'm being thoughtless again."

"Go home, Debra. Your husband is waiting for you." She might be her closest friend, but when push came to shove, Emily knew Debra's loyalty would lie with her brother.

"I can't leave you here like this."

Emily did something alien to her nature. She was rude and testy. "Will you go home? I want to be alone."

Debra's breasts rose and fell as she heaved an indignant sigh. "I am trying to be helpful." As she turned to walk away, she called over her shoulder, "I'll be in touch."

Emily watched the ten o'clock news and an old Humphrey Bogart movie before she went to bed, but she couldn't sleep. Where, she wondered for the thousandth time, had she failed her husband? That persistent question crowded every other thought from her mind and made even rest impossible. She put on a battered old robe, went downstairs, curled up on the couch with Boo, and tried to read. After a while, she leaned her head back and closed her eyes, listening to, but not hearing the sounds of the music playing softly in the background.

Larry found her on the couch at two-thirty in the morning. When she opened her eyes, he was shaking her shoulder. "Mom, wake up. You went to sleep reading."

Emily stirred. "Larry? Would you like something to eat?"

He yawned. "No. What I need now is rest." He raced up the stairs, taking two steps at a time. "See you tomorrow."

Emily called after him, "Kevin is coming for dinner tomorrow night. I want you here, too."

It was a dinner Emily didn't look forward to, and it rolled around all too soon.

Kevin was late, arriving a little after seven. As the doorbell sounded, Emily untied her apron and hung it on a hook. "That's your brother," she told Larry. "Let him in."

Emily made chicken fried steak and apple pie, Kevin's favorites. He came into the dining room and looked around before dropping a kiss on his mother's cheek. "Where's Dad?"

"He's not here." Emily pulled out a chair. "Sit down, both of you."

"I can see the old man's not here." Kevin sat at the table and turned to Larry. "Do you know where he is?"

Larry shrugged. "He hasn't been home all weekend."

"You shouldn't call your father the old man, Kevin." Emily laid her napkin across her lap. "Thank you for coming."

"I should have been here before now." He took a sip of water. "Are we waiting for Dad?"

"No. He won't be here. Eat before everything gets cold."

Larry forked a steak into his plate and covered it with cream gravy. "So, Kevin, how's the new job going?"

Kevin set his glass down. "Okay." He cleared his throat. "Why do I get the distinct feeling that something is wrong here?"

Emily looked into the expectant faces of her two sons and swallowed the tears that rose in her throat. "I have something to tell you. I don't know where to begin. It's not--"

Kevin's question cut across Emily's faltering explanation. "So, you found out? I was afraid this would happen."

"Found out what?" Larry looked more puzzled by the minute. "What were you afraid would happen?"

Emily chided, "Don't talk with food in your mouth."

"Who told you, Mom?" Kevin's jaw tightened.

"Told her what?" Larry swallowed. "Sorry, Mom."

Kevin's reply fell like a bomb into the quiet atmosphere. "The old man is screwing around with some young chick."

Larry jumped to his feet. "That's a lie." His chair tumbled behind him. "Take that back!"

Kevin lifted one hand. "Sorry, little brother, but it's the truth."

Emily anticipated some difficulty in breaking this news, but nothing like this. "Calm down, Larry." She had no idea Kevin knew about Robert and Susan. "Please, darling, sit down. It's not as bad as it seems."

Larry retrieved his chair and sat.

After a moment of tense silence, Emily asked Kevin, "How did you find out?"

"I saw them together about two months ago." Kevin's eyes clouded with pain. "They were in a restaurant. After that I made a few discreet inquiries. It's no big secret. A lot of people know."

Emily said, "Your father wants a divorce."

Kevin struck the table with his fist. "The sorry son--"

Emily's voice was level and firm. "That's enough. You may not approve of what your father is doing, but he's still your father."

"Tell him you forgive him, Mom," Larry begged. "Let him come back home. This is where he belongs."

"It's not my choice to make." Her young son's suffering added to Emily's pain. "Dad doesn't want to come home."

Kevin's hand tightened around his water glass. "You need to learn to play hard ball, Mom. Find a good lawyer and take him to the cleaners."

Why hadn't she seen this coming? She was so blinded by her own grief she failed to realize what a devastating effect Robert's affair would have on her sons. "Dad and I have settled on terms of the divorce. He's being very generous."

"Don't let him get away with this, Mom." Kevin shoved his plate back. "Don't let him treat you this way. Make him pay."

"Please," Emily begged, "settle down, both of you. I know this is hard for all of us, but let me tell you how I feel. Is that too much to ask?"

Kevin hung his head, "No, of course not."

"Larry?" Emily looked at her younger son.

Larry wiped his hand across his eyes. "Go ahead."

"I don't want Dad to come home if he doesn't want to be here. Can you understand that?"

After a heavy silence, Larry said, "Yeah, I guess I can."

"He will go on being your dad. You will still see him." Larry must not think his father was deserting him, too. "He will still be a part of your life, all right?"

"It's not all right," Larry answered vehemently, "I don't want you and Dad apart."

"You don't have a choice. This is a decision Dad has made, and I don't believe he's going to change it."

"I'm not hungry, Mom." A thin line of perspiration beaded Larry's upper lip. "May I be excused?"

She didn't want him to be alone, not now. "Please, stay a little longer."

Standing, Larry declared, "I need to be by myself for a while."

Kevin intervened. "Let him go, Mom."

Chapter Five

Emily watched her younger son hurry toward the stairs. As the sound of his feet racing up the steps died away, she turned to meet her older son's steady stare. She was surprised at the anger she saw there. "Kevin, we can't let this destroy our family."

"Family, Mom?" Kevin ridiculed. "What family? We're not a family anymore. Dad saw to that when he started messing around with some slut."

There seemed to be no way to salvage her marriage. Emily was striving to accept that fact and deal with it. She could not, would not, let the fallout from that tragedy tear her family apart, too. "Yes, we are. I'm still your mother. Larry is still your brother. We are still a family unit."

"And Dad?" Kevin asked bitterly. "What about the patriarch of our little clan?"

"He chooses to be with someone else." A determined note crept into Emily's voice. "We mustn't, we can't, let that fact ruin what we have left."

Kevin dropped his gaze. "I'm not thinking straight. I've known about Dad's philandering for a couple of months. I wanted to tell you." He paused and swallowed. "No, that's not true. I felt I should tell you. I couldn't bring myself to do it. I kept hoping he'd come to his senses. Sometimes I felt like I was a worse traitor than Dad."

Kevin's recent actions became clear. "Is that why you haven't been to the house for such a long time?"

Kevin hung his head "Yeah."

"I can understand your position." Her proud, protective Kevin must have spent the last two months in torment. She could relieve him of some of his guilt. "I respect your decision to keep quiet. I don't see how you could have done anything else."

He let out a long, whistling sigh of relief. "Thanks, Mom, for understanding."

Emily wiped her eyes with her napkin. "I have to stop thinking of you as a child. You're not."

"I'm glad you realize that."

This was even more difficult than Emily had expected. "I hope you're adult enough to understand what I am about to say to you."

"Don't defend my old man!" Kevin wadded his napkin into a ball and threw it across the table. "I can't stand it when you do that!"

"This is not about Dad. It's about me."

He leaned back in his chair. "Give him the dickens, Mom. Leave him without a dime."

Emily drew a long breath. "I don't want this divorce to disintegrate into a nasty name-calling, mudslinging mess. I want to behave as a Christian and come through this trial with my self-respect intact. Under the circumstances, I know that will not be easy. I am going to need your help."

"I never thought of it from that angle." Kevin's angry gaze melted into one of tender compassion. "What can I do?"

"Respect my decisions. Don't bad mouth your Dad to Larry or anyone else. Just try to be as neutral as possible."

It was a long time before Kevin answered. "I can do those things. I was afraid you would ask me to forgive Dad. That's the one thing I can't do."

""Forgiveness is a process we have to work through. You may change your mind later," Emily assured him with more confidence than she felt. "I must admit, it's a difficult thing for me, too.

"Maybe you can do it," Kevin pursed his lips, "but I doubt if I ever will."

"I don't intend to butt into the relationship you have with your father. You're both grown men. Larry is not that mature. He needs our protection." Her eyes locked onto her son's tortured face. "Don't judge your dad too harshly. I'm asking that, not for his sake, but for yours."

"I don't want to talk about the old fool." With a wave of his hand, Kevin dismissed the subject. "I would like to know if there is anything I can do for you?"

Emily smiled through her tears. "You can eat the dinner I cooked for you." She pushed her chair back. "I have to find Larry and talk to him."

"Mom," Kevin called as she hastened toward the door, "I agreed to what you asked. Now you can do something for me."

How could she say no? "Yes, Kevin?"

"I know an attorney, a very good attorney. He handled a case for a friend of mine last year. I'll give you his name. Will you go see him, or at least call him?"

"Thank you, Kevin." Emily put one hand on the stair rail. "I appreciate your concern."

When she came downstairs after a long, rather futile talk with Larry, Kevin was gone. A note was propped against the sugar bowl. On it was scrawled the name and telephone number of Thaddeus T. Thackeray, Attorney at Law. Across the top of the page, Kevin wrote, *I'll call you in the morning.* Emily folded the note and put it in her pocket.

Early Monday morning she called and made an appointment to see Thaddeus Thackeray the following Wednesday afternoon.

When she laid her phone aside, it burst forth with music. She picked up the instrument, expecting to hear Kevin's voice on the other end. Instead, Robert's baritone sounded over the wire. "Emily? How are you?"

Her chest tightened in an old, familiar way. "What do you want?"

His voice was tense and uncertain. "I want to know if you're all right."

"I am no longer your concern," Emily snapped. She was doing the very thing she vowed she wouldn't, being petty and vindictive. In a more conciliatory tone, she asked again, "What is it you want?"

"I would like to come by this evening and pick up my things." Uncertainty deepened his voice, "If that's all right with you."

"I packed them and put them in the garage. You have a key." If she saw him, she would be back in that same old heartache "The boxes are labeled. Lock the door when you leave."

"I need to see you, and talk to you."

"Whatever you have to say to me, you can say to my attorney," she told him coldly. "Mail your house keys to me. I don't want the expense of having my locks changed."

"You have an attorney?"

"I have an appointment for later in the week. Good-bye, Robert."

"Don't hang up Emily." He added a hurried, "Please."

Why, she wondered, did he keep hanging on? "What now?"

"I was wondering," his voice shifted to a lower key, "if you talked to Kevin and Larry?"

His concern was for his sons. She should have known. "Kevin came to dinner last night."

"And?" Robert prodded anxiously.

"He's looking well." She was not going to run interference for Robert with his children. "Good-bye, Robert. Don't forget to mail the house keys to me." She ended the call.

Her phone rang again immediately. Instead of answering, Emily walked from the room.

The remainder of the day passed in a blur of pain and ambivalence. One minute she didn't want to see Robert when he came for his things. The next instant, she was finding excuses to stay.

Over dinner, Emily explained to Larry that his father would be around later to pick up his belongings. "Maybe the two of you can visit for a while."

Larry's eyes glowed. "I'd like that. Are you going to see him, too?"

How could Emily answer that question? She didn't try. "Do you have homework?"

Larry wrinkled his nose, "Yeah, calculus and government."

"Why don't you do it in the living room?" Emily stacked dishes. "I'll be in when I'm finished here."

Larry pushed back his plate. "Maybe we can persuade Dad to come home." His young face was expectant. "We can ask."

She couldn't allow him to entertain false hopes. "You may ask him, if you like, but I doubt you'll get anywhere."

Larry stood holding onto the back of his chair, his eyes following Emily's every movement. "Kevin says Dad has a girlfriend. Is that true?"

Emily struggled for control. "Susan's not a girl. A young woman would be a more apt description." She was going to cry, and she didn't want to do it in Larry's presence. She lifted a stack of dishes in each hand, and headed for the kitchen.

Larry called after her, "Why, Mom? Why?"

How could she explain to her young son something she didn't understand herself? *This is Robert's problem. He has to deal with it.* "That's a question you'll have to ask your dad."

The doorbell rang as Emily was putting plates in the dishwasher. She heard voices mingling in conversation as she closed the dishwasher and turned the control to start. Should she go in? *No. Give Larry some time alone with Robert.*

The air exploded with the clash of loud voices and the slamming of a door. Before Emily could collect her scattered senses, Robert stood in the kitchen door glaring at her. "Is this your idea of revenge, trying to turn Larry against me?"

Emily wiped her hands on a dishtowel and hung it on a rack over the sink before she turned to ask, "Do you really believe I would stoop that low?"

His shoulders sagged. "No, I guess not. You've been rather decent about this whole affair."

Her eyes met his. She saw anger there, mingled with guilt and pain. Deep lines fanned out around his eyes and bracketed his mouth. Emily pointed to a chair. "Would you like to sit down?"

He sat on the edge of the chair and put his elbows on the kitchen table. "I didn't expect such an intense reaction from Larry."

"Larry's young. This is his first experience with heartbreak. He doesn't know how to cope."

"He asked me to come home." Twin splotches of red burned across Robert's high cheekbones. "When I tried to explain why I couldn't do that, he ran from the room."

"Running away is his way of dealing. He'll come around." *Why was she trying to spare the feelings of a man who had torn her world apart? For perhaps the first time, she recognized how difficult it must have been for Jesus to pray, "Father, forgive them."*

Robert shook his head. "I don't think he will. Not anytime soon, at least. Larry feels I've deserted him."

"Haven't you?" Emily asked, and then wished she hadn't.

Robert dropped his hands to his sides. "May I have a cup of coffee?"

This is no longer his home. "I just washed the pot."

"Could I have a glass of water?"

If he didn't want her for a wife, she saw no reason to be his waitress. "Help yourself."

Robert ran water into a glass, drank it, and set the empty glass on the counter.

Emily moved around him and walked toward the dining room.

Robert called after her, "Are you running away too?"

Emily stopped in the dining room door. "No." Without turning, she asked, "Did you get your things?"

Robert came to stand behind her. "Yes."

She felt his nearness, sensed the tenseness in his body. "May I have my house keys?" She turned and extended one hand.

He took the keys from his pocket and laid them in her palm. "I have to go."

Emily wrapped her fingers around the keys. "Good-bye, Robert." She looked around the door toward the living room. Larry was nowhere in sight. Thank goodness for that. The last thing he needed now was to see the animosity between his parents.

Robert lingered. "Will you see me to the door?"

Was he deliberately trying to torment her? Intentional or not, he was doing a fine job. "You know the way."

"I want a last word with you." Robert put his hands in his pockets and spread his feet apart. "I was hoping you could talk to Larry. He seems crushed."

"You're on your own to explain your behavior to Larry and Kevin." Emily stepped back into the dining room and moved aside. "Will you go, please?"

He took a tentative step toward her. "Have you told Kevin about...us?"

She drew a deep breath. "He already knew."

Surprise rippled across Robert's face. "Who told him?"

"He saw you with Susan in a restaurant a few months ago."

Under his tan, Robert turned an ash gray. "How did he react?"

"He's hurt and angry and feeling like a traitor because he couldn't bring himself to tell me." Emily moved toward the front door. "I'll see you out, after all. I need to take Boo for his walk." She whistled and Boo came bounding toward her, wagging his tail furiously.

Robert reached down to stroke his head. "I remember the day I brought this rascal home. He wasn't much more than a little ball of black fluff."

What did this man want from her? He had betrayed her with another woman and walked out of her life. He compounded that treachery by doing irreparable injury to her sons. Now he wanted to reminisce about, of all things, a dog? "Do you want custody of Boo?"

Robert stopped and stood very still. "I gave Boo to you. He was a birthday present."

"Everything else you gave me, you took back. Why not Boo?" She bit her tongue to stop herself. "I believe you were leaving."

Robert opened the front door. "Will you talk to Larry, try to explain to him?"

"I can't explain adultery to someone as naive and trusting as Larry. Don't ask me to try."

He flinched. "You are not making this any easier."

Emily reached for Boo's leash. "Is it supposed to be easy to desert your family?" She stooped and hooked Boo's leash to his collar. As she straightened, she said, "Move please."

Robert turned on his heel and walked away without looking back. He hurried down the steps, got into his car, and gunned the motor, spinning gravel as he sped away. When he was well down the road, Emily tightened her hold on Boo's leash and led him down the sidewalk.

Chapter Six

Emily returned from walking Boo some thirty minutes later to find Larry sitting at the desk in the living room with an open book before him. She hung the dog leash on a hook. "Are you still doing homework?"

Larry asked, "What made him change? He didn't used to be that way."

"We all change." It wasn't much of an answer, but it was all she could think of to say.

Larry closed the book. "He isn't coming back, is he?"

Emily sat on the couch and Boo curled up at her feet. "No, and we have to accept that."

Larry pushed his chair back and closed his book. "I'm going upstairs."

"You can't keep running forever." Emily called out, as he rushed past her. "Sooner or later, you have to face the truth and deal with it."

Larry stopped. "I can't, Mom. I can't face Dad leaving us."

"He isn't leaving you. He's leaving me." She got a grip on her emotions. "Only cowards run away from reality."

"I'm not leaving because I'm afraid."

"I think you are," she answered softly.

He retraced his footsteps and sat beside her. "You're right. I'm scared, really scared."

She knew what that admission cost him. "So am I, but running away from that fear won't change what is happening."

"It's not fair!" Larry struck the side of the couch with his fist.

"We can't expect fairness in this life. Jesus warned us about that." She was speaking to the child she considered a gift from God. He was no longer a little boy. He was a young adult, poised on the brink of manhood. She thought she could protect him from the pain of his parents' breakup. Now suddenly, sadly, she knew she couldn't. "It's not the end of the world.

God will give us strength and life will go on. Only not like it was before." It *was* the end of the world as she knew it.

Larry pleaded, "Tell me what to do, Mom."

"We will take this one day at a time. For now, you should concentrate on graduating high school and continue getting ready for college in the fall. I'm going to think about what kind of a future I want for myself."

"Maybe I could forget college." Larry's lower lip quivered. "You will need me here with you."

For one selfish moment she was tempted to agree, but only briefly. "I'm looking forward to being on my own." That was a stretch. She was forcing herself to look ahead. However, the thought of being without Robert terrified her.

"You don't want me?" Surprise lifted his voice.

She had to cut those apron strings. "I will always want you. You are my son. A single forty-two-year-old woman doesn't need an eighteen-year-old son in residence." She was being tough, but only because she loved him.

Larry tilted his head to one side. "I hadn't thought of it from that viewpoint."

"That's because you're not a forty-two-year-old woman." She patted his cheek. "Go to bed. It's late."

He paused at the door and turned to look back at her. "I love you, Mom."

"I love you, too." *More than you will ever know.* She watched as he vanished up the stairs.

Emily was scheduled to work at the library on Monday. Her first impulse was to call and cancel. By now several people knew Robert was divorcing her, and why. She didn't want to face being the object of gossip and pity. Words she said to Larry the night before came back to taunt her. *Running away is not the answer.* She decided to confront the situation and deal with it.

Emily not only showed up, she worked two extra hours.

Tuesday Emily visited Robert's Aunt Beth and met with the committee planning the high school senior prom.

Wednesday she canceled a meeting with the Historical Society, explaining that she had an important appointment. She suspected the chairperson thought she was lying.

At precisely three that afternoon, Emily was ushered into the presence of Thaddeus T. Thackeray, attorney at law. "This way, please." The receptionist opened a heavy paneled door that led to a richly appointed office.

The man sitting behind the massive oak desk stood when she entered. Thaddeus Thackeray was a tall, robust man with a shock of gray hair and a charismatic smile. He exuded self-confidence and charm that was at once arresting and intimidating. His piercing brown eyes swept Emily from head to toe in one assessing glance. "Mrs. Franklin." Coming around his desk, he extended his hand. "I'm Thad Thackeray." His thick fingers clasped Emily's cold hand. "Won't you sit down?"

Emily perched on a narrow chair. Thad sat on the edge of his desk, swinging one leg. "Shall we get down to business?"

Emily said, "I want to talk to you about a divorce."

Thad raised a bushy eyebrow. "That's a serious step. Are you sure?"

"I'm sure." Over the past few days, she had realized it would foolish to fight the inevitable. "Very sure."

Thad Thackeray drummed a pencil on his desk as his bushy brows pulled together in a straight line. "You're very sure you want to divorce your husband?"

"You misunderstand me." Emily's throat tightened with tension. "My husband is divorcing me. He told me I should engage legal counsel."

"Your soon-to-be ex is still telling you what to do?" Thad asked in a bland monotone, "Did he suggest you come to me?"

He was being both amiable and caustic and in the process he was making Emily feel like a simpering fool. "No. My son gave me your name."

"How long have you been married to this man who wants to divorce you?" Thad raised those expressive brows, looked straight into her eyes and waited for an answer.

Emily wanted to tell him that wasn't important. His piercing stare stopped her, "A long time."

"That's not what I asked."

A hot flush scorched Emily's cheeks. She answered his questions even though she didn't like the way he asked them. "Twenty-four years, eight months, and some days. Should I be more specific?"

"That's near enough and it is a long time. The better part of your life, I'd guess." Thad rubbed his chin with his hand. "And you, Mrs. Franklin? How do you feel about a divorce?"

"How do I feel?" Emily hesitated before blurting out the truth. "I love my husband, but I don't think it would achieve anything to try to hold onto him."

"Another woman?" Thad asked, again raising his shaggy eyebrows.

A band of uneasiness tightened around Emily's chest. "Isn't it always?"

"I assume you want to counter sue and fight the divorce?"

"Neither. Robert and I have agreed on terms for the divorce."

"Robert being your husband?"

"My husband's name is Robert Albert Franklin."

"You're still on friendly terms with this man who's leaving you for a younger woman?" He was being unnecessarily offensive.

Emily bit down on the urge to tell this man to mind his manners. "In a way. Yes, I guess you could say that."

Superciliously Thad asked, "Are you sure you need me?"

Emily met his calculating gaze. "Robert thinks I should have legal representation."

"And what do you think, Mrs. Franklin?" Thad moved behind his desk and sat in his chair. "What is your studied opinion?"

Emily fought to hold onto her self-control. "I want this over and done with. The sooner, the better."

Thad Thackeray sat for a few minutes, deep in thought. "I see." He tilted his head and stared at the ceiling.

Emily's aggravation moved up a notch. "Will you represent me?"

With studied indifference he asked, "Do you want me to?"

Emily's anger burst like a storm cloud. "Why do you think I'm here?" Her voice rose. "You could do with a crash course in manners."

A wide smile creased Thad's face. "Ah, that's what I wanted to see, a little fire, a little spunk. Shall we get down to business?"

Chapter Seven

Emily awoke suddenly, sat on the side of the bed, and dropped her head into her hands. A sharp pain shot from the base of her skull and traveled down her backbone. With wakefulness came a disturbing thought. As of yesterday, she was a divorced woman. She'd thought the divorce would be simple. How wrong she was.

She smiled, remembering how shocked Thad was when she told him she wanted no alimony. "I don't want to be dependent on Robert for anything."

Thad snorted in disbelief. "Are you kidding?"

"I mean it." Emily was adamant. "Not one cent."

Thad sighed. "You and your soon-to-be ex are both crazy." He paced across his office floor. "You won't accept the alimony he insists he wants you to have." He shook his head from side to side. "Why are you two divorcing?"

"You know why. Robert wants his freedom."

"If that's the case, why can't he let go?"

"Robert feels responsible for me." Emily shrugged. "It must be guilt."

"Take advantage of that guilt and make life easier for both of us," Thad pleaded.

Why couldn't she make anyone understand? She didn't want to be dependent on Robert. She wanted to stand on her own two feet. "I don't intend to change my mind."

Next came the long hassle over Robert's insistence that he pay Emily's health insurance premiums.

On that issue, too, Emily was adamant. "I don't want Robert's charity."

"Don't you think he owes you something?" Thad questioned on the end of a whistling sigh.

"I won't accept it. That's my final word. Robert wanted this divorce. He will have to live with the consequences."

"Consequences?" Thad almost shouted. He threw up both hands in exasperation. "You're making this far too easy."

Emily's voice lifted in surprise. "Do you think this is easy for me?"

"Not for you," Thad grunted, "for him."

"Maybe, but that's the way it's going to be."

When it became apparent that Emily didn't intend to give an inch, Thackeray was forced to yield once again. After that, things moved along at a faster pace. Now, she was a single person, a separate entity from the man who was her husband for almost twenty-five years.

Larry's graduation exercises were tomorrow evening. After that, she planned to look for a job. Last week she had, with a great deal of reluctance, resigned her volunteer position at the library.

Emily was vacuuming the living room when her phone rang. She switched off the machine and answered, "Yes?"

A feminine voice on the other end said, "One moment please."

Emily tapped her foot and waited impatiently.

A loud click was followed by Robert's voice saying, "I hope I didn't call at a bad time."

All Emily's times were bad. "What do *you* want?"

"I will be in your area this afternoon, showing some property. I'd like to come by and pick up the rest of my things. I'll be there between two and two-thirty."

"Robert, for Pete's sake." The court decreed he must remove his personal property from her premises as soon as possible. "There's no hurry. You can do it later."

"I'll be in the neighborhood," he replied. "Why should I make an extra trip later?" Before she could offer further objections, he hung up.

Emily was folding laundry when the doorbell rang. She took her time answering. When she opened it, Robert stood on the other side. "What took you so long?"

"I was busy." She stepped back. "Some of the boxes are in the garage, some are in your--the study." She recovered some of her self-control. "There are several boxes. I hope your car will hold them all."

He came out of the heat and into the cool room. "I'll get the things from the garage first."

She once believed this man would love her until the end of time. "There's fishing tackle and a box of tools in the shed in the back." It was time she let go of the myth of happily ever after.

"I have no place to put them." How apologetic he sounded. "If it's all right, I'll leave them for a while."

"That's fine. As I said, you can get them later." She wondered where he was living. Had he moved in with Susan? He was not her concern. *Not her concern, but he was her heartache.* She walked toward the kitchen. *She would get over this. She must, because she had no choice.*

Emily made iced tea while Robert loaded boxes, first from the garage and then from the study. "Would you like a glass of tea?" she asked as he carried the last box through the living room. She knew she should let him go, but she couldn't bring herself to do that. After today, it could be weeks, even months, before she saw him again.

"Let me get this last box stowed in my car, and I'll be back."

Emily poured tea into two frosty glasses and sat at the kitchen table. *Play it cool. It's over. Let him go.*

Robert stood in the doorway, staring at her. "You didn't have to go to all this trouble."

"It's no trouble." She nodded toward a chair. "Sit down and drink your tea."

He dropped into a chair and wiped his hand across his brow. After an awkward silence Robert blurted out, "Do you have an extra ticket to Larry's graduation?"

"You don't have a ticket? I was sure Larry put one in the announcement he sent you."

His hand gripped his ice tea glass. "I need two tickets."

She shot him a puzzled glance before understanding sharpened her gaze. "You're bringing Susan with you?"

With a defiant toss of his head Robert said, "If I can get my hands on another ticket."

His words were like a cruel blow. How could he be so insensitive? Slowly, because speaking was so painful, she said, "You could ask Larry. He might have an extra."

From what seemed to be a long way off, Robert's words intruded. "I'm having trouble communicating with Larry these days. I thought you might ask him for me."

She fought a rising anger. "If you want the ticket, you will have to ask him for it yourself."

Robert's hand tightened on his glass. "I never realized until we separated what a stubborn woman you are."

Emily shook her head, trying to clear her mind. "I've leaned over backward to be fair with you."

"Oh, have you?" he asked softly. "Do you call it fair when you refuse to take alimony, when you won't let me pick up the tab for your health care premiums? You want to punish me and make me feel guilty. You're being stubborn, Emily, stubborn and vindictive."

"You think I'm stubborn because I refuse to let you continue to run my life?" Emily's voice raised a few decibels. "You are no longer the master of this house. I make my own decisions now."

"I'm not trying to make decisions for you." He sighed wearily. "I'm trying to take care of you."

"You're trying to salve your conscience. There's no need for that. You gave up the burden of taking care of me when you divorced me."

Robert set his tea glass on the table. "I never thought of caring for you as a burden."

"Will you stop being such a hypocrite?" Emily's temper flared. "You feel guilty because you've treated me like dirt. You're upset because I refuse to allow you the luxury of buying peace of mind at the cost of my self-respect."

"Is that how you saw me?" he asked in a hushed voice. "As your master?"

She spoke with quiet dignity. "That's what you were. You were overbearing and selfish." She should stop. She was saying far too much.

"I resent what you're implying." The muscles in Robert's jaw tightened. "I never put my wishes ahead of yours."

"Oh, yes, you did." Memory liberated a host of old recollections. "All of my life you've been telling me what to do and I've been doing it. Even when we were children and played games or went to movies, you said what and where and when."

"I was older and better equipped to make decisions." He swallowed, making his Adam's apple bob up and down like an elevator. "I always did what was best."

"Best for whom?"

"You can't hold what we did as children against me." He took a quick swallow from his glass. "I always had your best interests at heart."

"When you decided we would marry, it had to be immediately. I wanted to wait and go to college, but you said no."

"I had finished college. I was ready to settle down. I needed a wife."

"I had, I was, I needed. Listen to yourself, Robert," she said dispassionately. "I, I, I."

"I thought it was the best for both of us."

"What did you think when I wanted another baby after Larry was born?" she asked softly. "I begged you for another child. You said no. When Larry started school and I wanted to enroll in college, you said no again. When I wanted to accept a paying job with the library, you wouldn't hear of such a thing. You didn't mind your wife volunteering, but she couldn't work and get paid for what she did. That was too much for your tender ego."

His face was ashen. "I had no idea you harbored such bitterness."

Emily's heart hurt and her throat was tight. "Neither did I until you left me for the kind of woman you never wanted me to be."

"That's not..." His voice trailed away and then revived. "You really do hate me, don't you?"

"I'm trying not to." She tasted the dregs of despair. "I allowed you to siphon my life away. You took, I gave, and when you had taken everything I had to offer, you walked away."

His nostrils flared. "You make me sound like a demon in human form."

"I'm merely saying I don't want you trying to tell me what to do, and don't keep coming around offering me crumbs. I am going to make a new life for myself. I don't need you to tell me how to do it."

He vaulted to his feet. "I really do care about you, Emily."

"If you had cared for me, you wouldn't have betrayed me with another woman. I have more affection for Boo than you have for me." She snorted her disgust. "Go back to Susan and leave me alone."

He swallowed and stood. "You don't paint a very pretty picture of me."

Never before had she been so brutally honest. She had wanted to get those things off her chest for months, maybe for years. She followed Robert to the door. "Shall I have Larry call you?"

He grasped the doorknob. "Larry?"

"About another ticket."

"No, that's all right." He looked at her in the strangest way. "I'll manage."

After much thought, Emily did speak to Larry. She told him Robert wanted another ticket and why.

Larry's young eyes flashed with sudden anger. "I don't want that woman at my graduation."

If she ever wanted to drive a permanent wedge between Larry and his father, this was her golden opportunity. She cast the thought aside. "She will soon be your father's wife. Don't you think it's time you accepted that fact?"

"He's going to marry her?" Larry's eyes widened in surprise.

"I expect he will. Why else would he want a divorce?"

"Do you think I should send Dad another ticket?"

"I think you should accept reality and deal with it."

Larry was reluctant. "Are you sure it's all right with you, Mom?"

Emily forced a smile. "I think it's the gracious thing to do."

Larry shrugged. "Okay, if you say so.

Chapter Eight

Emily tried to brace herself for the trauma of seeing Robert with another woman. For more reasons than she could name, she dreaded that encounter. It would make her an object of pity to their friends and Robert's family. Nevertheless, it was inevitable that sooner or later they would run into each other. Larry's graduation ceremony seemed as good a place as any. At least she wouldn't be taken by surprise.

Emily sat beside Kevin in the school auditorium. Robert came through the back entrance with a beautiful young woman clinging to his arm. Kevin reached for her hand. "Steady, Mom."

Emily gasped. Susan Barrett was tall and glamorous, with a mane of midnight hair and a figure that could have graced the pages of a fashion magazine. "She's so young."

Kevin's arm went around his mother's shoulder. "How can he do this?"

"It's all right," Emily said. But it wasn't all right. Inside she was dying.

"He's making a fool of himself." Kevin's fingers tightened around Emily's shoulder.

"Let's not spoil Larry's special evening," Emily begged, even though her own spirit plummeted to a new low. A soothing trauma took over her mind and body allowing her to function on the surface as a normal person. Looking back later, she would realize that she was in shock. It was nothing short of a miracle that she made it through the remainder of the lengthy ceremony without falling apart.

As the presentation of diplomas drew to a close, Emily whispered in Kevin's ear, "As soon as I congratulate Larry, I'll slip out the side door and go home." Robert's parents planned a family party after graduation. Since she hadn't been invited, she could only assume Robert was taking Susan there.

For once, Kevin didn't argue. "After I see Larry, I'm on my way, too."

"Aren't you going to Grandma's?"

"I should," Kevin whispered. "If for no other reason than to tell my old man what I think of him."

This was turning out worse than Emily imagined. "Promise me you won't say anything rude to your dad."

Kevin patted her arm. "I'm not even going to speak to that middle-aged Romeo."

After the ceremony Emily found Larry and offered her congratulations. "I'm so proud of you." She kissed his cheek. "I'm leaving now. Tell Grandma and Grandpa I said hello."

"Are you sure you don't want to go to Grandma and Grandpa's with me?" Larry looked at the crowd around him. "Where did they go?"

Emily didn't want to attend a family celebration that included Robert and his girlfriend. Nevertheless, she was hurt she hadn't been invited. How could Susan's feelings be more important than hers to Robert's family? She was pretty sure her ex-in-laws didn't want to run into her any more than she wanted to see them. "Not this time." Apparently, Larry was not yet aware that Robert had Susan with him.

As she turned to walk away, Larry called after her. "I won't be home until late. I'm going out with Gus after I leave Grandma's."

Emily waved without looking back. "I'll see you tomorrow." She hardly remembered the drive home. It was not until later, when she crawled between the sheets of her lonely bed, that the full impact of the evening's events hit her. She faced for the first time a truth she denied for months, Robert wasn't coming back, ever. She buried her head in her pillow and wept bitter tears. Lord, why did you let this happen to me, she asked. I did my best to be a good wife and mother. How could Robert treat me this way?

The next morning Emily did something she had not been able to do before. She slipped her wedding ring from the third finger of her left hand, and dropped it into the drawer of her nightstand. A part of her life, a large and important part, was over. "I can do all things through Christ who strengthens me," she whispered. Plenty of other women faced divorce and survived. So could she.

Some of her resolve vanished later in the day when Robert's parents appeared on her doorstep unannounced.

"I do hope we're not intruding." Clara Franklin's veined hand brushed a wisp of gray hair from her forehead. "I felt I had to see you and explain something."

Emily was fond of Robert's parents. "Of course, you're not intruding. Come in."

"Mama didn't sleep well last night." George Franklin patted his wife's arm. "I told her she worried too much, but you know how Mama is."

"Is there something I can do?" Emily had no idea where this conversation was going.

"We came to apologize for last night." Clara's lips pulled into a prim line. "We were so sorry we couldn't invite you to the house after the graduation."

"Robert thought it was best for all concerned if we didn't ask you," George hastened to add. "But Mama wanted to explain."

Emily brushed his words aside. "You don't owe me an explanation."

George Franklin intervened. "The situation is so awkward. Mama was upset. She still is."

"Robert brought Susan to meet us." Clara picked up where George left off. "It felt strange, having a family gathering without you there."

Emily's last wisp of hope died a painful death. Robert did intend to marry Susan. Why else would he bring her home to meet his family? "You will get used to it, Clara."

Clara's voice sharpened. "Why didn't you fight for Robert? Don't you love him anymore?"

"A part of me will always love him," Emily admitted, "but if he doesn't want me, it's pointless to try to hold on to him."

"Sometimes a virtue can be carried to a fault." Clara put her hand across her mouth as her eyes widened. "I'm sorry. I didn't mean that. I don't want to lose your friendship, but Robert is my son. I have to respect his wishes."

Emily wasn't the only person this divorce was hurting. "Of course, you do. I wouldn't expect anything else."

George's shaggy head moved from side to side. "We've known you all your life. You are very dear to us. You're like a part of our family."

Clara wore a tight smile. "It's not like you divorced us."

Through no choice of her own, she *was* divorced from them, in so many ways. "You will always be a part of my life. You're the grandparents of my children."

Clara breathed a sigh of relief, as George said, "See? I told you."

"But I'm no longer welcome in your home." Emily hated being so blunt, but she knew no other way. She despised having these two dear old people get hurt.

Clara began to cry. "Why did that woman have to catch Robert's eye? She's gone and spoiled everything."

George put his arm around his wife's frail shoulders. "We have to abide by our son's decision, Mama. But Emily has a side in this, too."

Clara and George left thirty minutes later. Even after Emily explained their relationship must have different guidelines now, Clara objected. "I don't like it, but I'll try to adjust."

After numerous assurances by Emily that she would call and the three of them would have lunch sometime soon on neutral ground, they took their leave.

The telephone's vibrating ring made her pull it from her pocket. To her utter surprise, Thad Thackeray was on the line. "Emily? How are you?"

Emily sighed into the telephone. "My ex-in-laws just left. Does that answer your question?"

Thad observed with grim amusement, "Just when you think the worst is over, up jumps the devil."

Emily laughed. "You sound like the voice of experience."

"Oh, I am. I've been through the trauma of divorce three times."

"How are you?" Emily asked, because she couldn't think of an appropriate response to his personal revelation.

"I'm in a quandary." Thad chuckled. "I have a problem that maybe you can help me solve."

His words caught her off guard. "What kind of problem?"

"I have suddenly fallen heir to two tickets to tonight's play at the Community Theater. I have no one to share my good fortune with unless you'd like to come along with me. We could have dinner somewhere first."

"You want me to go out with you tonight?" Emily gasped.

"I know it's a little sudden, but I didn't have the tickets until half an hour ago. What do you say?"

Emily didn't know what to say. "I don't know..."

His soothing voice probed, "Do you have other plans?"

He was giving her a chance to say no gracefully. "No. No plans."

"Then is it a date?" His question had all the trappings of a statement. "I'll pick you up around seven."

Emily hadn't been out on what could be considered a date in over twenty-five years. Given time to consider her rash act, she might have changed her mind. *It's too late now.* She pulled her dress over her head and with some difficulty, zipped the back, realizing as she did so Robert had always done her back zippers before.

Thanks to Thad, the evening was pleasant and enjoyable. He took her to a very fashionable restaurant for dinner. He was good company, witty and attentive and with some knowledge of any subject that came up for discussion. He was also thoughtful and considerate, holding doors for her, helping her off with her wrap, and listening attentively to her thoughts and opinions.

The play was a comedy, light and humorous. The dialogue was salted with sharp irony. Emily was caught up in the problems of the characters on stage. For the space of two hours, she was lost in a world of illusion.

As they pulled out of the theater's parking lot Thad asked, "Would you like to stop somewhere for a drink?"

"No thanks, I have an early appointment tomorrow for a job interview."

"Oh, really?" Thad glanced in her direction. "Where?"

"Downtown, at the main library, I've worked as a volunteer at the branch near my home for several years. I resigned last week. Yesterday, I got a call asking me if I'd be interested in a permanent, paying position."

Thad seemed genuinely interested. "Do you know what you'll be doing?"

"If they hire me, I'll be a library aide." It was good to be able to confide in someone. "I was offered that position several years ago, but I didn't take it."

The lights from a passing car played across Thad's somber face, "Why not?"

A little hesitantly, she admitted, "Robert didn't want me to work."

Thad's head swiveled toward Emily. "Did you want to accept?"

Their eyes met before he transferred his gaze back to the road. "I did, very much."

"Are there regrets now?"

Emily's soft "No" made him, once again, glance briefly in her direction. "Why not?" he asked as he deftly pulled around the car in front of him.

"I wanted to please Robert." Under the circumstances now that sounded inadequate.

Thad shook his head and continued to drive in silence. "We will have to do this again," his said as he pulled into Emily's drive. "May I call you soon?"

She wanted to tell him she had a wonderful time. That would have been a lie. The evening was pleasant and relaxing, nothing more. "That would be nice."

Emily got out of the car, unsure of what she should do or say. "Good night. Thank you for an enjoyable evening."

Thad smiled. "Relax; I'm not going to ask for an invitation to come inside. I'll call you soon." He shifted gears and sped out of the driveway, leaving a bemused woman staring after him.

After a restless night, Emily rose early, ate a skimpy breakfast, and dressed for her interview. She was more nervous than she cared to admit. A glance in the mirror brought some assurance. She had lost weight. In the new suit she bought for this occasion, she looked stylish and well-groomed. Her hair was longer now, highlighted by a rinse to accentuate the red-gold color and done in a sophisticated style.

Emily took a deep breath as she entered the massive downtown library. Her instructions were to report to the office of Lee Morgan on the fourth floor. She smoothed her hair and pushed the elevator button.

The elevator climbed upward before stopping with a lurch. Emily got out and hurried down the long corridor, searching for the office of Lee Morgan. Just as she spotted that name written across the glass of a closed door, a voice from behind her called out, "Emily? Emily Franklin?"

Emily turned. The face of the elegantly dressed dowager who stood in front of her was familiar. A name to go with that face eluded her. "Yes."

"Imagine seeing you here," the woman gushed, "and looking so lovely."

"Thank you." Emily searched through her memory, still trying to put a name to this aristocratic face.

"You don't remember me," the cultivated voice accused.

"Your face is familiar." Heat burned in Emily's cheeks.

"We met last summer at a Library Directors' board meeting."

How could she forget the name of so important a personage as Amelia Hamilton? This wealthy, influential woman was chairperson of the library's board of directors. "Mrs. Hamilton. I do recall. How nice to see you again."

"And I would certainly never forget you," Amelia Hamilton declared. "You gave such a magnificent presentation. All the board members were impressed."

"Thank you." Emily couldn't remember what her presentation was about.

"My office is just down the hall." Mrs. Hamilton pointed over her shoulder. "Do come and have a cup of tea with me."

"I'd love to, Mrs. Hamilton, but I'm here for a job interview."

"My dear, volunteers of your caliber are rare in this world." Mrs. Hamilton tilted her patrician nose a fraction of an inch higher. "I'm sure the interview can wait."

Emily explained. "This is for a paying position."

"You are no longer a volunteer?" Amelia Hamilton's eyes widened.

"Things have changed since I last saw you." There was no point in dodging the issue. "I was recently divorced. I need a paying job. So, you see--"

Before she could complete her statement, the office door opened and a tall, thin, middle-aged man stepped into the hall. "Mrs. Hamilton. I thought I heard your voice."

"Mr. Morgan." Mrs. Hamilton looked past Emily. "Come and meet Mrs. Franklin."

"Mrs. Franklin?" Lee Morgan came toward Emily with his hand extended. "I've been expecting you."

"You know Emily?" Mrs. Hamilton arched a painted eyebrow.

"No, but I'm anxious to meet her." He shook Emily's hand. "She and I have an appointment to discuss employment."

"How fortunate we are that she would consider being our employee." Mrs. Hamilton patted Emily's shoulder. "Do come by, my dear, after your interview and visit with me for a while." She nodded in Lee Morgan's direction. "Good-bye, Mr. Morgan."

Lee Morgan smiled as he held the door open for Emily. "How long have you known Mrs. Hamilton?"

Amelia Hamilton was the moving force behind half the benevolent organizations in the city. Emily squelched the impulse to infringe on her slight acquaintance with so powerful a figure. "I don't know Mrs. Hamilton personally."

Lee ushered Emily into his office. "She seems to think highly of you."

"I'm flattered that she would."

Lee pointed to a chair. "Do you know the other members of the library's board of directors?"

"Most of them by sight, none of them very well. As you must know, each branch library makes an annual report to the board. For the past several years, I've had a minor role in organizing and presenting that report for our branch." Emily eased into her chair.

"You must be familiar with the program that recruits, tutors, and monitors volunteers for the library system." Lee leaned against the side of his desk as his eyes scanned Emily from head to toe.

"That program was adopted from the system devised and used first at the Loftin Branch." Emily paused before adding, "That's where I was a volunteer."

"Who came up with the idea for the system used at Loftin?"

The idea had been hers, but Emily was reluctant to say so. "It sort of evolved."

"I suspect you're being modest." Lee studied her with avid interest. "How long were you a volunteer at Loftin?"

Emily did some swift mental calculating. "For fifteen years."

"Are you familiar with the computer network that connects the entire library system?"

"Oh, yes." Emily began to relax. "I was at Loftin when it was installed."

Lee moved to sit behind his desk. "Your resume shows you have some experience as a public speaker."

"Over the years I've been involved in numerous school and community activities. Last year I was president of the PTA, and program chairperson of the Band Boosters' Club at Woodrow Wilson High School. I'm vice president of the Historical Society."

Lee Morgan leaned back in his chair, "Which tells me that you are not afraid of hard work and you get along well with people."

"Where is this all leading?" Emily asked. "I thought this was an interview for the position of library aide at Loftin."

"It was originally, but that was before I saw you and learned of your acquaintance with Amelia Hamilton and the other board members." Lee splayed his hands in a conciliatory gesture. "There is another job opening which you might have the unique qualifications to fill. Do you have your own car? Do you know your way around the city?"

Emily's mind explored new possibilities. "Yes to both questions."

"Are you able to work flexible hours? There is a social aspect to this position. You will be called on to attend numerous social functions: banquets, receptions, luncheons, dinners, charity galas, fund raising events. Many of these occasions take place in the evening." He continued to scrutinize her carefully. "Do you have a family, Mrs. Franklin?"

"I have two sons. One is an attorney for Fenders and Grimes here in the city. The other will be going away to college this fall. My husband and I are divorced."

After an assessing moment, Lee asked, "Would you be willing to take this position for six months? At the end of that time, we will confer and review and decide if the appointment will be permanent."

Emily was completely mystified "I'm not sure what job you're offering me."

"It's a position, Mrs. Franklin." Lee leaned back in his swivel chair. "The official title is Public Relations Coordinator. You will be in charge of recruiting, training, and monitoring volunteers for all the libraries. You will also be active in raising funds and support for the library system. That's why it's necessary to attend so many social functions. At some of these events you will be expected to make speeches, expounding on the general operations and services of our system, or zeroing in on some specific branch or benefit, whatever the situation demands. Occasionally all you will do is show up and mingle."

A jolt of adrenalin shot through Emily. "It sounds exciting and challenging."

Lee nodded. "It is. But there's another very pedestrian side. You will be expected to visit each of the sixteen branch libraries once each month and then file a report with me about the status and progress of the volunteer program at each branch. It's a demanding, time- consuming task." He leaned forward. "What do you say?"

"What about salary?" Emily asked, thinking this was too good to be true.

Lee smiled. "Mrs. Franklin, something tells me you are definitely the woman for this job, excuse me, position." He quoted a figure that left Emily wide-eyed and staring.

When she could find her voice she said, "Mr. Morgan, you have just hired a new Public Relations Coordinator. When do I start?"

Lee rubbed his hands together. "Is now too soon?"

"Not at all." It was preferable to going home to an empty house.

"Come along." Lee stood. "Let me show you to your office."

Her own office. This was more than Emily had dared hope for. She was elated. It took away some of the lingering sadness that, of late, was her constant companion.

Chapter Nine

Emily smiled at the handsome man sitting across the table from her. "Thad, you are an incurable optimist."

Thad returned her smile. "Well, Buddy, you win a few and you lose a few."

Two months had come and gone since Emily's first date with Thad. He dubbed her buddy the night she kindly but firmly rejected his sexual advances. "I can offer you friendship, nothing more." They were parked atop Lookout Point, a strange place for a man of Thad's age and standing to bring a woman.

Thad took her refusal in stride. "You remind me of an old song." He began to sing, off-key. "*I only want a buddy, not a sweetheart.*"

"I'm flattered that you're attracted to me," Emily said, "but sex outside of marriage is against my principles as a Christian."

Thad laughed with good humor. "The word marriage scares the bejabbers out of me." He eyed her skeptically. "Do you really mean it about us being friends?"

"Yes, I do. I enjoy your company very much."

Thad rubbed his chin. "I never had a woman friend before. I never knew a woman before that I wanted for a friend, but now...all right, Buddy." He wiped one hand down the leg of his pants, and extended it in her direction. "It's a deal."

Emily shook his hand. "As one old buddy to another, I need to go home. I'm still trying to get accustomed to getting up so early in the morning."

After that brief but honest encounter, Thad stopped trying to get Emily into his bed. He continued to call once or twice a week and to escort her to some of the many social functions her new job demanded she attend. He also acquired the habit of meeting her for lunch each Wednesday at the restaurant across from the library.

As time went by they became good friends, discovering somewhere along the way that they had a great deal in common and shared a variety of interests. Emily found that beneath Thad's sophisticated, cynical exterior beat the heart of a sympathetic, disillusioned man.

Emily sought his advice for problems ranging from the name of a good auto mechanic to how to best structure her savings account. Thad, in turn, consulted Emily on matters such as the appropriate birthday gift for his teen-aged nephew. At the moment, he was regaling her with his misadventures collecting his fee from a wealthy divorcee.

"There I was listening to her plead near bankruptcy when a man I never saw before walked through the bedroom door. I didn't know if I should pretend I didn't notice or try to throw the rascal out."

Emily giggled. "You believed her when she said he was her cousin?"

"Would a woman who divorced three rich husbands in the past five years lie?" Thad glanced at his watch. "I have to run." He blew her a kiss as he hurried away. "I'll call you tomorrow."

Emily watched his departing figure. Thad was a kind, considerate man. How fortunate she was to have him for a friend. She sipped her coffee and lingered over dessert. Her mind wandered back over the past few months. How completely her life had changed. She loved her job. It was not only challenging and rewarding, but it kept her too busy to indulge in regret and self-pity most of the time. Rare moments of introspection still brought melancholy memories.

Her gaze roamed around the crowded restaurant. She felt alone in the midst of the crowd of people. Since her divorce, the pain inside her had reduced to an intermittent ache that returned to torment her at inopportune moments such as this.

In the periphery of her vision, Emily caught a glimpse of a man whose profile was so like Robert's that she gasped before looking away. This was not the first time she felt the sharp pang of recognition only to realize she was staring at a stranger.

When the man turned, Emily's heart skipped a beat. It *was* Robert. She was reaching for her handbag to make a quiet exit when she felt a presence and knew her ex-husband was standing behind her.

"Emily?"

She didn't turn. "Yes?"

"It's been a long time. May I sit down?" He came around the table, pulled out a chair and stood waiting for her to answer.

She prepared for that pang of hurt his presence brought. To her surprise, it never materialized. She shrugged. "Please yourself."

Robert took that for a yes and sat down across from her. "Are you sure you don't mind?"

He looked older, thinner. "I'm sure."

He scooted his chair nearer the table. "The last time I sat down at a table with you, I got the tongue lashing of a lifetime."

Remembering made her sigh. "Do you want an apology?"

Robert scooted his chair nearer the table. "Why should you apologize for telling the truth?"

"I *am* sorry." She dropped her handbag onto the table. "I was angry and hurt. That was no excuse for being unkind to you."

"I'm the one who should apologize." Robert signaled for a waiter and ordered a cup of coffee. "Would you like something?"

She would like to get out of here as quickly as possible. "No, thank you."

As the waiter set a cup of coffee before him, he asked, "Do you want it now?"

His presence played havoc with Emily's composure. "Want what?"

"My long overdue apology." Robert's eyes narrowed. "Emily, look at me, please."

She raised her eyes to stare into his face. She saw uncertainty there and something akin to regret. She couldn't deal with this, not now. "I have to go."

"Please," Robert pleaded, "this won't take long." She had never known him to be so humble.

Emily glanced at her watch. "Make it fast."

His shirt was wrinkled and he wore no tie. *What happened to the nattily attired Mr. Franklin who always dressed with such care and style?*

"Can you forgive me?"

What did he want forgiveness for? Betraying her, deserting her, tearing her world asunder? "You're forgiven." It wasn't entirely true. She didn't know if she could ever completely forgive him.

"Just like that." The air cracked with the snapping of his fingers. "Do you have any idea what I'm asking forgiveness for?"

She didn't. "Does it matter?"

"It matters to me."

Emily didn't want to have this conversation. She glanced over his shoulder toward the front door and safety. "I have to get back to work."

Determination etched itself into every line of his face. "When can I see you?"

"I don't want to see you, Robert." She would never heal if her ex-husband kept showing up, intent on probing old wounds. "We have nothing to discuss."

"You haven't forgiven me then. Maybe you never will." His voice was resigned. "Maybe you can't."

"Forgiving and forgetting are different things." Emily pushed back her chair, preparing for flight. "Is there anything else you want to say?"

Robert's jaw tightened. "I didn't think you could make it without my financial assistance."

Her eyes widened in surprise. "I'm managing quite well, thank you."

"I know that now." He took a quick sip of coffee. "Call it conceit, call it stupidity, but that's what I believed. I underestimated you in so many ways. I'm sorry."

She suspected his apology was nothing more than another attempt to ease his guilty conscience. "You can stop feeling guilty. I can make it on my own."

"So I observed. I'm also surprised at how soon you replaced me with another man." A touch of bitterness edged his voice. "You deserve better than Thad Thackeray."

"You don't know Thad."

"I know his reputation." Robert turned his cup around in its saucer. "You could get hurt, Emily."

Why did he insist on intruding into her life when he deliberately drove her from his? "It wouldn't be the first time." She grabbed her handbag and jumped to her feet. "I have to go."

"It's hopeless, isn't it?" Robert asked on a resigned sigh.

She had no idea what he was referring to and at this point, she couldn't afford to ask. "I'm afraid so." She left without looking back.

Once in her office, Emily put the incident from her mind. She worked steadily through the afternoon. By five o'clock, her monthly reports were complete. She was putting the last one into a folder when a knock on the door brought her head up. Kevin stood in the doorway, "Hi, Mom."

"Kevin! What a pleasant surprise. Come in. I was about to call it a day."

"Are you free for dinner?" He leaned against the doorframe and smiled down at her.

"As a matter of fact, I am. Larry is having dinner with the Carsons."

"Good. I have some news for you." When she lifted an eyebrow he added, "Some good news."

"You got the raise!" Emily exclaimed.

"That, too, but this is even better."

"What could possibly be better than a big fat raise?" Emily closed her desk drawer and shut down her computer.

"Come to dinner with me and I'll tell you."

His joyous attitude lifted Emily's spirits. "My mother's intuition tells me this has to do with affairs of the heart." She took his arm. "Am I right?"

"For an older woman, you're pretty sharp."

"Older woman indeed." Emily struck him playfully on his arm. "I will have you know I am in the prime of life."

"Looking at you now I can believe that." Kevin sobered. "You really are remarkable." The ghost of a grin pulled at his lips, "for an older woman."

They had dinner at a little seafood restaurant. Emily's suspicions were correct. They were scarcely seated at the table when Kevin said, "I've fallen in love, Mom. Her name is Stacy Morrison. She's beautiful and so sweet and loving. I want to spend the rest of my life with her."

The rest of his life, how blind could young love be? "How long have you known this woman?"

Kevin spread his napkin over his lap. "Not very long,"

Emily persisted, "How long is that?" Uneasiness challenged her sense of well-being.

Kevin kept his face behind his menu. "Four months. You should try the catfish. It's delicious."

"Four months!" Emily was flabbergasted. "Good heavens, Kevin, you can't be in love with someone you've known only four months."

"Yes, I can. I am." Kevin laid his menu aside. "I'm having the catfish."

Emily's overactive imagination conjured up visions of some *femme fatale* who had led her young son right down the garden path. "How old is this woman?"

He hung his head. "Almost nineteen."

"Almost nineteen," Emily echoed. "That means she's only eighteen-years-old. Eighteen is a child."

Kevin reminded her, "You were eighteen when you married Dad."

"Maybe you should listen to the voice of experience." A waiter appeared from nowhere to take Emily's order. She chose a seafood salad and waited as Kevin, after some hesitation, ordered catfish. As the waiter hurried away, she picked up the threads of their conversation. "I know now that I should have given myself more time to grow up before I jumped into marriage."

"Maturity is not a matter of age, Mom," Kevin argued in true attorney fashion, "it's a matter of experience and background. Stacy is mature."

It was not Stacy's maturity, or lack of it, that concerned Emily at the moment. Kevin was far too emotionally immature to be thinking about marriage. "I don't want you to rush into something you will regret later."

"Like you regret now that you married Dad?"

"I don't regret marrying your dad. We had some good years." She didn't want to talk about her failed marriage to her son, or to anyone else for that matter. "I'm only saying you should give yourself more time."

Kevin frowned. "I thought you would be happy for me."

The waiter reappeared with a tray of food. Not caring if he heard, Emily answered, "I am happy for you." She reached across the table and patted his hand. "Tell me about your Stacy."

Kevin's frown vanished. "As I was saying, she's almost nineteen. She's a student at City Business College. I met her through a mutual friend. It was love at first sight for both of us."

Emily's appetite diminished and threatened to disappear. "Does Stacy have a family?"

"Yes. I've only met them once, but they're very nice. I want you to meet them, too, and so does Stacy. She's dying to meet you."

Emily tried to match his enthusiasm. "Perhaps I should call Stacy's mother."

"Stacy's mother passed away some time ago." Kevin dumped catsup over his mound of fried catfish. "She lives with her father and her two younger sisters."

Emily asked, "Would you like me to invite them to the house some evening?" She couldn't shake a feeling of apprehension.

"You're really being nice about this, Mom." Kevin said between bites. "I was afraid you'd give me a bad time." He touched his napkin to his lips. "Stacy and I have talked about introducing our families to each other. We think it would be best if my family came to her home. Can we set a date for some time this week? I'd like to do it before Larry leaves for college."

Why did she feel she was being manipulated? "I have to know a few days in advance. I have so many evening commitments. Going out requires planning."

Chapter Ten

Without a moment's hesitation, Kevin asked, "How about next Tuesday evening?"

Emily nodded. "I could manage that. I don't know about Larry."

"I've talked to Larry." Kevin's relief was evident. "Tuesday is fine for him."

"Oh?" Emily lifted an eyebrow. So, her sons were co-conspirators in this little scheme.

"Larry knows Stacy." Kevin's voice gained momentum. "They went to high school together. He thinks Stacy and I were made for each other."

"Larry thinks anything you do is perfect." Emily pushed her salad away. "You are his big brother."

"I don't take that lightly," Kevin assured her. "I'm not much of a role model, but I'll have to do now that he has no father."

Emily swallowed her outrage. "Larry does have a father. He sees Dad every other weekend."

"We're talking about role models, Mom." Kevin snorted his disapproval. "Not some middle-aged playboy."

Emily was appalled her older son would think such a thing, let alone voice that opinion. "I hope you haven't been saying things like this to Larry."

"I don't have to tell Larry how I feel about the old man. He knows."

It was an ill wind that blew no good. Their parents' divorce had brought Larry and Kevin closer. Since she'd promised herself she wouldn't interfere with Robert's relationship with his sons, Emily tactfully changed the subject. "Shouldn't you give me Stacy's address?"

"Larry knows the way." Kevin couldn't hide his elation. "You can ride over with him."

"I may have to drive directly from work."

"She lives at 241 Oakdale Drive. That's over in Northern Heights." Kevin scribbled the address on a napkin. "It's the house behind the Oakdale Community Church." He gave Emily the napkin. "Stacy's dad is the Reverend Dennis Morrison."

Reverend Morrison was a well-known and highly respected minister with a reputation for being very civic-minded. "Stacy's father is Dennis Morrison?" Emily couldn't keep the surprise out of her voice.

"Does that bother you?" Kevin asked.

"No." Emily couldn't believe that her son, who had always been, to say the least, on the wild side, would look twice at a minister's daughter, let alone contemplate spending the rest of his life with her. "Not if it doesn't bother you."

"It did, at first." Kevin admitted with a self-effacing grin.

"And now?"

"Is this some kind of third degree?" A note of agitation sounded through Kevin's bantering tone. Emily got the message. It said, don't intrude.

"I look forward to meeting Stacy and her father and her sisters." She tried to sound pleased. "I have to go. Larry will be home and wondering where I am."

Kevin helped her from her chair. "Mom, be happy for me."

"I am, Kevin. Truly, I am."

"Then try to sound like it. I'll see you Tuesday evening." He gave her arm a pat before saying good-bye.

Was she worrying needlessly? A little prod of apprehension wouldn't go away. Even from her skewed point of view, Kevin was an unlikely candidate for marriage, and to a minister's daughter who was only eighteen-years-old? The next day over lunch, Emily voiced her misgivings to Thad, who listened patiently and then suggested she adopt a wait and see attitude. "Sometimes those things that loom largest on the horizon of the future never come to pass."

Good advice, Emily decided, but she had trouble following it. Doubts kept creeping in at the oddest times and in the most unlikely places, like the following Friday evening.

Emily stood in the midst of a group of chattering people, munching an hors d'oeuvre, as her mind wandered back to her last conversation with Kevin. He had no qualms about what the future held. How could any human being be so sure about anything?

"Emily, I've been looking for you." Lee Morgan's voice brought her back to the present. He pushed his way through the group of people and stood beside her. "There's someone here I want you to meet." He took her arm.

They were half way across the floor, threading their way through the crowd, when Emily saw the profile of a tall man standing near the door. She sucked in her breath. "That's Robert."

"Who's Robert?" Lee slowed his advance.

"Robert is my ex-husband. He's here." He was the last person she'd expected to see.

"This is a cocktail party given by the Greater Chamber of Commerce." Lee moved through the crowd. "Everybody who is anybody is here."

Emily shook hands with the man Lee introduced as Mac Evans, as Lee explained, "Mac is a filmmaker. He does short films for Public Service ads on TV. He has some ideas he would like to talk over with you."

Mac looked more like an aging cowboy than a filmmaker. He held onto Emily's hand. "I'm scheduled to make some public service films spotlighting the city's libraries. I'd like your help."

Emily glanced at Lee before looking back to face the man she'd just met. "I can supply you with any information you need, Mr. Evans."

"Please call me Mac. Mr. Evans makes me feel like an old man." Mac dropped her hand. "No need to bother giving me information. Set a date to come to my studio. You can provide the information to the audience."

Emily looked again at Lee. He was smiling. "Mac heard you speak at the Rotary Club luncheon last week. He was impressed."

"Mac, please call me Emily." How did she gracefully refuse? "I am accustomed to public speaking, but I've never been on television."

"No need to worry," Mac assured her." You are a photographer's dream." He reached into his shirt pocket, pulled out a card, and held it in his extended hand. "Call me sometime next week and make an appointment." He smiled, revealing a row of beautiful white teeth. "Good-bye. See you soon."

Emily took the card and slipped it into her handbag. "I'll do that."

"Good job, Emily." Lee turned to go. "Thank you for agreeing to be a part of the commercial."

Emily hadn't agreed to anything. She had been railroaded into appearing in a TV commercial. When she went for her appointment with Mr. Evans, she would set him straight on several issues. She mingled with the crowd, and chatted with friends and associates, all the while wondering if Robert's being here was a coincidence. She had caught glimpses of him in a few other places during the past two months. *Don't be stupid.* She continued to circulate.

Much later that evening, Emily found her hosts, then Lee and said her good-byes.

She was opening her car door when the figure of a tall man emerged from the shadows and walked toward her.

The man was Robert. As he came nearer, she frowned. "You scared me."

"That was not my intention. We have to talk." His shadowed countenance was grim. "Since you refuse to answer my phone calls, this seemed my only alternative." He extended one hand. "Please don't run away."

Emily had no intention of running away. "We can't talk here." She couldn't imagine what he wanted, but it was becoming increasingly evident that he was not going to stop following her until she agreed to listen to what he had to say. "Name a time and a place and I'll be there."

"What's wrong with here and now?" He pointed toward her automobile. "We can sit in the car."

Maybe that was best. Anything to get this conversation over with if it had to take place. She got in the car, reached across, and unlocked the other door.

Robert came around the car, opened the door, and sat in the front seat beside her. "I feel like a fool, going to such lengths just to have a conversation."

"Is Susan inside waiting for you?" Emily put her key in the ignition. Why had she asked that?

Beams from a streetlight played across Robert's set features. "What I have to say has nothing to do with Susan."

Emily was skeptical. "Whatever it is, it must be important. You've been stalking me for weeks."

"That's ridiculous. I'm not a stalker." He rested his arm on the back of the seat.

"Do you deny you've been following me?"

"It's a free country." He turned his head and stared through the windshield. "I can't reach you at work. When I call your phone, I go straight to voice mail. You refuse to have anything to do with my family. You have cut me out of your life completely."

He was making it sound as if she left him. "As I recall, you are the one who wanted a divorce."

He stared at her with his eyes narrowed. "For more than a quarter of a century you have been a part of my life. A divorce doesn't mean we can't be friends. I hoped that after a while, we could let bygones be bygones and patch up our differences."

"If I'm not good enough to be your wife, why would you want me for a friend?"

Robert's voice was resigned. "It wasn't a question of being good enough."

"What was it?" she asked bitterly.

"We drifted apart. You had other interests that filled your life. Sometimes I felt like a chore you never quite got around to doing."

His words cut like a knife. She realized there might have been some truth in what he said. "Are you saying that I neglected you and took you for granted?" She fought a nagging suspicion she was guilty on both counts.

The muscles in Robert's face tightened. "I am not blaming you for what happened."

"But you said--" Emily began.

He interrupted her before she could complete her sentence. "I know what I said. It was not meant as a criticism. I admit I am the one who destroyed our marriage."

It didn't feel right to let him shoulder all the blame. "I suppose there are a lot of things I could have done better as well."

He smiled the saddest, most hopeless smile she had ever seen. "How tragic it is when something that once was alive and beautiful slowly dies away."

Was he telling her, as gently as he could, that the love he once had for her was gone forever? He was offering her friendship, but that was all he could give her. "We are not the first couple to fall out of love. We won't be the last."

After an awkward silence, she reached to turn on her ignition. "I have to go. Larry will worry."

Robert made no effort to get out of the car. "How is Larry doing?"

"He's okay." Emily dropped her hand. "Looking forward to college. He leaves next week."

"Does he? It seems like only yesterday that he was a toddler, walking around demanding that I carry him on my shoulders. Now he's ready to go off to college. Children grow up so fast."

"Too fast sometimes." Emily's hands rested on the steering wheel. "Larry's off to college and Kevin is thinking of getting married. Our sons are adults now."

"Kevin is getting married? I didn't know that." Robert's gaze sharpened. "When did this happen? Who is the woman?"

Emily assumed he did know, even though he and Kevin were no longer on speaking terms. "He's considering it. Didn't Larry tell you?"

"Larry doesn't talk to me anymore." There was resignation in Robert's voice and a touch of reproach, "Not about anything of importance anyway."

"Well..." Happy to be on safe ground again, Emily explained, "It seems Kevin met this woman, girl really. She's only eighteen. He says they're in love."

The tension between them lessened as Robert asked, "You don't believe they are? In love, I mean."

As she spoke, Emily realized that for the first time in a long time, she and Robert were communicating instead of firing words at each other. "I haven't met the girl. Her name is Stacy Morrison. She's a minister's daughter."

"You haven't seen them together?" Robert asked, "How can you be so sure they aren't in love?"

"She's young and apparently naive. You know how wild Kevin has always been and how fickle." That was a cruel assessment of her own flesh and blood. "After the newness wears off, he may find he acted hastily. I'm afraid he still thinks attraction is love."

"Are you going to try to dissuade him?"

"That would only make matters worse." If she had learned anything over the past few months it was that people did what they wanted to do, regardless of what anyone around them said or did. "I hope Kevin doesn't do something he will regret later."

"Sometimes a man is caught between a rock and a hard spot." There was a note of sadness in Robert's voice. "I miss my sons very much. I miss being a part of their lives."

"I know you must. I'm sorry."

"Are you, Emily?" he asked softly, doubtfully.

"You know I am." Robert's relationship with his sons was only one of the many things she would change if she could.

Robert's fingers played along the back of the car seat. "Maybe you would consider helping me win them back?"

"I don't know what I could do." Caution whispered in Emily's ear. His ever-moving fingers grated on her nerves. "Please move your hand. You're annoying me."

She saw in his expression the intent to argue. Instead, he moved his arm. "Sorry, maybe you can suggest something I can do."

Emily hesitated. "You know the old adage, give advice and buy a foe."

He slid his nervous fingers through the sides of his hair. "Are you refusing to help me?"

Did he think she was that spiteful and unfeeling? She wasn't, or at least she didn't want to be. "The first step would be getting them to accept Susan." It took every ounce of control she had to speak so calmly about his other woman. "Now that you and she are married, things have to change."

Moisture gathered in Robert's eyes. "My marriage to Susan didn't work."

Those words hit Emily like a thunderbolt. She wanted to ask why. She didn't. "But it's been less than a year."

"Nevertheless, it's over." He closed his eyes. "Susan is out of my life for good, or will be when our divorce is final."

Emily wondered if she ever knew the man who sat beside her. He tore the fabric of his life to shreds and lost so much he held dear for Susan Barrett. Now they were breaking up? So soon? "I'm sorry."

"Really?" He opened his eyes and looked at her. "I thought you'd be glad."

Why would she be glad to see him suffer? If he felt half the pain she experienced when he left her, he must be in agony. "Maybe there's hope for a reconciliation. If you're still in love--.".

"Love," he snorted. "I don't even know what the word means anymore."

"Perhaps..." Emily began.

"Drop it, Emily." Robert ordered. "Just let it go."

"I honestly am sorry things aren't working out between you." Was she out of her mind, offering sympathy to the man who betrayed her and walked out of her life without a backward look? Probably. She'd been told more than once she had too soft a heart.

Robert swallowed. "I'd like to mend the rift between me and my sons."

That was something Emily wanted, too, though more for the boys than for their father. "I'd like that, too."

"Do you think things can ever be the way they were before?"

She didn't. After another painful silence, she said, "No, but that doesn't mean they can't get better than they are now." *Things could hardly get worse.*

"What do you suggest I do?"

"Be patient. This estrangement didn't happen overnight. It will take time to mend."

Robert's voice quivered. "I have the rest of my life."

"It may take that long to reconcile with Kevin. Larry is not nearly so antagonistic toward you."

Robert reached out his hand as if to touch her and then let it fall to his side. "Have you and I resolved our differences?"

"As well as we ever can, but don't ask me to run interference for you with your sons. I don't want to get involved."

Robert leaned nearer. "We are talking about your children and their father. You are involved. You always will be."

After a moment's reflection, Emily was forced to agree. "What do you have in mind?"

A shadow of a smile crossed Robert's face. "Maybe we could demonstrate to Larry that we are on friendly terms again."

Her love for her son won over her fear of being hurt again. "You can come to dinner some night soon."

"I have a better idea. Do you remember how we drove to Austin with Kevin and helped him settle in his dorm?"

Nostalgia pulled Emily backward in time. "We were so proud of him and he was so excited."

Robert ran his hand along the back of the car seat. "Maybe we should do the same for Larry."

Emily pushed down an inner voice of caution. "I don't have time for-_"

"Not even for your son?" Robert's eyes held hers for a long moment.

"Why don't you take him? It will give you a chance to iron out some of your differences."

"The idea is to show Larry you and I are on friendly terms." He knew where she was most vulnerable.

"All right. I'll go."

"Thank you, Emily. I know I have no right to ask for your help, not after all I did to you."

She didn't need his sympathy. "Not all the recent changes in my life have been bad ones. I have a new career now and a new life."

Robert's voice was accusing. "You make the divorce sound like a blessing."

"Well, in God's hands even bad things work together for good."

"Do you still believe all that stuff we were taught as kids?"

"I do." Was he hurt or relieved? She couldn't tell. Pride brought her chin up and strengthened her voice. "In many ways my life is better than it ever was before. I've discovered I'm a very resourceful person. I can make it on my own."

He kept his face averted. "I hope that's true, but I worry sometimes. I don't want you to be hurt again."

Once again, she reminded him, "I'm no longer your concern."

From out of the blue, he blurted out, "You can't trust a man like Thad Thackeray."

She could have told him Thad was only a friend. Why should she? By his own admission, Robert's love for her died a slow death. It soothed her battered self-image to have him believe another man might care. "I've learned not to expect too much from any man."

"I have no right to intrude into that area of your life, but--"

"That's right, you don't," Emily interrupted. "You're stretching the limits of friendship."

He shifted again and stared at her. "So, you do think we can be friends now?"

Emily squared her shoulders. "I hope so, for our children's sake."

In the dim light, his profile was grim. "Friendship is more than I have any right to expect." His hand rested on the door handle. "I'll call you next week."

Without saying good-bye, he got out of the car and walked away. Emily watched as he faded into the shadows. *What have I let myself in for?* She turned the key in the ignition. The car sputtered to life. She shifted gears and drove off into the night.

As she sped along the familiar freeway, a new doubt arose. Was she asking for more heartbreak? She turned off the freeway and onto a tree lined street. Her baby was going away to college. If she could see him start with some peace of mind, whatever the cost, it was worth it.

Emily pulled into the driveway and stopped the car. The lights in the living room were on. Larry was home. She took a deep breath, got out of her car, and walked toward the house.

Chapter Eleven

Dinner with the Morrisons was a pleasant occasion. Stacy was a charming young woman. Her sisters Amy and Kim were a delight. They were twins, barely thirteen years old and as alike in appearance as two peas in a pod. However, Emily soon discovered they were very different in temperament and personality. The Reverend Morrison was the perfect host, thoughtful and considerate, going out of his way to make them feel wanted and welcome. She doubted Dennis Morrison had the capacity to be unkind to anyone. Why then, did she feel uncomfortable in his presence? She tried to pinpoint the reason for her unrest. She couldn't. Those feelings were more a result of intuition than logic.

After an enjoyable meal Kim and Amy challenged Larry to a game of Stump the Wizard and dragged him off to the den. Stacy and Kevin decided to walk to the corner drug store to pick up a bridal magazine. Emily suspected they wanted some time alone. She couldn't blame them, but being left with Dennis Morrison, even for a short time, was awkward. Maybe she could make a quick exit as soon as Kevin and Stacy were gone. "If I'm gone when you return," she told Stacy, "I want you to know I had a lovely time."

"Thank you, Ms. Franklin. We loved having you." Stacy preceded Kevin out the door, leaving Dennis and Emily alone in the cozy living room of the parsonage.

Emily stirred restlessly. "They make a nice couple, don't you think?"

The Reverend was an exceptionally big man with a commanding presence, and none of the clumsiness that often plagued men of his size and stature. His natural elegance and warm personality added to his charm. He was also a disciplined man. No male Dennis Morrison's age stayed in such fine physical condition, or carried himself with such ease and grace, without a conscious effort to do so. "Kevin is not the kind of man I envisioned Stacy marrying." The words were spoken with bland indifference. Why then, did Emily perceive them as a rebuke?

"Doesn't Kevin measure up to your expectations?" Who was this man to find fault with her son?

"I have no doubt Kevin is a fine young man, Ms. Franklin. I worry more about the obvious differences between the two of them than I do about any character flaw Kevin might possess."

He did have a point. If the shoe was on the other foot and her very young daughter was contemplating marriage to a man of Kevin's age and background she would be concerned. "Perhaps you are worrying needlessly. There isn't a wide disparity in Kevin and Stacy's background. They are both Protestants. They are of the same socioeconomic status."

"Perhaps I am being an overprotective father." Dennis ran his hand through his silvery gray hair and smiled. "I've been accused of that. Since Ellen's death the girls are all I have."

"Ellen was your wife?" Emily could sympathize with someone who lost a mate.

"For almost twenty years," Dennis replied. "She died four years ago."

Emily's annoyance evaporated. "You still miss her, don't you?"

"Not a day goes by that I don't think of her."

Would she still be missing Robert four years from now? She empathized with the melancholy man sitting across from her. "Those poignant recollections come at the most unexpected and inconvenient moments."

The Reverend nodded his head in understanding. "Stacy told me of your recent divorce. It sounds trite I know, but the first year is the hardest. The first few months after Ellen's death, I almost lost my mind. Every birthday, every holiday, every special occasion was a cross to bear. I finally sought counseling to help me cope."

Here is someone who understands. "I'm discovering that, but I'm learning to take things one day at a time. It helps to have a friend I can talk to." Not for the first time, she was thankful for Thad. Debra hardly spoke to her anymore, and the couples she and Robert used to socialize with had nothing to do with her after the divorce. "I have a new job and of course, there are the boys."

Dennis tented his fingers and stared over them into Emily's troubled face. "Even surrounded by work and family, there are times you feel completely alone."

For the first time in a long time Emily was talking to someone who knew her pain from experience. "Sunday afternoons are the worst for me." She was wallowing in self-pity. "Forgive me. I didn't mean to sound maudlin."

"Sunday afternoon can be a maudlin time if you're alone." A minute ticked by before the Reverend added, "Ms. Franklin, Emily--may I call you Emily?"

"Please do."

"You must call me Dennis." He smiled, untented his fingers and leaned back in his chair. "We're almost related."

"Dennis it is."

A smile spread across his face. "Emily." He spoke her name slowly. "I lead an encounter group of recently divorced and widowed partners. We meet in the recreation hall of the church every Sunday afternoon. Would you like to join us next Sunday?"

"I wouldn't want to impose."

He smiled. "I'm really not that formal and you wouldn't be intruding. We would love to have you."

It was all the encouragement Emily needed. "I'd love to come. Robert, my ex-husband, and I are driving Larry to Austin next weekend. I'll make it a point to be back for the meeting. What time does it start?"

"We meet at three o'clock each Sunday afternoon." Dennis smiled. "I look forward to you being there."

"I look forward to attending," Emily told him sincerely. She welcomed a chance to make new friends and visit new places.

Thirty minutes later, when Larry came back into the room, she suggested they go home.

Larry was reluctant to leave. "How," he asked Dennis, "can two little girls look so much alike and be so different? Amy is a genius at answering literary questions, and Kim is a math and science whiz."

"Ah, son, you don't know the half of it, in every way Kim and Amy are as different as day and night."

Larry and Emily said their polite good-byes and took their leave. They were in the car driving home when Larry commented. "It would have been nice to have a younger brother or sister when I was growing up."

A lump rose in Emily's throat. "I agree."

"Why didn't you have more children after me?"

"When we had you, we decided we'd come as near to perfection as we could get. We quit while we were ahead."

"Ah, Mom." Larry turned his head to one side and smiled. "That's not an answer."

It was all the answer he was going to get. Emily changed the subject. "Are you ready to go to Austin?"

"This is only Tuesday. We don't leave until Saturday. I have plenty of time." Larry stopped for a red light before glancing in Emily's direction. "I'm glad you and Dad are coming with me. Dad says you will be staying in Austin overnight. Does that mean--?"

Emily interrupted. "It means I have to take Boo to the boarding kennel Saturday morning."

The light changed and the car moved forward. "Mom, you know what I'm asking." Larry's knuckles whitened on the steering wheel. "Are you and Dad...did you and Dad *really* make up?" A ruddy blush stained his cheeks. "I thought maybe--"

She couldn't allow him to hold on to false hope. "Dad and I have rooms at the Ambassador Motel, separate rooms."

"But Dad left his--" Larry paused before saying, "Dad said Susan is divorcing him."

"That doesn't mean that he and I are together." The kindest thing she could do was make Larry understand that his parents were not going to reconcile. "We aren't and we never will be again."

Larry's shifted gears with a vengeance, "Never?"

"Darling, try to understand. Susan wasn't the only problem between Dad and me."

Larry pulled into the driveway and stopped his car. "Don't you love Dad anymore?"

Emily's heart ached for her son. "There are so many factors involved in a marriage. I--" How inadequate she felt. "We both love you very much and we always will."

"But do you want Dad back?" Larry persisted.

She didn't know the answer to that question. Maybe she never would. "I don't know." That was as near to the truth as she could get at this stage in her life. "When I know more, I'll give you a definite answer."

Larry unfastened his seat belt. "Kevin said you don't. He said you couldn't, not after the terrible things Dad did to you. I didn't believe him."

"Don't judge your father." *He broke my heart and shattered my life.* "When a marriage ends, there's blame on both sides. "

"You don't hate him?" Larry's voice lifted in surprise. Her young son did have a way of cutting to the heart of a problem.

"I could never hate Dad." She kept her tone light. "We have settled our differences. We're friends, but that's all."

Larry sniffed. "You aren't unhappy now?"

She wasn't unhappy. She couldn't say she was happy, either. "I am content. I have a job I love, two fine sons and my health. What else could I ask for?"

Larry said, "I'm glad we had this talk. I can tell Kevin now that you're happy, because you are, aren't you?"

"I count my blessings every day." Emily opened her car door. "Let's get inside. I have a million things to do."

Emily pondered Larry's question far into the night, making sleep difficult. Her life was changing. She wasn't sure of so many things. One thing she did know for certain. She would never again depend on a man to define her.

Chapter Twelve

In the bright light of the next morning as Emily prepared breakfast, she thought back over the night before. Larry's question about happiness made her come to grips with no longer knowing what she felt for Robert.

Larry called from the other room, "Mom, I can't find my baseball cap." He stuck his head around the door. "I've looked everywhere."

"Even on the hook in your closet?"

A wry grin spread across Larry's young face. "The one place I forgot to look." He pulled out a chair and sat at the table. "What are you doing?"

"Making coffee," Emily replied, "and thinking about last night."

"Did you like the Morrisons?"

"I thought they were very nice." What a moth-eaten statement that was.

Larry poured cold cereal into a bowl. "Kim and Amy said I was the first college man they had ever known personally."

Emily smiled. "Made you feel important, huh?"

"Yeah, sort of." He spooned sugar over his cereal and reached for the milk. "I should be home early today. Do you want me to start dinner?"

"If you'd like." She threw Larry a kiss. "See you tonight."

Once inside her office, Emily put her personal problems aside and applied herself to the tasks at hand. The morning flew. Before she knew it, lunchtime had arrived. This was Wednesday. Emily felt a tingle of anticipation. Thad would be waiting for her at the diner.

She found him seated at what they had begun to refer to as their table. When she entered the restaurant, he waved to her.

Emily waved back, feeling a little surge of happiness as she did so. Thad was good for her morale. She slipped into the chair across from him. "It's good to see you."

He smiled. "Howdy, Buddy. I ordered for you. The house special today is veal cutlets. I know that's one of your favorites."

"Thank you." Emily settled back in her chair.

They talked, as they always did, of events and happenings from the past week. Thad told Emily of an especially exciting court case he won and provided some sketchy details about a wild encounter with a crooked judge. His vivid descriptions left Emily in stitches. When she could stop giggling, she declared, "You make up these stories, or at least heavily embroider them."

Thad raised his right hand. "Upon my oath as an honest man, I swear." His hand dropped to his side. "How was your dinner with the Morrisons?"

"It was nice and it got better." After describing her evening with Dennis Morrison, Emily told Thad of her meeting with Robert. She finished by adding. "Susan is divorcing Robert. I gather she dumped him."

Thad didn't pull any punches. "Is that why the two of you are going away for the weekend?"

"We aren't going away for a weekend." Emily's mind lingered briefly over the last time Robert took her away for the weekend. "No more weekend trips with Robert, ever."

"You're staying overnight." Thad inclined his head and widened his eyes.

"That's only because we are spending the entire day with Larry. Robert thinks it would be better to rest overnight and drive back the next morning."

"Don't you think you might be tempting fate, staying overnight in the same motel as your ex-husband?"

Emily smiled. "Robert wants nothing more from me than friendship."

Thad cut into his steak. "How can you be sure?

"He told me so." Emily's smile vanished. "Robert doesn't love me. I sometimes wonder if he ever did. I'm not sure whether or not I love him anymore."

"Do you want my opinion?" Thad chewed thoughtfully.

"I put great store by your opinions and your advice."

"I don't think he ever stopped loving you, and I wouldn't be surprised to find you care for him."

Emily almost choked on her food. "Don't be absurd."

Thad shrugged. "Sorry if I hit a sore spot." He laid his fork on the table. "So, what else is new?"

"So much for your flawless opinions," Emily teased. "I still put great stock in your advice, some of which I need now."

"Shoot." Thad held up one hand. "I didn't mean that literally."

Again, Emily laughed. "What would I do without you?"

"Hire an attorney?" Thad quipped with a quizzical lifting of his shaggy eyebrows. "Without you, I would have to begin writing Dear Abby again."

When their laughed died down, Emily asked in sober tones. "How much is my house worth at present market prices?"

"You're thinking of selling?" Thad pushed his plate back and reached for his dessert. "Are you moving into an apartment?"

"I'm not the apartment type and neither is Boo. I want a smaller house, one nearer the city, but in a good neighborhood."

"Boo?" Thad stuck a fork in his sticky dessert before pushing it aside, "Your dog?"

"It may sound silly and sentimental, but I am very fond of Boo."

"Sentimental, yes. Silly, no. You are such a paradox. Do you want me to help you sell your house?"

She wasn't about to ask him why he thought her a paradox. He would tell her and it might not be something she wanted to hear. "Do you know the name of a reputable realtor?"

"Isn't Robert a realtor?"

She knew he knew the answer to his question. "I don't need my ex-husband's help to sell my home."

Thad glanced at his watch. "Okay, Buddy. I'll see what I can do. I have to run now." He waved to her and was gone.

True to his word, Thad called the next evening. "I tentatively listed your house with Mercer Realty. It's a very reputable firm. All you have to do is go by the office, sign the necessary papers, and leave a key. You're in luck. Houses in your area are in great demand right now. They would like permission to start showing the place immediately."

"I can come in the first of next week." The thought of actually giving up the house that had been her home for so many years was a little scary. "Is that all right?"

Perceptive Thad picked up on her doubts immediately. "If you're sure that's what you want to do."

She couldn't retreat now. "I'm sure." After she put away her phone, Emily stood for a long time staring into space. For the first time in her life, she made a big decision independently and then acted on it, but not without calling her choice into question. Was she doing the right thing? *I'm selling a house, not making some life-or-death determination.* She squared her shoulders. "I'll go in the first thing Monday morning."

Emily spent Saturday morning helping Larry sort through the odds and ends he didn't want to take to Austin. The two of them carried several boxes to the attic. As she stared around the cluttered room, a sobering thought hit her. When she sold the house, she would have to do something with this collection of relics from the past.

"Mom," Larry's voice impinged on her straying thoughts, "I asked a question."

Emily put her hand to the small of her back and stretched. "Sorry, what did you say?"

"Do you want me to stack these boxes in that corner?" He pointed to a space at the far end of the attic.

"No." Emily shook her head. "Leave them where they are."

"Won't they be in the way?" He set his boxes on the floor.

"Not for long." Emily surveyed the cluttered attic with mild disdain. This mess had to go.

"I hope you aren't thinking of trying to straighten this place after I'm gone." Larry turned an empty crate on its end, and sat on it. "You shouldn't be lifting all these heavy boxes and trunks."

Emily's heart expanded with love. "Don't worry, if--I mean, *when* I clean the attic, I'll find someone to help me."

"Do you promise?" Larry scrutinized the attic and shook his head. "This place is a mess."

"I promise. Let's get ready to go to Austin. Dad will be here soon."

They were ready and waiting when Robert arrived. It took some time to load Larry's things into Robert's car. Emily made iced tea and they sat around the kitchen table, sipping tea and reminiscing. It was almost as if they were a family again.

Emily opted to sit in the back seat for the long drive to Austin, insisting that Larry share the front seat and the last hours with his father before he took up residence in another city.

The trip was pleasant enough. So was the long day they spent with Larry. As the time drew near to say good-bye, Emily braced herself for this last parting. By the time the last farewells were said and the final admonitions and reminders exchanged, she was as taut as a bowstring.

Robert was silent during the drive to the motel. Did he feel as nervous and uncertain as she did?

They were parking before a row of motel doors when Robert asked, "Are you all right?"

"I'm tired," Emily admitted, "and feeling let down. It wasn't this hard to let Kevin go."

"Things were different then." Robert opened his car door. "You should get straight to bed. This was a trying day."

"Kevin was different." Emily spoke her thoughts, "Not nearly as vulnerable and naive as Larry is." Also, she'd never expected to be alone in an empty nest.

"Larry will manage." Robert got out of the car, and came around to open her door. Emily thought that strange. He had never opened doors for her, not even when they were dating.

Emily got out of the car. "I'll feel better tomorrow, after I've had a good night's sleep." She opened her handbag and retrieved her key card. "Good night, Robert."

He took her arm. "I'll see you to your room."

"That's not necessary." She didn't try to pull away from him.

"I happen to think it is." He guided her toward her door.

Emily was too tired to argue. "Do you really think Larry is going to be all right?"

"I'm sure of it." Robert took the card from her and inserted it in the slot. "I'm not so sure about you." The door opened with a little click. He ushered her inside. "Sit down. I'll get your overnight bag."

When Robert returned, Emily was on the bed with pillows propped behind her back. She had kicked off her shoes and let her hair down. "Put the bag on the dressing table. I'll rest for a moment before I dress for bed."

Robert stood in the middle of the room, staring at her. "You've lost weight."

She was surprised he noticed. "Not too much, I hope."

"No. You look...no. Not at all." Uninvited, he sat in a chair. "Your hair is longer, too. Why did you decide to let it grow?"

She combed her fingers through her thick tresses. "A desire for change, I suppose."

"It looks very nice." His glance slid over her slim figure. "You look nice."

His unexpected compliment caught her off guard. Robert Franklin was not a man given to flowery speeches or pretty words. "I'm glad you approve." For the briefest moment their eyes met. Emily looked away. "I hope Larry doesn't get too homesick."

Robert's voice was gruff. "Larry will be making new friends and meeting challenging demands. He will soon adjust to his new routine."

"I'm going to miss him," Emily said. "I'm so used to having him underfoot. Home won't be the same without him around."

Robert settled back in his chair. "I hate to think about you rattling around in that big old house all alone."

"I won't be for long." Should she tell him she was going to sell the house?

Under his tan Robert turned a pasty white. "What does that mean?"

He would disapprove. So what? "It means I'm not going to be living alone in that big house much longer."

"Don't tell me the elusive Thaddeus Thackeray popped the question."

It took a while for his words to sink in. "Do you think I would marry a playboy like Thad?" Emily laughed. "When pigs fly."

"You're going to live with him without benefit of matrimony?" Robert's brows met in a scurrilous frown. "I would have thought better of you."

Surprise tilted her voice. "I'm not going to live with Thad, period." She swung her feet to the floor. "Is the pot calling the kettle black?"

Robert ignored her insult. "Do you know the kind of reputation Thad Thackeray has? Emily, you're not the only woman the man is seeing."

Sudden anger took her. "The last time we were alone in a motel room, you told me you were seeing another woman. We weren't divorced then. We are now, and you are finding fault with *my* behavior?" Before the words were out of her mouth, she repented of having said them. She put her hand to her forehead. "That was uncalled for."

His mouth thinned. "I asked for it."

How many times had she promised she would not be unkind? "Let's forget Thad and talk about something else."

Robert offered an apology, of sorts. "I didn't mean to be offensive, but when you said you weren't going to be living alone, I assumed you would be living with Thad."

"I'm not going to be living with anyone, except Boo." Emily took a deep breath. "I've listed the house. I'm going to sell it and buy a smaller place."

Chapter Thirteen

Robert leaned forward in his chair and gasped. "You're going to sell our home?"

"*Our* home?"

Robert cleared his throat. "Excuse me. Your home. I know how much you love that house. You always said it was perfect."

"It was, when I had a family. I'm alone now." When would he realize that she was capable of making her own decisions?

"Maybe you won't always be alone."

What could he possibly mean by a statement like that? "I'm going to sell the house," Emily told him with a stubborn lift of her chin.

"Maybe you should think about it for a while first."

"I have thought about it. My mind is made up."

On a resigned sigh, Robert asked, "Why didn't you list the house with me?"

"Because I knew you would do what you're doing now, try to talk me out of selling."

"Which, obviously, I can't do," he observed with a touch of bitterness. "Who has the listing?"

"Will you stop giving me the third degree? Thad says it's a very reputable company."

For a moment she thought he was going to yell at her. "You went to Thad Thackeray who knows nothing about the real estate business when you could have come to me. Why?"

"For all the obvious reasons, the main one being, Thad's a friend, you're my ex-husband."

He shot back angrily, "You said we could be friends."

The sudden harshness of his voice startled her. "We can be." It would be useless to try to explain. "Friends should respect each other's decisions.

Obviously, this is another one of the things we can't talk about rationally. Good night, Robert."

He didn't stir. "Does Larry know you're selling the house?"

"Not yet. I didn't want to upset him further."

Robert's anger seemed to evaporate, only to be replaced with concern. "Larry was upset? About what?"

"Nothing important," Emily assured him.

"But you *are* going to tell me what that 'nothing important' is?" He glared at her. "Right?"

Maybe she owed him that much. "When I told Larry about our plans to come to Austin with him, he jumped to a lot of conclusions. He thought because we were staying overnight we would be staying together."

Robert's brows pulled into a frown. "What made him think that?"

"It was more a hope than a thought. I assured him it was not going to happen. He was upset at first. I explained that we no longer loved each other, but that we both loved him very much." She shook her head. "Sometimes I wish Larry could be a little tougher and a little more pragmatic."

"A little more like Kevin?" Robert asked.

How well he read her thoughts. "Yes. A little more like Kevin."

"Speaking of Kevin, Larry said the two of you met Stacy Morrison." Robert ran his fingers over the beginning stubble on his chin. "What do you think of her?"

"She's a very nice young woman," Emily answered, happy to change the subject. "A little more mature than I thought at first."

"And her family?" Robert asked anxiously, "What are they like?"

"They're very nice, too." Once again, Emily leaned back and relaxed against the pillows. "She has thirteen-year-old twin sisters who completely charmed Larry. The Reverend Morrison seemed almost formidable at first. I don't think he approves of Kevin."

Robert hung onto her every word. "Did he say that?"

"No. It was just an impression."

Robert asked, "Do you like the Reverend?"

"I don't know him. I suspect that much of what Dennis Morrison projects to the casual acquaintance is a façade acquired from years of meeting and dealing with people when they are at their worst both emotionally and spiritually." The shadow of a smile pulled at Emily's lips. "What he lacks in charisma, he makes up for in appearance. He's incredibly handsome."

Robert put his hands on his knees and narrowed his eyes. "When did you start noticing handsome men?"

"When I was about twelve and I began to notice you." Reminiscence made her smile.

For the first time since he came into her room, Robert smiled, too. "I never knew that."

"You would have if you had stopped to look around you. It was the summer our parents rented a house on Padre Island. You were seventeen and too busy being the heart throb of every teenage girl on the beach to notice me."

"I did notice you, later."

"How much later?" Emily asked.

"The year you were sixteen and I came home from college for the summer. I couldn't believe my little sister's skinny freckled-faced friend had turned into a ravishing red-haired beauty."

He never told her that before either. "I never knew."

Robert sighed. "Even then we didn't communicate very well."

They were communicating now. How sad that love had to die before understanding could take root. Warmth flooded into Emily's cheeks. "I hated all those buxom, bikini-clad teenage beauties you hung out with."

"As much as I hated Andrew Rawlins?" An ironic grin stretched Robert's lips.

She had forgotten about Andrew. "I thought I was in love with Andrew. When he dumped me for Cynthia Connelly, I cried for days."

Robert settled back in his chair. "When I asked you about Andrew, you told me you dumped him."

"I was too proud to admit the truth." Emily put her hand over her mouth to stifle a yawn. "Cynthia was willing to 'put out' as Andrew so crudely put it. I wasn't."

"I thought you slept with Andrew," Robert admitted with a rueful smile. "I was surprised when I discovered you were a virgin. We were great together back then." His voice caught. "Where did we lose the magic?"

She wished she could pinpoint the exact time his love for her died. "Maybe it began when we started taking each other for granted." Was there anything more heart-rending than perfect hindsight?

He lifted his head to stare at the ceiling. "At first, I blamed you because our marriage failed. The night I came to the house for my things, you laid that idea to rest forever. What you said forced me to take a long hard look at myself. I didn't like what I saw.

Their marriage died, not with a bang, but a whimper. There seemed no point in poking around in the ashes of a dead fire. Emily yawned again. "It's very late."

Sudden tension rose and crackled between them.

Robert's voice was taut. "It's too late, isn't it?"

Emily kept a tight rein on her emotions. Maybe there had been other affaires besides the one with Susan, a topic she did not wish to explore. Her feelings for Robert were like Humpty Dumpty, shattered with parts missing. "I don't have answers anymore."

He pushed himself to a standing position. "Is there any way I can persuade you not to sell the house?"

"I wish you wouldn't try." Despair filled her heart. He had shed his past as a snake sheds its skin. Why should she be shackled to hers? Troubled by the painful look in his eyes, she added, "For goodness' sake, it's only a house."

His shoulders slumped. "Whatever." Without another word, he went out the door and closed it behind him. She listened to his fading footsteps until they were swallowed up in the sounds of a city night. Sleep was a long time coming.

Chapter Fourteen

The drive home from Austin was surprisingly pleasant. Neither Robert nor Emily mentioned their conversation from the night before. They talked instead of Larry and Kevin, the weather, current events, and even reminisced a little about old times.

As they turned off the main thoroughfare Robert asked, "Would you like to stop somewhere for lunch?"

Emily glanced at her watch. "I can't. I have a two-thirty appointment."

"With Thad?" Robert asked. Before she could answer, he added, "I shouldn't have asked that."

"It's not with Thad." Emily stared out the car window. "The Reverend Morrison invited me to a church function."

Without the slightest hesitation Robert asked, "What kind of a church function?"

Emily shifted in her seat. "Reverend Morrison leads an encounter group each Sunday afternoon at his church." She thought he would ask what kind of encounter group. He didn't.

They rode several miles in silence before Robert asked, "When is the meeting over?"

"Around five." What did he want now?

"Are you free after that?"

"Why do you ask?"

"Would you like to come with me to visit Mom and Dad?"

Emily hadn't seen George and Clara in months. Still, she was reluctant. "I would feel out of place there now."

"You shouldn't. They ask about you often." Robert's voice was persuasive. "They miss you."

Against her better judgment, Emily acquiesced. "I guess so. All right."

A note of triumph sounded in Robert's words. "I'll pick you up around six."

Emily got home just in time to make preparations to leave again. She showered and dressed, wondering which was worse, a lonely Sunday afternoon or one laden with stress from an overloaded schedule. She arrived at the church just as the encounter group's session was beginning.

Dennis hurried toward her as she came into the room. "We were about to start without you." He grasped her hand in a warm handshake. "Come in and I'll introduce you to the group."

The meeting was not what Emily expected. It was more like a social gathering than a structured therapeutic session. The participants sat in a semi-circle, talking freely about a variety of subjects, with Dennis facilitating. Emily was impressed with his ability to guide a conversation unobtrusively.

The openness of the group members surprised Emily. "If I'd been as nice to my first wife as I was to my second wife, I never would have had a second wife," a balding man commented.

There was comfort in realizing she was not alone when a woman talked about her husband leaving her for someone younger.

All too soon the meeting was over. As the participants drifted out the door, Dennis caught Emily's arm. "Stay for a few minutes, if you have the time. I would like to talk to you."

Emily glanced at her watch. "I was wondering how I was going to kill the next thirty minutes." She leaned against a kitchen counter and watched as Dennis adroitly herded two gushing women across the room.

After smoothly curtailing what could have been a lengthy good-bye, he ushered them out the door, came back across the room, and leaned against the counter beside Emily. "I thought they'd never go."

Emily's eyes sparkled with humor. "You've had a lot of experience at this, haven't you?"

Dennis feigned a frown. "At what?"

A mischievous smile pulled at Emily's mouth, "At fighting off aggressive females."

His laughter rippled out into the room. "It's all a part of being a pastor. Would you like more coffee?"

"Yes, please." The Reverend Morrison had a knack for putting her at ease.

Dennis poured coffee into two Styrofoam cups. "There's more cake. Would you like another piece?"

Emily took the cup from his hand. "No thanks."

"Shall we sit down?" He pointed to a table in the corner and waited until she was seated before he slipped into a chair across from her. "How was your trip to Austin?"

It was a question she hadn't expected. "All right, I suppose."

"Only all right?" His hands wrapped around his coffee cup. "I take it there's no reconciliation in the offing?"

From anyone else that question would have been intrusive. From Dennis Morrison it seemed quite acceptable. "No. That part of my relationship with Robert is over."

"How can you be so sure?" His grip on his coffee cup was the only sign of some inward tension. "In the meeting you mentioned his marriage to the other woman is breaking up."

Emily stared down at the bare third finger of her left hand. "My feelings for Robert have changed. It's very confusing. I'm hoping someday to forgive him, but I cannot forget. I've really struggled, wondering if it's my Christian obligation to take him back. But I can't trust him with my heart again. I suspect he is still in love with Susan."

Dennis raised one eyebrow. "Did he tell you that?"

"He didn't have to." Emily took a quick sip of coffee. She found it so easy to open up and talk to Dennis. "I've known him since we were kids."

"Obviously he 'played around' at least once." Dennis observed.

Emily shook her head. "That's the point. I don't think he was playing around."

Dennis's smile invited confidence. "Middle-aged men often get caught up in trivial infatuations that don't last."

"Not Robert." Was she defending her ex-husband? No, she was telling the truth, as she knew it. She paused, uncertain whether to bare her soul to this man. "I have a suspicion Robert may have had a fling or two in the past. But this time he broke up our family and married Susan. That proved he had no plans to come back to me."

"If he had, would you have taken him back?" Dennis asked softly.

Emily tried to put her thoughts in order, and failed. "Maybe, if he'd come back immediately, while I was so vulnerable. Not now. If it had been a middle-aged infatuation, that would make me feel better, but I don't believe it was. I do feel sorry for him occasionally." She pushed her cup back. "Most of the time I'd like to give him a swift kick in the rear."

"If Robert is set on winning Susan back, why isn't he pursuing her instead of spending his time trying to get back into your good graces?"

"Our divorce caused quite a rift between Robert and his sons, especially Kevin. He's trying very hard to win them back. He thinks I can help him do that."

"Do you feel he's using you?"

That candid question stung, since it precisely summed up Emily's suspicion. "Maybe he is. Anyway, our marriage is over but we're trying to be friends."

"You are one complicated lady." Dennis reached across the table and touched her hand. "He was a fool to let you go." His fingers wrapped around her wrist. "I have something of a personal nature to say to you."

Emily's heart beat a little faster. "Is this about Kevin and Stacy?"

His fingers tightened. His touch was warm and comforting. "I'm trying to find a way to ask you to go out with me. It's been so long since I asked a woman for a date that I seem to have forgotten how."

Emily was at once flattered and flabbergasted. "You want a date with me?" Dennis Morrison could ask any one of a dozen women out and be rewarded with an immediate yes. "Why me?"

Dennis released her hand. "I like you and I admire you." He fitted his broad shoulders against the back of his chair. "I'm receiving an award from the Houses for Humanity Organization for my part in helping raise money to build houses for homeless families in this area. I would consider it an honor if you would accompany me to that ceremony."

Emily studied his handsome face before scanning his muscular physique. At least he wasn't the type to try getting her to go to bed with him. "I'd like that, too. When is this gala event to take place?"

"The first Saturday evening of next month. Can you make it?"

"I think so. I usually have Saturday evenings free." Emily looked at the clock on the wall. "I have to run."

"One other thing..." Standing, Dennis pushed his chair back. "Stacy and Kevin will be attending the banquet also. Are you comfortable with that?"

Emily blinked. "I don't know how Kevin will feel about his mother dating his future father-in-law."

"I was thinking of it more as a family outing." After some hesitation, Dennis said, "The twins will be with me, too, and I'd be pleased if you'd bring Larry."

Emily was beginning to understand why he asked her to go with him. Where else could he find a woman willing to go out with a man who insisted on taking his entire family and a prospective in-law along on a first date? "I'll talk to Kevin."

"Kevin thinks it's an excellent idea." Dennis flashed his charming smile. "So does Stacy, and the twins are elated."

She was going to be late for her appointment with Robert. Emily picked up her handbag. "I'm very pleased you invited me."

Somewhere down the hall a door slammed. Over that disconcerting sound, Dennis asked, "You will go, won't you?"

Emily backed toward the entrance. "I'd be happy to go with you and your family. Good-bye, Dennis. Thanks for a most interesting afternoon."

Chapter Fifteen

Robert's car was parked in front of her house when Emily pulled into her driveway. Before she could set the brake and open the door, he was out of his vehicle and striding across the lawn. "I was beginning to worry about you."

Emily stepped onto the driveway. "I visited with Dennis for a while after the meeting." She glanced at her watch. It was only six-ten. "Have you been waiting long?"

"About ten minutes." He took her arm. "Are you ready to go?"

If she went inside, Robert would go with her, which she didn't want. "I'm ready."

George and Clara's restrained greeting made Emily sense they were expecting her. Later, in the kitchen, she asked Clara, "Did you know I was coming out here with Robert?"

Clara straightened from putting dishes in the dishwasher. "Robert called earlier. I hope this means my son has finally come to his senses."

Emily didn't want Clara entertaining false hopes. "We have agreed to be friends for the boys' sake. Robert wants to resolve his differences with his sons. He thinks I can help him do that. I'm doing this for my sons." *Was she? How long would she be in this confused state before she got her life back on an even keel?*

"I was hoping that you and Robert were getting together again." Clara's eyes, so like Robert's, filled with tears. "Since you claim to be a Christian, I know you don't believe in divorce. Am I prying where I shouldn't?"

"I know you mean the best, Clara, but yes, you are." Emily had only spoken the truth. Why did she feel as if she had committed a crime?

"I won't interfere again, my dear. But that doesn't mean I will stop hoping." Clara untied her apron and laid it on the counter. "Shall we go into the living room?"

The remainder of the evening passed swiftly. They were in Robert's car and pulling from his parents' driveway when he asked, "Did you enjoy the evening?"

"There were a few uncomfortable moments. I suppose that was to be expected."

"My parents still think of you as part of the family."

It occurred to Emily that her ex-in-laws were only concerned about their son. What she wanted was the least of their priorities. "They will get over that, eventually."

Robert glanced briefly in her direction. "Why should they?" He turned his gaze back to the road.

Going with Robert to visit Clara and George was a mistake, one she knew she should not repeat. "Because we are divorced and you are married to someone else." She covered her mouth to stifle a yawn.

Robert asked, "Are you tired or just bored?"

He was terribly touchy. "I'm tired. It's been a long day."

They were pulling into Emily's driveway when Robert asked, "Do you want me to go inside with you?"

That was the last thing she wanted. "I'm too tired to entertain a visitor tonight."

Robert was bent on arguing. "I'm concerned about you going into a dark, deserted house alone at this hour of the night."

"The house is locked." Emily felt around in her handbag for her keys. "Boo is inside."

Robert scoffed. "Boo wouldn't bite a biscuit."

"I go into the house alone every night." Why couldn't he believe that she could manage on her own? "I'm not afraid." She reached for the door handle. "Good night, Robert."

"Good night, Emily. I'll see you soon."

No, he wouldn't. She would see to that.

*****

106

Early Monday morning Emily sent Larry an e-mail telling him of her decision to sell the house. Later she called Kevin's office. The realtor's ad would appear in Wednesday's newspaper. She didn't want it to come as a surprise to either of her sons. "Do you have time to talk?" she asked Kevin when she got him on the line.

"I'm up to my neck in work." Kevin answered. "Can I call you back?"

Emily wouldn't be in her office for the rest of the day. "Better still, why don't you come to the house for dinner tonight?"

Impatience sounded in his reply. "I have a date with Stacy tonight."

"Bring her along," Emily suggested. "I'd love a chance to get to know her better."

"Actually..." There was an infinitesimal pause. "I'm going to Stacy's house. She's babysitting her sisters tonight. Her father is going out."

"Bring the twins and Stacy along with you." The thought of having teenagers in the house again was a pleasant one. "I'd love to have them."

Kevin seemed hesitant. "Are you sure? It wouldn't be too much trouble?"

"I'm looking forward to it. I'll see you this evening around six." Emily hung up before Kevin had time to argue.

Through the remainder of the day, Emily looked forward to the evening. She missed Larry and his noisy, boisterous friends. She made a list. There wouldn't be time to cook, but that didn't matter. Young people loved fast foods and take-outs.

The dinner menu was a combination of French fries, hero sandwiches, and soft ice cream. Emily had the deli throw in a vegetable salad for good measure. She made the drive home in record time and was putting the ice cream in the freezer when the doorbell rang.

She opened the front door to see Stacy and her sisters standing on the front porch. "Ms. Franklin." Stacy looked over Emily's shoulder and into the living room. "Kevin said we should meet him here. Are we too early?"

Emily swung the door open. "Not at all. Kevin should be here any minute. Won't you come in?"

Stacy came inside, followed by Kim and Amy. After a moment of awkward silence, Emily asked, "Won't you sit down?"

Boo, who had been asleep on the rug beside the couch, raised his head and wagged his tail.

Kim screamed with delight. "A dog! What's his name?"

Emily snapped her fingers and Boo came to her. "His name is Boo. Would you like to pet him?"

Kim stroked Boo's shiny coat. "He's so beautiful. How did he get the name Boo?"

"It's a long story," Emily replied, grateful that Boo was an ideal icebreaker. "He was a birthday present. At first, we had some idea of him being a watchdog. That was before we discovered that if someone said boo to him, he tucked his tail between his legs and ran away."

"I like him." Kim announced.

"May I pet him, too?" Amy asked.

"Of course, you may."

Stacy smiled at her sisters. "The twins love animals, especially dogs. They've always wanted one, but Dad doesn't think they're old enough for that kind of responsibility yet."

"Maybe you'd like to take Boo into the backyard and play with him?" Emily suggested as the twins continued to stroke Boo and talk to him.

"Could we?" Kim asked. She was halfway out the door.

Amy turned as she followed her sister outside. "Thank you, Ms. Franklin."

Stacy was still smiling when she asked, "May I help you in the kitchen?"

Over the sound of Kevin's car stopping in the driveway, Emily answered, "Everything is ready."

Dinner was relaxed and pleasant. The twins were delighted to have hero sandwiches and French fries for dinner.

Afterward they offered to help Emily clear away the dishes. "That was an awesome meal, Ms. Franklin." Kim remarked as she dumped paper plates into the waste can. "Our housekeeper never makes sandwiches for dinner."

"I'm glad you enjoyed it." Emily put lids on half-filled containers. "Why don't you call me Emily? Ms. Franklin makes me feel positively ancient."

"I don't think Daddy would approve," Amy answered.

"I'll be almost family when Stacy marries my son," Emily said. "I don't think your dad would object. If he does, I'll explain I prefer to be called Emily."

"All the same, we'd better ask first," Kim chimed in.

Kevin and Stacy disappeared into the living room. Kim looked around to make sure they were out of earshot before she asked, "Ms. Franklin, I mean Emily, what are you wearing to the awards ceremony?"

"Kim!" Amy scolded.

"It's all right." Emily put silverware into the dishwasher. "I hadn't thought about it. Maybe I'll buy a new dress."

"Daddy says Amy and I can have new dresses." Kim followed Emily as she moved around the kitchen. "Stacy wants us to get dresses that are alike, but we don't want to do that because we're not alike."

Emily smiled over her shoulder. "Don't you like dressing alike?"

"It was all right when we were kids," Kim said. "But since we've grown up, we'd rather be thought of as individuals instead of twins."

Emily remembered Larry's remark about the great difference in the two girls. "Have you tried explaining this to Stacy?"

"Do you have a big sister?" Kim questioned.

"No," Emily answered, "but I see your point."

Amy looked around before she whispered, "Older siblings can be terribly opinionated."

"You are so right." Kim winked at her sister. "I have a great idea. Maybe the three of us could go shopping together, Ms. Franklin. Emily. That way Stacy wouldn't have to be there at all."

That idea appealed to Emily. "We'd have to clear it with your father."

"He'd agree." Amy put a bowl of salad on the kitchen table. "He likes you."

When Stacy and Kevin returned to the kitchen, Kim and Amy sent each other knowing looks and fell silent.

Now was a good a time as any. Emily told Kevin, "By the way, I'm putting this house up for sale."

She expected him to object. Instead, he surprised her by saying, "That's a great idea, Mom. This place is too big for one person."

Emily breathed a sigh of relief. "The listing will be released tomorrow." After that she relaxed and enjoyed the remainder of the evening.

Later, as Emily prepared for bed, she thought that she was not the only one who thought the evening to be a huge success. Kevin was more relaxed than she had seen him in weeks.

The next day over lunch, Emily related the events of the past evening to Thad. "It was such fun having teenagers in the house again. I'm taking the twins shopping next week now that I have permission from their father."

Thad was not his usual happy self. "That's nice," he answered halfheartedly.

"You sound down," Emily observed. "Is there a problem?"

"Truth." Thad's brow wrinkled. "I have a problem of gigantic proportions."

Emily studied his troubled face. "Can I help?"

"There ain't no cure for what ails me." His flippant answer couldn't cover his somber mood.

"Are you ill?" Emily laid her fork on her plate.

"Love sick. Would you believe it?" Thad's voice was derisive. "I've gone and fallen in love."

"You?" Emily swallowed to keep from laughing. "The invincible Thaddeus T. Thackeray has fallen in love?"

Thad smiled as he said, "It's not funny."

"I'm not laughing." Emily bit her bottom lip.

"No, but you'd like to." Thad frowned. "It would be funny if it wasn't so downright depressing."

"Being in love shouldn't depress you. It should make you deliriously happy."

Thad pushed back his half-filled plate. "I'm having a hard time convincing Lucy I'm serious. Considering my track record, that shouldn't come as any surprise."

Thad was serious. Lucy must be his latest conquest. He hadn't mentioned her before. "Tell me about her."

"Lucy and I met by accident. I ran into her, literally. I backed into her car. After she lectured me about looking where I was going, I learned she lives on a farm north of town. She's a widow with two grown children.

"For me it was love at first sight." Thad's fingers pleated his napkin. "Lucy refuses to believe that."

"She'll come around." Emily wasn't too sure that was true. She added a qualifier, "Eventually."

"I don't want eventually. I want now."

"Instant gratification," Emily chided. "Thad, that's childish."

"Hang it all, I feel childish. I feel like a teenage Romeo who has just met his Juliet."

Emily asked, "Is there anything I can do?"

"There's nothing anyone can do," Thad answered. "I'm almost fifty years old and for the first time in my life, I'm more in love with a woman than she is with me. It's like I waited until I was middle-aged to come down with some childhood disease." He grimaced. "There's something else. We have to stop meeting like this."

"You mean our weekly luncheons?" How much Emily had grown to count on Thad's friendship. "Lucy objects?"

"Lucy doesn't know. If she did, she wouldn't understand. I'm still trying to explain that Daphne means nothing to me and it's over between me and Rochelle."

"Poor Thad," Emily sympathized. She had never seen him so troubled.

111

"It's my own fault. If I didn't have such a rotten reputation, Lucy might believe that you and I are only friends."

"But you do and she wouldn't." Emily patted Thad's hand. "I understand. I'll miss you. Maybe later, after you prove yourself to Lucy, we can all be friends."

"I'd like nothing better." Thad tossed his napkin on the table. "This is good-bye, for now at least." He stood. "You listen better than any friend I ever had. It's too bad you're a woman." Shoulders slumped, head bowed, he turned and walked from the restaurant.

Emily finished her meal and walked back to her office in a cloud of gloom. She'd lost her friendship with Debra because of her divorce. Now romance was taking Thad away from her. She would miss him.

Remembering her coming shopping trip with the Morrison twins lifted her spirits. It wasn't the end of the world. She had survived worse things than losing a close friend to another woman. She opened her office door and went inside.

Chapter Sixteen

Over the next few days, Emily had very little time to concentrate on anything beyond her regular office duties and a host of social events. Friday night she was the keynote speaker at the annual Downtown Merchants' dinner. Saturday, she attended a luncheon and benefit held by the Literacy Council. If her job did nothing else, it kept her too busy to be bored. As she pulled into her driveway late Saturday afternoon, her one objective was to shower, crawl into bed, and sleep for the next twelve hours.

She was surprised to see Robert standing on her front porch. A dozen thoughts crowded into her head, most of them worrisome. She hurried up the walk as she braced herself for the worst. "Has something happened to Larry? Is George ill? Tell me what's wrong."

"Does something have to be wrong for me to come calling?" Robert pointed to the paper bags in the front porch glider. "I brought dinner."

"You came without bothering to call?" Emily snorted her disapproval. "How do you know I'm free tonight?"

"I didn't." Her reprimand didn't seem to faze him. "Free or not, you have to eat dinner."

Emily snapped, "I could be going out to dinner."

"Are you?" he asked bluntly.

"No." She put her key in the lock. "What did you bring?"

Robert smiled, "Barbecue, salad, hot rolls, and pie." He lifted a bag in each arm, and followed her inside.

Emily wasn't especially hungry, but she was curious. She couldn't shake the feeling that Robert had some ulterior motive in coming here. After a strained, silent meal, she pushed her plate back. "I have soft ice cream in the fridge. Would you like some with your pie?"

Robert laid his napkin on the table. "No." He spooned sugar into his coffee. "Have you talked to Larry lately?"

"Not since Monday evening. He called to say he wouldn't be home this weekend."

"Do you still miss him?" Robert stirred his spoon around in his coffee.

"Of course, I do," Emily admitted, "I miss having his friends underfoot. I miss his loud music. I even miss picking up after him and helping him with his homework."

"You never know how much you will miss someone until they aren't around anymore." Robert laid his spoon in his saucer and stared into space. "Even the things that once annoyed you become precious memories."

Did he want sympathy from her because the woman who took him from her walked out on him? "I don't dwell on Larry being gone. I have other things to occupy my mind."

Robert took a quick sip of his coffee. "I saw Thad Thackeray at a cocktail party last night. He was with a woman he introduced as his fiancée."

So, Lucy had succumbed to the irrepressible Thackeray charm. "Her name is Lucy." Was this what Robert came to tell her? "I didn't know she had agreed to marry him, but I'm glad for them."

Robert's coffee cup halted in midair. "You don't mind that he dumped you for another woman?"

That was what happened, but not in the way Robert thought. "There was never anything serious between Thad and me."

"You weren't thinking of marrying him?"

"I'm not thinking of marrying anyone. I'm satisfied with my life the way it is."

"You don't have to pretend with me. I came here tonight to offer a shoulder to cry on." Robert lifted his coffee cup in a salute. "Here's to a speedy recovery."

"You don't believe me?" Emily studied his expressionless face. She didn't know which annoyed her more, his insincere sympathy or his arrogant assumption that she was lying.

"You're well rid of him." Robert's concerned gaze searched her face.

It was more than Emily could bear. "You're judging my behavior by your situation, not mine. I'm not mourning the loss of Thad Thackeray."

Robert reached across the table, and touched the back of her hand with his fingers. "You're better off without him."

"I doubt that." She pulled her hand back. "He was a good friend."

"I'm here for you now," Robert offered. "Why not think of me as your new friend?"

His words struck like an arrow through her heart. The last thing she wanted from Robert was friendship based on pity and false assumptions. "How can you be a new anything? We have a history, a past. We can't blot that out."

Her rebuff rolled off him like water off a duck's back. "Perhaps we can rebuild and redeem the close friendship we once had."

Her natural caution prevailed. Did he think he could use her again? "I have to be able to trust my friends, and I expect them to believe what I say."

He was unmoved by her derogatory insinuation. "In time you will learn to trust me again. I know when someone leaves it creates a void. I could help fill that empty space."

He was asking for her confidence and trust. She couldn't give him either. "You could never take Thad's place."

Robert read all the wrong meanings into her words. "You *are* hurt. I understand how you feel."

"Losing Thad's friendship is not the end of the world. I'll get over it."

"I'd like to be around to make it easier for you." Robert's fingers once again reached for her hand. "Maybe we can see each other now and then."

This time she didn't pull her hand away. "You do see me. You're seeing me now."

"I want you to be a part of my life again. We'll put your affair with Thad behind us." He squeezed her hand.

"I *don't* want to be a part of your life." Emily pulled her hand from his.

"We still share so much and have so much in common." There was strangeness in his voice, a shifting nuance that made her frown.

"What do we have left to share?"

The corners of Robert's mouth turned down. "Twenty-five years of being man and wife."

Emily pushed her chair back and stood. "Don't come here again without calling first, and don't ever ask me to go with you to visit your parents again."

She read in his expression the intent to argue. He looked away. "They will be disappointed."

"They will adjust." Emily studied his downcast face. The past year must have been torment for him. He'd lost Susan. Now he was, out of sheer loneliness, asking to see his wife, correction, his ex-wife from time to time, whatever that meant.

"Kevin still refuses to speak to me." Robert ran his fingers through his hair. "Have you seen him lately? How is he?"

"He's fine. He was here for dinner earlier in the week. Stacy and her sisters were with him. I wanted to tell him I was selling the house before the realtor put the sign in the yard. I thought he would object, but he said it was an excellent idea."

"Would it have made any difference if he objected?" A note of belligerence found its way into Robert's voice.

"I wouldn't want to upset my family." Emily pushed her chair under the table.

"What about Larry? How does he feel?"

"He approves." She walked toward the living room.

Robert followed her. "If they had objected, would you have changed your mind?"

She sat down on the couch. "I might have."

Robert sat beside her. "It doesn't matter to you that I object?"

"This house belongs to me. You don't have the right to object if I want to sell it."

His expression hardened. "I suppose I don't. Nevertheless, I feel compelled to say, you are making a mistake. From a practical standpoint, have you thought about how difficult this will be for you?"

"I don't need your advice. I do need you to pick up your boxes stored in my shed. Make arrangements to take them elsewhere. Most of what's in the attic is junk. Kevin says the Salvation Army will be glad to come and haul it away."

Robert took a deep breath. "Surely you're going to let me look through what's in the attic before you toss it out?"

"Why?" Emily frowned. "There's nothing up there but junk."

"Just the same, I'd like to look."

What could she say? What was up there was as much his as it was hers. "If that's what you want, go ahead. Do it as soon as possible. The moment this place sells, I'm out of here."

"Have you found another place yet?"

Emily didn't want to discuss her plans with him. "It's late. You should go."

She saw the hurt in his eyes as he stood and shoved his hands into his pockets. "I asked out of concern."

"I don't need your concern. Can't you understand? I have moved on."

His anger surfaced swiftly. "What's personal about finding a new house, for goodness' sake?"

Emily stared him down. "I can manage it on my own."

"I was not implying--" Robert paused then snapped, "Forget I asked."

They had been together less than two hours, and already they were arguing. Emily's voice softened. "You really should go. It's very late and I have a busy day tomorrow."

Robert moved toward the door. "I'll call you sometime next week. We can set a time for me to pick up the rest of my things and go through that stuff in the attic." He opened the door. "Lock up after I leave."

Emily considered telling him, once again, she could take care of herself. She didn't. "I'll do that." She watched him walk down the drive and get into his car before she shut and locked the door.

Chapter Seventeen

Emily dumped her packages onto the couch and sank beside them. "This has to be the shopping spree to end all shopping sprees." She watched as Kim and Amy exchanged amused glances and then burst into happy giggles.

Kim ran her fingers over her hair. "Thank you, Emily, for the new hair style. Now everyone can tell me from Amy."

That was certainly true. "I hope your father approves." After a moment's consideration, Emily added. "Maybe we should have asked him first."

"He won't mind," Amy assured her. "I love my new style."

Emily hoped Dennis would agree. When she offered to treat the twins to a trip to the beauty salon in the mall, she had no idea Kim would decide to have her long hair cut into a short style, and Amy would opt for a curly perm. When the girls asked what they could have done, Emily foolishly said, "Don't change the color. Past that the sky's the limit." They took her at her word. Over the chiming of the grandfather clock in the hall, Emily said, "We will know soon enough what he thinks. He should be here any minute."

Amy patted the top of Boo's sleek head. "May we take Boo for a walk?"

Were the twins reluctant to face their father? She was apprehensive herself. "Maybe that would be a good idea. Why don't you go out the back way?"

The twins found Boo's leash and led him toward the back door. "We won't be gone long," Kim called as they hurried outside.

Emily laid her head on the back of the couch and closed her eyes. Maybe she had overstepped the bounds of her friendship with Dennis. If she had, she hoped he would forgive her. She didn't want to lose his good will, and she certainly didn't want to do anything to cause problems for the twins. The more she was around Kim and Amy, the more she was drawn to these two bright, vivacious children.

The sound of the doorbell brought Emily to her feet. The Reverend was here. She took a deep breath and opened the front door.

Dennis stood on the other side, holding his hat in his hand and frowning. "I'm a little behind schedule. I was held up by a minor emergency. Are the girls ready to go?"

"They took Boo for a walk." Emily stepped back. "Won't you come in?"

Dennis came through the foyer. His glance swept quickly around the large living room. "I didn't know you collected antiques."

Emily extended her hand toward a chair. "I don't. Would you like to sit down?" She sat on the couch. "Robert was the collector. I prefer something a little less staid and a little more modern."

Dennis pushed aside packages and sat in the chair. "Was there no room for compromise?"

She had never thought about it before, but Robert didn't ask her opinion about how the house should be furnished. Maybe when he began to buy antiques, she should have said she preferred something more modern. She hadn't, but that was water under the bridge now.

Dennis laid his hat on the coffee table. "I saw your realtor's sign outside. Don't tell me you're going to sell this lovely place."

Emily smiled. "I already have. At least, I'm in the process. A buyer has put up earnest money. After the deal is closed, I have thirty days to get out of here and I haven't even begun to look for another place."

"What are you looking for?"

"A smaller house in a good neighborhood," Emily answered. "And it definitely has to be one story. I'm tired of climbing stairs."

Dennis leaned back and crossed his legs. "There's a house two doors down from the parsonage that fits that description to perfection."

"I'll have to look into that." As concerned as Emily was about a house, she was more worried now about what Dennis would say when he learned about the twins' little escapade at the beauty salon.

An uneasy silence settled between them as Emily waited for Dennis to ask about her shopping expedition with Kim and Amy. When it became evident that he wasn't going to do that, she ventured, "I enjoyed taking the twins shopping."

Dennis tented his fingers and looked over them. "That's nice. They're very fond of you. I'm sure they had a grand time, too."

"I like them so much. I never had a daughter and I always wanted one." Why had she said that, and to Dennis Morrison, of all people? "I treated Kim and Amy to a trip to the beauty salon in the mall. I hope that's okay."

Dennis chuckled, "They must have loved that."

Emily tensed. "They did, but I don't know what you're going to say about the results."

"Don't tell me my daughters now have shaved heads or purple hair." Dennis's handsome face relaxed in a wide grin.

"Oh, no, nothing that drastic." Dennis didn't seem upset. Emily breathed a sigh of relief. "Kim had her hair cut. Amy now has curls. Things got a little out of hand. I hope I didn't overstep some unseen boundary by letting them do this without your permission."

Dennis's smile blossomed into a belly laugh. "Don't look so anxious. I know my girls. You drew parameters and they pushed them to the limits, maybe a little farther."

Emily was greatly relieved. "You know them well. I very foolishly said, 'don't change your color, past that, the sky is the limit.' They took me at my word. I was afraid you might be angry."

Dennis shook his head "I'm not a tyrant. I don't dictate to my daughters how they should style their hair any more than I would have told my wife how to decorate and furnish our home."

The inference was that Robert was a tyrant. Emily was set to refute that assumption when she realized that in some ways, Robert actually was dictatorial and unyielding. "You're a very understanding father. I see now why your twins are so outgoing and well-adjusted."

"Someday I may need them to be understanding of me. What better way to teach them tolerance and understanding than by example?" Without a change in his voice, he added, "Your ex-husband must be a very selfish man."

Emily wanted to tell Dennis *he* had overstepped a boundary. That would be unkind, considering how well he took her news about his daughters' new hairstyles. "I'm sorry if I gave you that impression. He wasn't." She corrected herself, "Isn't."

"It wasn't just what you said. Kevin is very antagonistic toward his father. Most of my conclusions come from what he said." He smiled at her. "Kevin speaks very highly of his mother. I'm beginning to understand why."

The twins came bounding into the room with Boo at their heels. They sang out hellos to Dennis and regaled him with episodes from their day with Emily.

Dennis smiled and nodded as they pulled packages from bags to show him their loot from the shopping trip.

"Slow down, girls," Dennis admonished. "Try talking one at a time." From across the room, his eyes locked into Emily's bemused gaze. "You put up with this all day? You deserve a medal."

"I loved every minute of it." She didn't want the twins and Dennis to leave, not yet anyway. "Why don't you stay for dinner? That is, if you don't mind taking pot luck."

In concert, the twins pleaded. "Please, Dad. Can we, Dad?"

For a moment Dennis looked as if he might refuse, then he smiled and relented. "We'd love that, wouldn't we, girls?"

From a culinary perspective, the dinner wasn't much. Emily and her guests dined on hot dogs and tossed salad, with soft ice cream for dessert. From the standpoint of sheer enjoyment, it was a huge success. The conversation between the twins and their father was relaxed and cheerful. Dennis did have a way of drawing out the reticent Amy and at the same time curbing some of Kim's untamed exuberance.

After dinner, Kim and Amy insisted on doing the dishes. "You old folks go into the living room and relax," Kim said, with a wave of her hand. "Amy and I can take care of the kitchen."

Dennis raised an eyebrow, "Old folks?"

"Kim didn't mean old, as in years." Amy came to her sister's rescue. "She meant old as in wise."

Kim made a superficial apology. "Sorry about that."

Dennis offered Emily his arm and said with mock formality. "Shall we retire to the living room?"

Emily took his arm and walked with him to the living room. "Amy's such a diplomat. Has she always been like that?"

Dennis released Emily's arm and waited until she sat on the couch before easing his big frame into a chair across from her. "Oh, yes. Amy is so like Ellen. She always thought of others first. Amy has that rare quality also. I think it must be a gift from God."

After all this time, it still hurt to remember his wife. Emily wanted to chase that haunted look from his eyes. "Who is Kim like?"

A wry smile touched Dennis's lips. "Like me, I'm afraid. When I was her age, I was very much like Kim is now."

"They're both adorable," Emily said. "Raising twins--" Music from her cell made her lift it from a nearby table.

She hardly had a hello out of her mouth when Robert's strident voice sounded in her ear. "You sold the house two days ago. I thought you were going to call me. Why didn't you?"

"Why should I?" Emily shot back. She muted the phone and whispered to Dennis. "Sorry."

Robert ranted, "You said you'd let me have a look at the things in the attic. Have you already thrown them all away?"

She didn't want to quarrel with Robert with Dennis so near, hearing every word she said. "I have dinner guests. Call me tomorrow." She closed her phone and laid it on the table.

Dennis ran his forefinger around his cleric's collar. "If that's an important call, feel free take care of business. The twins and I will be leaving soon anyway."

"It wasn't important." Emily turned her full attention to Dennis. "As I was saying, raising twins must be quite a challenge."

"That it is," Dennis agreed.

Dennis and his daughters left thirty minutes later with the promise that they would see Emily the night of the awards banquet.

"I look forward to it," Emily said as she shut and bolted the front door.

Later, she prepared for bed. Her day with the twins was an eye-opener. They stirred a maternal instinct she thought had vanished with the passing years. The evening was enjoyable, too. She had almost forgotten how good it felt to be included in a family.

The Morrisons were special. The twins were devoted and affectionate daughters. Dennis was a wonderful father, and obviously he had been a caring, loving husband.

Emily switched off the light and stretched out on the bed, when her phone rang. Shortly after Robert moved out of the house, she'd received a series of crank calls that bordered on being obscene. Warily, she checked to see who was calling. It was Robert.

She turned on a lamp. Her first impulse was not to answer. A mixture of curiosity and fear made her change her mind. She pressed 'talk' and said, "What do you want?"

Robert's voice sounded loud and clear. "I want to apologize for my earlier call. My only excuse is that I was upset about Dad. I should look over any papers you sign, before you sign them, to make sure everything is in proper order."

"Forget it." Emily brushed his apology aside. "What happened to George?"

"He had another heart attack this morning. Fortunately, Debra was at the house when it happened. She and Mom rushed him to Southwest General."

"How bad is it?" Emily clutched her sheet with a hand.

"It's been pretty much touch and go. Debra and Mom haven't left the hospital since they took him there." Robert added matter-of-factly, "I thought about calling you, but I wasn't sure you'd want to be bothered."

That was a rotten thing to say. Emily wanted to reply with some stinging remark. Instead, she asked, "Do Kevin and Larry know?"

"I spoke with Larry. He's standing by." Robert made an explosive noise under his breath before adding; "I doubt that Kevin would talk to me if I called him."

Emily offered, "Do you want me to call Kevin?"

"Maybe you should."

Emily had known George Franklin all her life. "Is he going to be all right?"

"We don't know yet. He's still in intensive care."

"When you know will you call me?"

Robert's voice was accusing. "You said you didn't want to visit Dad and Mom again."

"He's not going to..." Emily couldn't say the word 'die.' "He is going to be all right, isn't he?"

"I don't know." There was weariness in Robert's voice and a touch of fear. "The doctor says if he makes it through the night, he has a fifty-fifty chance."

"How is Clara?" Against her better judgment, she asked, "Do you want me to come to the hospital?"

"Would you?" Robert sounded surprised, but pleased. "I know that's a lot to ask, but Debra and Mom need someone now."

"I'll call Kevin and then I'll be there."

Chapter Eighteen

An hour later Emily hurried into the hospital waiting room to see Clara huddled in a chair near the far wall. She sped across the room. "I came as soon as I knew."

Clara stood and grabbed Emily in a bear hug. "Oh, Emily, I'm so scared." She held the younger woman from her. "Did Robert call you?"

Emily helped Clara back into her chair and sat beside her. "Yes, about an hour ago. I called Kevin and came right over."

"I'm so glad Robert got in touch with you." Clara took a tissue from her sweater pocket and wiped her nose. "I was afraid he wouldn't."

Emily scolded, "You should have let me know sooner. Why didn't Debra call?"

Tears glistened in Clara's eyes. "Robert asked us not to." She laced her cold fingers through Emily's warm ones. "Please don't be angry with him. He thought he was doing the right thing. Will you pray for George?"

"I have been, and I will continue." Emily glanced around the deserted room. "Where are Debra and Robert?"

Clara clung to Emily's hand. "They went to have a bite to eat."

"When did you eat last?" Emily studied Clara's lined face. She looked near the point of collapse. "Maybe you should have gone with them."

Clara tried to smile and failed miserably. "I couldn't leave George." She squeezed Emily's hand. "Thanks for coming."

"I should have been here hours ago."

"You're here now and that's what's important." Clara wept softly. "I'm so afraid George will die. For over fifty years he's been my world. What would I do without him?"

Emily put her arm around Clara's shoulder. "Do you remember when Debra, Robert, and I were children, how we loved to play scrub baseball?"

"Those were dear golden days." Clara smiled through her tears. "George was always the umpire."

"He always said, 'the worst thing you can do is give up,' remember?"

"That's my George." Clara gave Emily a wobbly, watery smile. "He wanted to instill in all of you the will to keep trying regardless of the odds."

"Do you think George has given up?"

Clara straightened her shoulders. "Not my George."

"He wouldn't want you to, either."

Clara dried her tears. "I won't." Suddenly, impetuously, she grabbed Emily in a tight embrace. "I'm so glad you're here, Emily, so very glad!"

Emily returned Clara's hug and held the older woman from her, pushing a strand of gray hair from her forehead. "Try to relax."

"Good advice," Debra echoed as she appeared from the recesses of a dark hall with Robert following close behind. She sat beside her mother. Over Clara's head, her eyes met Emily's. "Thanks for coming."

Robert stood in front of his mother, offering her a sandwich and a cup of hot coffee. "You have to eat." He acknowledged Emily's presence with a nod. "Did you call Kevin?"

"Yes." Emily shook her head. "He wasn't home and so I left a message."

Robert knelt before his mother, opened a food carton, and put it in her lap. "This is your favorite, grilled cheese." He gave her the coffee before moving to sit in the chair beside Emily. He looked like death warmed over.

Emily folded her hands in her lap. "I asked Kevin to call me when he gets my message."

Through the long hours of a dark night, the four people kept an anxious vigil. There was some sporadic conversation about trivial incidents and familiar happenings, little things that strengthened the invisible bond that tied them together. For Emily it was a time of mixed emotions. Robert's family had been a part of her life as long as she could remember. The divorce changed everything.

The first rays of a weak sun bleached the eastern sky before a tired physician delivered the news that George had survived the night and, miraculously, taken a turn for the better.

Clara sobbed. "Thank God!"

Debra and Robert, in unison, breathed a sigh of relief.

As the doctor turned and walked back down the deserted corridor, Emily glanced at the clock on the waiting room wall. "It's almost six o'clock. Clara should go home and try to rest."

Debra slipped her arm around her mother's shoulder. "That's where I'm taking her. That is, if I can impose on you one more time, Emily."

Emily stood, and smoothed her wrinkled skirt, "Of course -- anything."

"We came here in the ambulance with Dad. If I take Robert's car, will you see that he gets home?"

Before Emily could answer, Robert protested. "I can grab a taxi."

Debra argued, "I know, but your apartment is on Emily's way home." She patted Robert's hand. "Mike and I can bring your car to you later."

Debra was right and Emily said so. Second thoughts made her add, "Unless Robert doesn't want me to take him home."

"That would be nice of you." Robert gave his mother a peck on the cheek. "I'll call later." Turning to Emily, he snapped, "Let's go."

Emily had never driven with Robert as a passenger before. She expected him to give instructions, or offer advice. He did neither.

She was pulling from the hospital parking lot before Robert uttered a sound. "Kevin didn't call. Do you think he got your message?"

"He will, eventually. Give him time."

Robert fastened his seat belt. "Maybe he won't."

Emily pulled onto the deserted Sunday morning street. She had no idea where Robert lived. "I need directions to your apartment."

"Turn left on Ridgemont Avenue." Robert turned in his seat. "It was plain rude of Kevin not to return your call."

Who was Robert to find fault with Kevin's behavior? "Don't be so quick to jump to conclusions."

"I'm not accusing him of anything. I do worry about him."

Emily slowed for an intersection. "Are you afraid he may follow in his father's footsteps?" She was sorry before the words were out of her mouth. Should she apologize? For what? Speaking her mind? She negotiated the turn onto Ridgemont Avenue, "Where to now?"

Robert pointed. "Two blocks down on the right. Turn under the sign that says Armstead Apartments." He ignored Emily's snide remark. "Do you think Kevin was with Stacy?"

Emily didn't think that was likely. "I doubt it. Dennis wouldn't allow Stacy to stay out all night."

Robert speculated, "Maybe he didn't call or come to the hospital because he didn't want to risk seeing me."

Emily made a right turn under the sign. "Try not to worry about Kevin. Eventually, he will forgive and forget."

"Not if he's like his mother." Robert unfastened his seat belt. "If you'd like to come in, I'll make some coffee and cook breakfast." He pointed toward a slot at the far end of the drive. "You can park there."

"I wouldn't want to intrude." If someone else was living with Robert, Emily didn't want to know about it.

"There's no one else in the apartment. There never has been. I live alone."

Emily pulled into the parking space and stopped her car. "I didn't know you could cook."

"I'm not good at it, but I can make an omelet and put bread in the toaster." He opened his car door. "Let's go inside."

Emily protested, "I'm tired and hungry. I should go home."

"For Pete's sake, Emily, I'm not going to pounce on you, and I owe you something for being there for Mom and Debra."

Not without reservations, Emily got out of the car and fell in step with Robert. The apartment was small and surprisingly neat. She followed him into the tiny kitchenette. "Do you need help?"

"I can manage." He measured coffee into a coffee maker. "Would you like some orange juice?"

"No thanks." Something Robert said in the car nagged at Emily. "I really am trying to forgive you." A need for self-justification made her add, "When your world is torn asunder, it takes time."

Robert took a bowl from the cabinet and set it on the counter. "I did a fair job of destroying my own universe, too." He set a skillet on the stove and took eggs from the refrigerator. "I didn't intend what I said about Kevin as a criticism. I don't want him to do something foolish. My conscience bothers me because I'm not there for him."

Emily could have told him that was his own fault, but she didn't. Robert was doing a good enough job of beating up on himself. He didn't need any help. "He wouldn't listen to you."

"I feel the need to warn him, all the same." Robert broke eggs into the bowl and stirred them with a fork. "I don't want him make a mistake now that he will regret later."

"We all make mistakes we regret later." Emily took cups from the rack behind the coffee maker. "The sad truth is we regret, but we keep making the same mistakes over and over again." Her life was a long, linear line of repeated blunders.

Robert poured the omelet into the pan. "I like to think I've changed over the past year."

"For the better, I hope." Emily clamped down on her desire to say more. She concentrated on pouring just-made coffee into two cups.

"Maybe I should say my perspective has changed."

Emily poured cream in her coffee. "In what way?"

Robert turned the omelet with a spatula. "The world seems different when you're on the outside looking in."

It was a cryptic answer. Emily suspected Robert would explain if she asked him. She didn't. "If I could change Kevin's perspective, I would."

Robert flipped the omelet onto a plate and put bread in the toaster. "Was Kevin upset that I called you last night?"

It took a while for the question to register. "Kevin wasn't there when you called."

"You said you had dinner guests, and you sounded as if you couldn't talk. I assumed it was because of Kevin." Robert buttered toast, not looking in Emily's direction.

"Dennis Morrison and his young daughters were there. I spent yesterday afternoon at the mall with Kim and Amy." Was that only yesterday? It seemed now she took the twins shopping a decade ago.

"The handsome preacher." Robert put omelet and toast on two plates and pushed one toward Emily. "Has he taken Thad Thackeray's place?" After a quick sip of coffee, he lifted one hand. "There I go again. Sorry."

Emily tasted her omelet. It was delicious. "This is good." She took another bite. "Where did you learn to make an omelet?"

"I found the recipe on an egg carton."

They ate a silent meal. As she watched Robert spread marmalade on a slice of toast, Emily wondered how two people who were once so close could have drifted so far apart. She looked up to see Robert staring at her. "I must look a mess."

"You look beautiful."

Emily opened her mouth, set to refute his words. The expression on his face stopped her. She pushed her plate back and dusted crumbs from her lap. "Thank you."

Robert turned his head to one side. "You have changed, too."

She wanted to ask how. Remembrance of past rebukes stopped her, even though she had the distinct feeling Robert wanted to pursue the subject. "I'm another year older."

"It's more than that." Robert laid his fork across his plate. "I'm discovering depths in you I never knew existed before. Maybe I never really knew you in the first place."

"You've known me all my life." She felt his need to connect, to find and anchor to those things that had once been sure and steadfast. That kind of an intimate conversation would put her right back in that same old cycle of regret and rejection. Emily stacked her cup and saucer in her plate. "I really should go."

Robert was on his feet. "You have plenty of time. It's early yet."

"I'll help with the dishes first."

"I can manage the dishes. It will give me something to do. Sunday afternoons can be incredibly dull."

Emily knew the desolation that came from being alone on a Sunday afternoon. She wanted to put her arms around him and comfort him, as she had when he was ten years old and mourning the loss of his runaway dog. She couldn't risk being that close. There were some things she could do to lift his spirits and still keep a safe distance. "I'll visit George tomorrow after work. I'll see Aunt Beth sometime this week, too."

"Aunt Beth will be so happy to see you." Robert turned away to stack dishes in the sink. "She asks about you often."

Guilt overtook Emily. "I've hurt people I love. That's a terrible thing to do. That's a good example of failing to learn from past mistakes."

Robert came from across the little kitchenette and pulled her to her feet. "You're tired and overwrought." He put his arms around her, and drew her close. "Things will seem better after you get some sleep."

She slipped, without a second thought, into his embrace. "Is there anything worse than self-deceit? For what I tell myself are good reasons, I can be selfish and mean."

Robert's breath was soft on her face. "You could never be either of those things."

In the strength of his embrace, the truth spilled out, "I could and I was."

What began as a sympathetic gesture moved toward an intimate encounter. Her first impulse was to surrender, but then common sense kicked in. She pulled away, "Robert, no." Any desire she felt, died a swift and sudden death. She refused to be a substitute for another woman.

Robert's hands fell to his sides. "I'm sorry." He closed his eyes and swallowed.

Emily put her fingers to her temples and rubbed gently, before folding her arms across her chest.

"Can you forgive me? I didn't intend my embrace to be..." He stopped.

"Sexual?" Emily questioned. "I'm not some innocent girl. I understand the needs of a man who doesn't have access to a woman all the time."

Anger bubbled in Robert's words. "Not just any woman would appeal to me. It's not that impersonal." He rammed his hands into his pockets.

"I'm a poor substitute for the woman you really want." The words were out before her mind could master the pain that squeezed like a fist around her heart.

"Is that what you think? You couldn't be more wrong." Robert sat on the edge of a chair. "Will you give me a chance to explain?"

He could explain until the end of time and she wouldn't be reconciled to him leaving her for Susan, a woman whose loss he obviously still mourned. "That's not necessary."

"It is if we ever hope to bridge this terrible gap between us. Please, I want to tell you."

"I don't want to hear it." This conversation had to stop. "It's not important anymore." Emily picked up her handbag and started toward the door. "I'll call you after I talk to Kevin."

Robert stood with one hand extended. "Don't let a moment's indiscretion destroy what we have salvaged over the past few months."

Salvage was an apt word. They had reclaimed the dross left over from a once blazing passion. With odd detachment, she reasoned that dross was better than nothing. "Old habits die hard." Emily swung her handbag over her shoulder. "Forget it happened."

As she turned to go, he called after her, "I won't make unwelcome advances again."

Emily nodded her head and without looking back, closed the door behind her. She hurried down the steps, taking them two at a time. Never again would she open herself to the hurt and rejection loving Robert Franklin could bring.

Chapter Nineteen

The next few days passed in a flurry of activity. The paperwork to close the sale of her house was completed on Monday. Emily took time from an overloaded work schedule to meet with the realtor and the new owners to complete the transaction. She was hard pressed to make time to visit George, but she managed. Then she drove to the nursing home and sat for a while with Aunt Beth. She called Kevin's office and left a message with his secretary, telling him of his grandfather's heart attack. A few hours later, Kevin called back. "Mom, would you like to go to lunch with your older son?"

Emily asked, "Did you get my message?"

"I've been to the hospital. Why didn't you let me know sooner?"

"I called you Saturday night," Emily answered, "and left a message."

"I turn off my phone when -- Stacy and I didn't want to be disturbed."

She hoped he didn't mean what she feared he did. "I see."

"No, it's not what you think. Stacy and I were discussing our future and making plans."

Why would that necessitate turning off his phone? She didn't understand Kevin when he was a child, and she didn't understand him now. She changed the subject. "When I saw George this morning, he seemed much improved."

"He looks like warmed over death to me. Seeing him that way was quite a shock." Kevin asked again, "Can you meet me for lunch?"

Emily glanced at the calendar on her desk. "I'd love to but I have an appointment at noon to meet with a realtor to look at a house."

"You sold the house already?" Kevin's surprise sounded in his voice

"I signed the final papers this morning."

Kevin paused before saying, "I really need to talk to you, Mom. Maybe I could drive you to your appointment with the realtor.

"That sounds like a plan. Meet me in front of the library. Be here by twelve-thirty. I don't have a minute to spare."

"See you then." Kevin hung up the phone.

Despite her instructions, Kevin was five minutes late. He waved as he stopped at the curb. "Sorry I wasn't on time. It's been one of those days." He reached across the seat, and opened the car door. "Where are we going?"

Emily got in and fastened her seat belt. "The house is in Northern Heights. It's very near the Reverend Morrison's church, just a few doors down from the parsonage."

"I know the place." Kevin pulled away from the curb.

Emily leveled a steady gaze in her son's direction. "What's wrong?"

"I never could fool you, could I?" Kevin frowned. "Seeing Grandpa lying in that hospital bed, so weak and sick really knocked me for a loop. Until this morning I assumed he'd live forever."

Emily put her hand on her son's arm. "He's going to be all right."

"This time maybe, but he has a bad heart." Kevin's jaw tightened. "How much longer before this happens again?"

"Don't borrow trouble. We can deal with that eventuality when it happens."

Kevin's hands tightened on the wheel. "You are a strong woman, Mom, but too good for your own good. Aunt Deb and Dad had no right to ask you to come to the hospital and stay up all night with them, but they did and you went."

"I volunteered to go and it wasn't for Debra or Robert. I went for Clara. She needed me." Emily turned her gaze from her son to the rapid flow of moving traffic. "Clara has been like a second mother to me."

They rode for several minutes in silence before Emily turned to study her son's grim face. She wondered what thoughts lurked behind that bleak countenance. Had he seen Robert at the hospital? That might explain his anger. Casually she asked, "Have you talked to your dad?"

"No. I haven't talked to him, nor do I intend to."

Kevin was too old for such juvenile behavior. "Are you going to wait until your own father is lying on his death bed before you decide to make things right with him? What makes you think you'll have that last minute opportunity?"

Kevin's voice rose. "How can you defend that man after all he's done to this family?"

"I'm not defending your father, I'm stating facts. What happened between Robert and me doesn't have to ruin your relationship with him."

Kevin protested, "Yes it does--"

Emily cut him short. "No. It doesn't. Our divorce is none of your business. To set the record straight, the breakup of our marriage was partly my fault. I neglected your father, taking him for granted. We shouldn't be surprised that he went looking for warmth and companionship with someone else."

"Warmth and companionship? Mom, come on. Dad had a cheap affair with a younger woman, who you might be interested to know is taking him to the cleaners in their divorce." Kevin waved a hand. "You were a good wife."

Once Emily had thought that was true. Now she wasn't that sure. "If I had been a success as his wife, he wouldn't have found someone else."

Kevin frowned briefly in her direction. "I can't believe you're blaming yourself and defending him."

"I'm trying to put what happened into some perspective, and that's what you have to do. Regardless of what he's done. Robert is the only father you will ever have."

"You really mean that, don't you?" Kevin glanced briefly in her direction before shifting his gaze back to the street.

"Every word," Emily declared.

"But, Mom," Kevin argued with all the fervor of injured youth, "he slept with another woman while he was still married to you."

Emily put her arm on the back of the seat and leaned toward her son. "That's the most devastating thing that can happen to a woman. Still, I refuse to let what happened in the past rob me of my future, or you of a relationship with your father."

"Don't you feel some urge to make him pay for what he did to you?"

Maybe she had once. Those feelings were gone now, well almost gone. "I'm going to say this once. After that, let's consider this a closed issue. Your father and I both made mistakes, but what happened is between the two of us. If we can settle our differences--and we have--that's all that counts. Butt out, Kevin, and get on with your own life."

Kevin snorted, "You think I'm being childish, don't you?"

"Somewhat." She was being tough, but she needed to get her point across. "You're a man. Start acting like one."

Belligerence tightened Kevin's features. "I'm not going to run to my old man and try to make things right between us."

"Maybe he feels the same way," Emily told him. "You haven't exactly been a dutiful, supportive son."

"You don't pull any punches, do you?" Kevin turned off the interstate and onto a residential street.

"Kevin, darling." A pleading note crept into Emily's voice. "I'm not saying these things to hurt you, but to keep you from being hurt. I love you, and I want the best for you. Don't you know that?"

"I know." Kevin slowed for an intersection. "What do you think I should do, Mom?"

Emily thought for a moment. "Maybe the two of you should meet on neutral ground and give yourselves a chance to get past some of your differences. Your dad wants to go through the things in the attic before I have Goodwill take them away. Would you like to drop by the house while he's there and say hello?"

"I don't know." Kevin hesitated before saying reluctantly, "Maybe."

Emily pushed down her own misgivings. "Good. I'll let you know when he'll be at the house."

Kevin pulled his car into the driveway of the compact brick house with a 'for sale' sign in the front yard. "The realtor is here. Let's have a look around."

Emily liked the house. The rooms were spacious and airy. One of the three bedrooms could easily be converted into an office and the kitchen was roomy and recently updated.

When she opened the back door and saw that the backyard was fenced, Emily smiled at the portly realtor. "I'd like to make an offer."

From behind her, Kevin questioned, "Are you sure this is what you want, Mom?"

"I have to have something. This looks good." Emily had never before made such a weighty decision on such short notice. It was time she stopped being so cautious. "Let's discuss details. I have to get back to work."

It was Thursday before Emily found time to phone Robert at his office. She spent several minutes on hold before he answered. "Sorry to keep you waiting." He sounded distant and cold. "I had about decided you weren't going to call me."

Emily matched his stilted tone. "I've been busy." She wondered if there was someone in the room with him. Was it Susan? "I talked to Kevin earlier this week. He's visited his grandfather twice since then."

"Dad told me." Robert answered brusquely.

"I talked to Larry last night." Stung by his cool reserve, she added in even more stilted tones. "He'll be home over the weekend."

"That's nice." Impatience clipped Robert's words. Emily made one more overture toward congeniality.

"I signed the final papers on my house last Monday."

The voice on the other end of the line was as remote as the hills. "I know."

Of course, he knew. He was a realtor. "I bought a little house on Oakdale Drive in Northern Heights."

"You got a good deal."

He knew that, too. "Can you could come out Sunday and take what you want from the attic? I'd like to have the Salvation Army truck pick up the rest on Monday."

"What time?" He didn't intend to give an inch. Two could play that game. Coldly Emily intoned, "Any time that's convenient for you."

"I'll see you around four Sunday afternoon. Good-bye." Robert hung up the phone.

Emily shrugged before she put the phone aside, and wondered aloud, "What got into him?"

Her mind quickly moved to more pressing matters. Larry would be home soon and to be welcomed by utter chaos. His room was bare, except for the bed and one straight-backed chair. Half of Emily's belongings were in crates and boxes. The other half lay in piles on the floor or draped over disassembled furniture. In less than twenty-four hours she had a date with Dennis. To be more exact, she and her family would be going out with the entire Morrison clan. Emily sat on the couch and kicked off her shoes. Boo settled on the cushion beside her and laid his head in her lap.

Thirty minutes later Larry came through the door. Boo ran to meet him, his tail wagging furiously. Emily was curled up on the couch, half-asleep. Larry laughed and ran his fingers through Boo's thick fur. "Some watch dog you are."

Emily stirred and muttered, "I must have dozed."

Larry looked around him. "It looks like a hurricane hit this place."

Emily stretched and yawned. "Wait until you see your room."

"I've spent the last three months in a dorm." Larry tossed his bag on the cluttered floor. "I can manage."

He keeps changing. Emily studied her younger son's composed face. *He's been away only three months and already he's different.* She said, "I hung the tux I rented for you in your closet." She viewed Larry's muscular chest and trim waist. "I hope it's not too small."

Larry lowered himself into the only vacant chair in the room. "I've been working out twice a week. Where is the rest of the furniture?"

"I sold the antiques and one load of my belongings has already gone to the other house." Emily frowned. "Maybe you should try that tuxedo on."

"After dinner." Larry stroked Boo's head. "Tell me about this banquet. I talked to Kevin on the phone Wednesday. He's really excited about us all going out together."

Emily was afraid Kevin might have reservations about going out with his mother and his younger brother. "Dennis, the Reverend Morrison, is to receive an award from a group that builds houses for the homeless. From what he and the twins say, it's quite an event."

The mention of the twins brought a smile to Larry's face. "How *are* Kim and Amy?"

"Great, both of them. They have new hairstyles. You can tell them apart now."

"I already could," Larry answered. "The moment Kim opens her mouth I know who's who."

Emily laughed as she stood. "Everyone can tell them apart now before Kim utters a sound. Come into the kitchen. I'll make you a sandwich."

Chapter Twenty

The next morning Larry tried on the tux. Fortunately, it fit. Emily breathed a sigh of relief. She wouldn't have to worry about an exchange. That was good news because her schedule for the day was already too full. She had a luncheon to attend and some packing to do before the movers came for another load around five.

She kissed Larry on the cheek. "I'll be home by three o'clock."

Larry hung his cummerbund over a chair. "When did you start working on Saturdays?"

"I don't usually, but today I'm speaking at the Elk's Club's annual fund-raising luncheon." Emily slung her handbag over her shoulder. "Your dad will be out tomorrow around four, but maybe you'd like to call him today and say hello."

Larry shed his shirt. "I'm meeting Gus and Rocky at the mall around eleven. I'll see Dad tomorrow."

Throughout the luncheon and even as she drove home, a little fizzle of excitement bubbled through Emily's veins as she anticipated her coming evening out with her sons and the Morrisons. Even though she felt a sense of pride in her newfound independence, she had never lost the sense of isolation that came with her divorce from Robert and the severing of her close ties with his family. A sobering concern took her. Was she risking another possible rejection and subsequent heartache by becoming so involved with the Morrison family? Her excitement dampened, leaving a residue of concern.

Some of the excitement returned that evening when Emily caught a glimpse of herself in the bathroom mirror. Her hair, done in a simple upsweep, gleamed like copper in the soft light. The dress she bought the day she went shopping with Kim and Amy was the exact color of the yellow flecks in her eyes. The bodice hugged her waist, leaving the skirt to fall in elegant folds around her ankles. She gave her hair a last pat and checked her makeup before going downstairs.

"Guess what?" Larry called as she swept into the living room. He stopped and whistled through his teeth. "Mom, you look awesome!"

Emily scanned the figure of her younger son. "So do you."

He smiled. "We should look our best for this occasion. Reverend Morrison hired a limo to take us to the banquet."

Emily's eyes rounded in surprise. "He did?"

"Yeah, Kevin just called. They're on their way now." Larry offered Emily his arm. "Something tells me this is going to be a great party."

Emily tucked her hand into the crook of his arm. "Our coach will soon arrive. Shall we go?" They exchanged smiles as they walked toward the door.

The ride to the banquet was a celebration. The twins were ecstatic over their first trip in a limo, and delighted to see Larry again. Even the usually shy Amy warmed in his presence. Kevin sat with his arm around Stacy, looking handsome and proud as he smiled at his younger brother and gave his mother a sly wink.

Emily silently thanked Dennis Morrison for making this possible. She leaned near him, and whispered, "This is wonderful."

By the time the limo stopped in front of the banquet hall, Kim and Amy were arguing over who would sit beside Larry. He assured the arguing girls that he had two sides and each twin was welcome to one of them.

The table reserved for Dennis and his guests was front and center of the hall, and set on a slightly raised dais. Dennis looped Emily's hand through his arm. "It looks as though we're to be on display for the evening. Do you mind?"

"I don't mind in the least if you don't."

Dennis escorted Emily to the table and helped her sit down. As he pushed her chair forward, his hands rested on her shoulders. "I'm more than pleased to show off my handsome family."

In his own way Dennis was as isolated and alone as she was. Emily laid her hands over his and smiled up at him. "Shall we enjoy our fifteen minutes of fame?"

The meal, served in several courses, was surprisingly good. The conversation around the table was constant and affable. Kevin was in rare form, regaling the others with tales of his past week in court as he held Stacy's hand and occasionally raised it to his lips to kiss her fingertips.

Stacy, her eyes aglow with love, said Kevin must be the most brilliant lawyer in the state.

Larry told of his first days at the university and how he spent more time looking for classes than he had attending them. Kim insisted that Larry was the bravest man she knew, to go off all alone to school and be able not only to survive, but to excel. Amy smiled in agreement.

Emily watched as Kevin squared his shoulders and Larry glowed. Maybe all any man needed to be happy was the support and adulation of a caring woman. She laid her hand on Dennis's arm. "Dennis deserves a word of praise also. He's being honored tonight for his tireless efforts to help the less fortunate. That, too, is a noble feat."

Suddenly, they were all laughing. Dennis raised his glass, "A toast to us, one big happy family." Of one accord seven voices chimed in unison, "Here, here" as they touched glasses and drank.

After dinner, Dennis was introduced in glowing terms, lauded for his tireless efforts in helping the homeless and presented with a plaque. As he rose to walk to the podium, Emily observed, once again, what an incredibly handsome man he was.

Dennis's acceptance speech was an oratorical accomplishment. He spoke in simple terms, giving sympathy and tenderness to complicated concepts and abstract ideas. By the time he completed his speech and returned to the table, Emily doubted there was a dry eye in the house. She caught both his hands in hers. "You were wonderful."

Dennis held on to one of her hands. "Can we discuss this in detail later?"

Warmth flowed from Emily's hand and up her arm. "I'd like that very much."

"I'll call you soon."

All too soon the evening ended. The happy group crowded into the limo to go home. Emily leaned her head against the upholstery and listened as Larry asked Dennis's permission to take Kim and Amy to a baseball game tomorrow afternoon. She raised her head. "Your father is coming by tomorrow."

Larry shrugged. "The game won't last that long."

Emily turned her gaze toward Kevin. "You are coming by to see your dad, aren't you? He's coming for the last of his things."

Kevin nodded. "I'll be there, but I can't stay long."

Emily didn't pursue the matter. It was enough for now that Kevin agreed to show up and talk to his father.

Later, lying in the king-sized bed she had once shared with Robert, Emily had second thoughts about getting Kevin and his father together. Maybe she should let well enough alone. The problem with that was, as things stood, there was no "well enough." There was only a wrenching rift between father and son. If someone didn't intervene, it might never be breached. She wished for Thad's comforting words and sage advice. Turning over, she pulled the covers up under her chin. Dennis was a counselor. Maybe she could talk to him. With that comforting thought, she closed her eyes and drifted off to sleep.

Emily awoke the next morning to the sound of rain on the roof. This would hamper the movers. She slipped into a robe and hurried to look out the window. Toward the west, the clouds were breaking.

She put on battered old jeans and a baggy sweatshirt, and went downstairs. She was frying bacon when Larry came through the kitchen door. "Something smells good."

Emily pointed her spatula toward the table. "Sit down and eat your breakfast."

Larry sat, and heaped his plate high with eggs and bacon. "This looks delicious. I miss your cooking, Mom." He shoveled a forkful of scrambled eggs into his mouth. "I miss you, too. I'm getting over it, but I was homesick for a long time." He chewed thoughtfully for a moment before asking, "Will you miss this place when you move?"

Emily poured coffee into a cup and sat down across from her son. "Maybe at first, but I'll get over it, just like you did."

"Would you like me to stay over an extra day and spend the first night with you in your new house?"

His thoughtfulness was touching. "That's sweet of you, but I can handle being alone."

"I gotta go." Larry stood and pushed back his chair. "I promised Kim and Amy I'd pick them up at noon, and I don't want to be late."

It sounded more like he couldn't wait to get away. "I thought you said the game doesn't start until one."

"We're going to McDonald's for a quick lunch." Larry glanced at his watch.

Emily wondered how her son could eat lunch after the breakfast he had consumed. She hadn't realized it was so late. "I miss the clock in the hall chiming out every hour."

"Cloudy days can fool you." Larry's face splintered into a wide grin. "You should have slept late. You didn't get to bed until after two this morning."

Ignoring his comment, Emily followed Larry into the empty living room. "Your dad will be here later this afternoon. Try to be back in time to visit with him."

Larry stopped his headlong dash for the door. "Why should I?"

"Because he's your father and he wants to see you."

Larry's shoulders sagged. "Dad doesn't really care that much."

"Yes, he does." This she would have expected from Kevin, but not Larry. "He cares very much."

Larry turned toward his mother with a look of patient forbearance on his young face. "We're not important to Dad anymore. Why can't you see that?" There was no bitterness in his words, only a stoic acceptance of what he must perceive as an honest assessment of how things were.

"Larry, please..." Emily began.

Larry made a sweeping gesture with one hand. "I've accepted that and learned to live with it. There's no point putting things I want to do on hold to please Dad." He headed for the door. "Bye, Mom."

Emily spent the remainder of the morning packing the last of her personal belongings. Then she took Boo for a walk.

When the movers came at noon, she had them bring all the clutter from the attic and pile it in the vacant living room.

Sitting on the floor, she opened the box nearest her. It held baby clothes. She picked up one of the little garments. It was a tiny, beautifully embroidered baby dress that was a gift from Aunt Beth. Both Kevin and Larry wore that tiny, exquisitely stitched garment home from the hospital.

Nostalgia, like a tidal wave, swept over her. She closed the box. These dusty, oblong crates held her past. A little segment of her life was stored inside each container. She had neither the emotional stamina nor the physical strength to poke around in what was, and contemplate what could have been. She closed the lid. Finding an old quilt the movers left behind, she spread it on the floor and lay down. As soon as Robert came and took what he wanted, she would close this chapter of her life. She would shut and lock the front door for the last time, go to her new home, and start over.

Boo curled up on the quilt beside her. Emily stroked his head. "Are you ready for a new beginning, pal?" Boo wagged his tail and yawned causing Emily to arch an eyebrow. "Are you talking back to me?" Boo put his head between his paws and thumped his tail against the floor. That seemed a clear enough answer. Emily curled up beside him and thought about a comforting promise, "I will never leave you nor forsake you."

Chapter Twenty-One

Emily was somewhere between the wakeful world of reality and that restful realm of repose when the doorbell pealed. She sat up, and called out, "Come in." Larry must have decided to come home early.

It wasn't Larry, but Robert who came through the door. The sight of him brought Emily to a standing position. "I thought you were Larry."

Robert closed the door with his foot. "Obviously you were mistaken."

What is his problem now? Emily recalled their last phone conversation. He was cross as two sticks then. From the tone of his voice, his mood hadn't improved. She smoothed her hair back with her hands. "I didn't realize it was four already. I miss the grandfather clock."

Robert frowned as his eyes scanned the room. "It's only three-fifteen. I'm early."

Emily considered asking him what made him so short-tempered. She'd made a point of telling Robert to say out of her personal life. She could ill afford to butt into his. She waved toward the boxes, barrels, and crates that filled a good portion of the room. "I had the movers bring the clutter from the attic down here. Take what you want."

Robert looked around him. "Where's the furniture?"

"I sold the antiques." Emily sat back down on the quilt. "Everything else is at the other house." She pulled her knees up under her chin and wrapped her arms around her legs.

"It looks so...empty."

He made her nervous and she didn't know why. "Has George taken a turn for the worse?"

"Dad's doing as well as can be expected. He's home now." Robert's gaze kept wandering around the empty room. "Who bought the antiques?"

"Some dealer over on Market Street." A sobering thought took Emily. "Did you want some of them?"

"It's a little late now to ask that, don't you think?"

149

It was. "You knew I was going to sell them. You should have said something."

"It's not important." His voice was sharp.

In the past, that tone of voice always made her feel guilty. It was liberating to realize it was one of the many devices he used to manipulate her. "Do you want to tell me why you're so irritable?"

Before Robert could frame an answer Larry burst through the front door accompanied by Kim and Amy, "Hi, Mom, Dad."

Boo bounded to greet the twins. They stroked his head and talked to him.

Over the hubbub, Larry introduced Kim and Amy to Robert. "Kim, Amy, this is my dad, Mr. Franklin."

Amy smiled and nodded a greeting.

Kim dropped her hand from Boo's head. "I thought your dad was dead."

Larry turned a dull shade of red. "Whatever gave you that idea?"

"I can't imagine anyone leaving you and Kevin and Emily if he didn't have to."

"Kim!" Amy poked her elbow into Kim's ribs.

Completely unabashed, Kim shrugged. "Did I say something wrong?"

"Never mind." Larry suppressed a chuckle. "Let's make some popcorn." He moved toward the kitchen. Kim, Amy, and Boo followed him.

As the three disappeared into the kitchen, Emily said, "I hope Kim didn't offend you. She takes some getting used to. Seeing her for the first time you can't tell, but--"

"I've seen Kim before," Robert interrupted. His gaze followed the departing figures. "I saw her last night at the Homes for Humanity Banquet."

Emily blinked. "You were there?" Of course, he was there. How could he have seen Kim if he hadn't been? "I didn't see you."

Robert pulled his hard gaze back to Emily's face. "You and my sons were too engrossed in Reverend Morrison and his daughters to notice anyone else."

Like a match struck in the dark, the reason for Robert's anger flared through Emily's brain. He was jealous of his sons' relationship with the Morrisons. Maybe he feared Kevin saw his future father-in-law as a replacement father figure. "Why didn't you come over and say hello?"

"I thought you were snubbing me."

"You know me better than that. I'm not a snob."

Robert sighed and leaned against a stack of boxes. "I don't know what you are anymore. I'm beginning to wonder if I ever did."

The front door knob rattled. Kevin stuck his head around the jamb and asked, "Anybody home?"

He could not have chosen a worse time to put in an appearance, but she *had* asked him to come. Pasting a smile on her face, Emily hurried toward her son with both hands extended. "Kevin! Come in."

Kevin pushed the door open and stood back for Stacy to enter. Tension in the room rose and snapped like an exposed electric wire.

Robert's husky voice fell out into the strained silence. "Hello, Kevin."

Every muscle in Kevin's body tensed, "Hi, Dad." Emily introduced Stacy to Robert. She took her time, hoping the interval would ease some of the tension.

Robert stepped around Emily and extended his hand to Stacy. "It's a pleasure to meet you. Emily has told me a lot about you."

Stacy's long lashes fell to cover her eyes. "I'm pleased to meet you, too."

After another period of strained silence Kevin said, "We came to pick up Kim and Amy. Are they here?"

"They're in the kitchen with Larry." Emily moved toward the kitchen. "I'll get them."

Stacy followed after her. "I'll go with you."

Once in the kitchen, Emily asked Kim and Amy to pop more popcorn. Her aim was to give Robert and Kevin some time together. Fifteen minutes later the five of them emerged from the kitchen carrying a bag of popcorn. "We're ready to go," Kim told Kevin, as she gave Boo's head one last pat.

Kevin and Robert stood glaring at each other. A fist of tension clenched in Emily's stomach. When she spoke, her voice sounded high and unnatural. "Kim and Amy popped some popcorn for later this evening."

Kevin broke his stare and took Stacy's arm. "Larry's going with us, Mom. Dennis invited us to dinner tonight."

"You're invited too, Emily." Stacy called over her shoulder as Kevin guided her toward the door. "Dad says there's no way you can fix a meal in your new kitchen. We're going to evening services first so dinner will be late. Is nine all right for you?"

Emily was too distracted to do anything but nod. "Nine is fine. I'll be there."

"Can we take Boo with us?" Kim pleaded. "Amy and I will take him for his evening walk."

"Sure, why not? You can put him in the backyard of my new house afterward." Some of Emily's composure returned. "His food is on the back porch. You can give him his dinner too." After a flurry of hurried good-byes, Emily closed the front door and turned to face Robert. His set expression told her to expect the worst. She steadied her voice before asking, "How did it go?"

"Do you have time to listen?" Robert leaned against the wall, hostility written in every line of his tense body, "Now that you've attended to everything of importance?" He ran his fingers through his hair. "I'm sorry, Emily. That seems to be all I say to you anymore. I keep apologizing and you keep exacting another pound of flesh. Haven't you punished me enough?"

He was angry with her and she didn't know why. She sat on the movers' quilt, and looked up at him. "I break my neck to arrange a meeting between you and Kevin and then clear the way so you can talk to him. You thank me by finding fault with my efforts?"

Robert drew a long breath, and sat on the far edge of the quilt. "I'm not talking about today. I'm grateful for a chance to talk to Kevin. He's about as approachable as a mountain lion, but at least we're speaking to each other now."

Emily was completely perplexed. "What *are* you talking about, then?"

"I'm talking about the way you have treated me since the day I chased you down and begged you to let me be a part of your life again."

"I've done everything you asked me to do." Her mind sorted through recent encounters. "You said you wanted to win your sons back. I offered to help. You said you wanted us to be friends and I agreed."

Robert jumped to his feet. "Let's keep our facts straight, shall we?" He paced the room like a caged panther. "You are the one who said we could be friends."

"You agreed," Emily countered. "Since then, I've intervened with Kevin, gone to see your parents, and visited Aunt Beth."

Robert drew a jagged breath. "I'm not talking about what you've done for my family. I'm talking about how things are between you and me." He lifted his head and stared at the ceiling. "I don't know how to reach you anymore. You reject my every overture."

Emily's mind leaped backward in time. "Are you talking about what happened in your apartment last week?" Her irritation warred with a sudden surge of sympathy. All men had biological urges. Robert was no exception. "I'm finding it difficult to offer you comfort and sympathy because the woman you left me for walked out on you."

Robert dropped his head and stared at her. "Is that what you think?" His eyes narrowed. "That Susan walked out on me?"

Surely, he hadn't left Susan, not after all he gave up to be with her. "Didn't she?"

"No," he declared emphatically. "I left her."

Emily was too surprised to be anything but honest. "You told me you were in love with her."

"I told myself the same thing. My only defense for such a stupid assumption is that I couldn't admit that I was in the throes of a foolish middle-aged infatuation." His voice was heavy with self-derision. "I thought I was above such things."

For the space of a few breathless seconds, she believed him. Then common sense moved in. "Then why did you insist on a divorce?"

"I divorced you, but I couldn't let go. At first, I told myself I was hanging on because you needed me. You soon put that idea to rest. That's when I began to realize I had thrown away my marriage for a shallow, superficial emotion that wasn't going to last. By the time I came to grips with what a mistake I had made, you had taken up with Thad Thackeray. I decided to bide my time because I was sure Thad didn't want a serious relationship. Sooner or later, you'd find that out. I could wait. When I learned he'd dumped you, I came rushing back, crawling and begging, with my pride in tatters. Fool that I am, I thought you'd welcome me with open arms. That's when I discovered you didn't even want me for a friend. I became desperate."

All that Emily had assumed to be settled and true was called into question. "Desperate?" That wasn't a word that described Robert Franklin. "Aren't you being a little melodramatic?"

"I'm trying to be honest." The pulse at the base of his throat beat erratically. "I knew how much you love our sons. I used that love to get back into your good graces. I wanted a chance to be near you." He shook his head. "I'm saying this all wrong. I don't mean to imply that I don't want to patch things up with Kevin. I do."

That was the one thing Emily had always been sure of. "I never doubted that."

"Do you doubt what I'm saying to you now?"

There was doubt, and a vast amount of caution. "Can you understand why I might be a little hard to convince?"

Robert rubbed his sleeve across his face. "After what happened in my apartment last Sunday, I thought I'd ruined everything. I should have known I couldn't handle being alone with you. Once again, all I can say is I'm sorry."

"There is no need to apologize." Her smile was ironic. "I suppose I should be flattered." She would have been if she had thought what he had felt had been anything more than a basic biological urge.

"You accused me of using you for a substitute." He swallowed, painfully. "Believe this even if you can't believe anything else I say. I never made love to you and thought of another woman. If you wanted revenge for my past actions, you had it last night. Seeing you with Dennis Morrison was as near hell I ever want to get. I realize he's a formidable rival. Morrison is no Thad Thackeray. I'm sure his intentions are honorable."

He thought there was something between her and Dennis. He also thought that she and Thad had been lovers. Emily could set him straight on both issues. "There was never anything between Thad and me. Dennis and I are friends, that's all." As an afterthought, she asked, "Why are you prying into my personal life?"

"Because I want another chance." His gaze locked into hers. "I have every intention of winning back your heart."

On an expelled breath, Emily asked, "Why? So you can break it all over again?"

Robert's answer echoed across the empty room. "Why? Because, I love you that's why. I love you enough to forgive your affairs with Thad and Dennis. All I want is for us to be together again."

Chapter Twenty-Two

Anger erupted inside Emily, and ran like molten lava through her veins. This man cheated on her and shattered her self-confidence. Nothing in her life would ever be the same again. Now he had the audacity to say he was willing to forgive *her*? Rage pushed her to her feet and propelled her across the room. "You two-timing heel!" The words exploded from her mouth.

"If it makes you feel better to call me names, go ahead." Robert studied her with calm detachment. "You wouldn't be so angry if you weren't still in love with me."

Emily turned to stare out the window as she tried to master her emotions. One by one the memories of past year played across her senses, bringing pain so acute it was physical.

Robert cried, "Emily, talk to me."

Emily turned to meet his searching gaze. "It seems all I ever say to you is 'I'm sorry' and we've worn that trite little phrase threadbare."

Robert's face contorted. "We had a good marriage once. Given time we will again."

Emily swallowed around the knot of tears in her throat. "Don't threaten me with your love. I lived through that torment once."

This time it was Robert who turned away, put his hands in his pockets, and hunched his shoulders. "I need you, Emily."

She suddenly saw the man she had known for so long, and thought she knew so well, in a different light. He had little thought for her feelings. His concern was for himself. "I've changed. I'm not the woman you left over a year ago."

"I've changed, too. I'm not the fool I was a year ago." He turned, determination written in every line of his face. "It's not too late. I won't let it be."

Light slanting through the bare window cast long shadows across the room. The afternoon was far spent. *It's later than you think. In fact, for us it's too late.*

Emily's hands were awkward appendages with no place to go and nothing to do. She clasped them behind her. "I'm leaving now. Take what you want. The Salvation Army will get the rest."

"Are you throwing all this away?" Robert nodded toward the stacks of crates and boxes.

Those containers held Emily's past. "There is nothing here I want."

Robert's voice was husky. "I hoped we could go through the pictures together."

Emily would rather have a root canal. "I'm going home." This house was her home for more than two decades. She amended her statement, "To my new house."

Robert's plea echoed across the space between them. "May I call you some time?"

Emily pointed to the kitchen. "I have one more box to put in my car."

"Is that a yes or a no?"

She would always have ties to this man. He was the father of her two sons. "Don't push me."

His voice impinged on her flagging senses. "Do you enjoy watching me die a little more each time you spurn my every effort to make amends?"

This scenario was playing out like the final scene from a bad movie. Emily hurried to the kitchen.

She returned a few minutes later, carrying a box in her arms. Robert sat cross-legged on the floor with an opened carton beside him. "Do you need help loading your car?"

"I can manage." Outside the rain fell in sheets. Emily paused in the doorway for a final good-bye to the house that was her home for so many years.

She stepped out into the cold rain. Without looking back, she put the box in the back seat of her car, got behind the wheel, backed from the driveway, and turned onto the rain-drenched street.

When she drove into the driveway of the house on Oakdale Drive, Kim and Amy sat in the front porch swing. They waved and shouted greetings as she stopped her car. The rain had slowed to a fine drizzle. Emily ran from the car to the front porch. "What are you doing here?"

"We stayed with Boo until you got home," Kim explained, "and we wanted to remind you again that you're coming to our house for supper after services."

Emily unlocked the door and invited them inside

They refused. "Evening services start in an hour," Kim said, as Amy waved good-bye.

Emily stepped across the threshold. A bone-chilling cold had settled over the cluttered room. "What a mess." She couldn't face trying to make order from this chaos, not after all that had happened today. Instead, she showered and went to evening services.

She found a seat on the back pew just as the strains of the last hymn died away. Dennis stepped to the podium. She was struck as always by his magnificent physique and commanding presence.

As he spoke, Emily's mind drifted back to the events of the afternoon. Robert's declaration of his love for her came out of left field. How could he love her if he thought her promiscuous and a liar?

The discovery that she wanted to put her past behind her and forget Robert, had hit with the force of an earthquake. Now the aftershocks set in, leaving her shaken by tremors of uncertainty. She wanted to believe again, to trust again. Did forgiving her ex-husband mean she had to return to being his wife? Was that what God expected of her? Wisdom, an abstract from the pain of Robert's betrayal, made her doubtful. She folded her hands in her lap and listened to Dennis's eloquent discourse extolling the virtues of forgiveness. For the first time in months, she concentrated on the words coming from the pulpit, considering how to apply them to her life.

Dinner with the Morrisons was a welcome reprieve from the stress of the day. By the time the meal ended, Emily was relaxed and rejuvenated, Larry was all smiles and Kevin told stupid, pointless jokes that made everyone laugh.

Larry left immediately after dinner, explaining that he had to drive back to Austin tonight. As his car pulled out of sight, Emily said her good-byes to Kevin and the Morrisons and began the short walk to her new home.

A brisk north wind had blown the clouds away. Stars as bright as diamonds littered the night sky. She was almost to her front door when she heard someone calling, "Mom, wait up." Turning, she saw Kevin hurrying toward her.

He caught up to her. "I want to talk to you."

The catch in his voice told her this was something serious. She wasn't up to another soul-searching conversation. "I'm very tired."

"This can't wait." Kevin followed her onto the front porch.

Emily put her key in the lock. "Is there a problem?"

Kevin leaned against a porch post. "That's what I'm here to find out."

That was a strange statement. Emily flipped the light switch and took her key from the door. "The house is a mess."

"It's like an igloo in here." Kevin closed the door behind him. "Where's the thermostat?"

Emily pointed to the square box mounted on the wall in the hall. "It's there but it's not working." She rubbed her hands along her upper arms. "It's not usually so cold this time of year."

"It needs to be turned on." Kevin lifted the little glass lid and turned a knob inside. "Does it seem odd being here in this strange house instead of home?"

Emily welcomed the warm blast of air that filled the room. "You didn't come here to talk about my new house." She gestured toward a chair stacked high with boxes. "Put those boxes on the floor and sit down." She sat in the only empty chair in the room, folded her hands, and waited.

Kevin looked around the cluttered living room. "Is this house big enough for you?"

"Now that I am rid of a lot of excess baggage, Boo and I should be very comfortable here."

Kevin stretched his feet in front of him and stared at the toes of his shoes. "What in the world is going on between you and Dad?"

Emily was aggravated that he would ask such a personal question. Her laugh didn't quite cover her annoyance. "No one could accuse you of being subtle."

Kevin asked again, this time more emphatically, "What is going on between you and Dad?"

Chapter Twenty-Three

Emily didn't owe Kevin an explanation, but she half-heartedly offered one. "What has always been going on, Robert and I have a long history and mutual concerns."

Even her not-so-observant Kevin recognized her deceit. "Today when we came into our old living room, the air was tense enough to ignite. Is Dad giving you a bad time about something?"

"Certainly not," Emily crossed her fingers. "Your father and I are on good terms." Kevin's scowl made her add, "Is it so hard for you to believe that a divorced couple can be friends?"

"Friends," Kevin hooted. "You two aren't friends. I'm not the only one who sensed something was wrong today. Stacy noticed, too."

"You are both making too much of an awkward moment," Emily declared with more conviction than she felt. She wanted to add that her relationship with her ex-husband was certainly none of Stacy's business. Prudence made her hold her tongue.

"Maybe we were, but I don't think so, and neither does Larry."

"Larry?" Emily echoed. "You talked about this with Larry?" She didn't like the idea of her sons discussing her.

"He's the one who brought it up." Kevin smiled wryly. "He said he thought you and Dad were quarreling."

Her sensitive Larry was the one who picked up on the obvious. "Why didn't you take an ad in the newspaper?"

Kevin grimaced. "We thought about confronting you and Dad together. Then Dennis pointed out that--"

Annoyance plunged headlong into full-blown anger. "What goes on between Robert and me is none of your business, nor is it any of Larry's concern. Dennis Morrison is way out of line even listening to such gossip from the two of you. That he would offer advice is outrageous."

Kevin argued with practiced lawyer-ease. "Dennis is almost a part of the family, since I'm engaged to his daughter. He's also a certified counselor. Besides, he didn't pry. We asked for his advice."

"This is certainly an about-face," Emily observed, caustically. "I didn't know you were so fond of Dennis and I suspect that he disapproves of you."

"He did at first. He's changed his mind."

"That was after he got to know you," Emily taunted.

"No. It was after he got to know you. Dennis likes you, Mom. He likes you a lot."

Dennis told her sons he liked her? She was pleased, and more than a little flattered. "That doesn't give him license to interfere in my life."

Kevin raised an eyebrow. "And how about Larry and me? Don't we have some rights? You are our mother."

He was striking where Emily was most vulnerable. The last thing she wanted was to hurt her sons. "Robert is your father," she asserted, striving for dignity and not quite achieving it.

Kevin straightened his back and crossed his legs. "I showed up and talked to him, like you asked me to. It wasn't much as conversations go, but we are on speaking terms now."

Emily bit her tongue to keep from asking what they had talked about. "That's a start."

Kevin's voice was resigned. "Don't go looking for miracles, Mom. Things between Dad and me will never be the same as they were before he left us."

"Your dad didn't leave you. He left me."

Much to her annoyance, Kevin said, "That's not the way it seems to me, but Dennis agrees with you. That's one of the things he told us when we talked."

Maybe it was good that both Larry and Kevin could talk freely to Dennis. She asked, even though she knew she shouldn't, "What else did Dennis say to you?"

"Several things, some I didn't want to hear." Kevin leaned forward. "Confound it, Mom, I still haven't figured out what happened to Dad." He was on his feet and pacing among the boxes in the room. "Just about the time I come to terms with what happened and accept that he's gone, he comes back, wanting to be a part of our lives again." He stopped pacing and ran his hand through his tousled hair. "My forgiveness doesn't extend that far. I don't want him messing up everything and upsetting everybody all over again."

"Sit down, Kevin," Emily extended one hand.

Kevin returned to his chair and sat down. "He's a sly dog. The full impact of what he was trying to do didn't hit me until I started talking to Larry and Stacy."

Although she disapproved of her son's behavior, his pain was very real. Emily was torn between a desire to comfort and a need to reprimand. "Don't call your father names."

Kevin bounded to his feet again. "Dennis says that middle-aged men sometimes get involved in affairs that don't last and then they have second thoughts." He came to stand directly in front of his mother. "Promise me you won't let him screw up your life again."

Emily pushed herself to a standing position. How could she fault her son when she shared his sentiments? "I appreciate the thought behind your concern, but you are prying into things that you have no right to call into question."

"I didn't mean to sound dictatorial." Kevin stepped back. "I've been a little overwrought. It helped us to talk to Dennis this afternoon."

Emily raised an eyebrow. "And who is us?"

"Larry and Stacy and me." Kevin glanced at his watch. "It's late. I have to go."

Emily wanted to assure Kevin that he could trust his father not to hurt him again. How could she when the same doubts and fears that Kevin voiced plagued her like a persistent itch? "Give this some more time and see how everything goes?"

Kevin shook his head. "You think time heals all wounds. This time, it won't."

Tomorrow Emily intended to call Robert and find out what he said to Kevin that upset him so badly.

After that, she was going talk with Dennis. Maybe a more objective view would help her settle some of her doubts. "Good night, Kevin. Try not to worry. Things will work out."

"My mother, the optimist," Kevin mocked as he closed the door behind him.

Emily stared at the bare walls of her living room. Her life was like her house, messy and strange and cluttered with useless items, while some of the essential elements had been lost in the chaos of change.

After a while she called Boo from the backyard and spread a mover's quilt in the corner of her bedroom for him. She went to bed, but it was a long time before she slept.

The next few days were busy ones. Emily phoned Robert and asked him to call her. Several days slipped by and Robert didn't answer her call. Early Friday afternoon she received a text message from him. *I will see you this evening.*

Emily had neither the time nor the inclination to ponder over his cryptic message. She was comforted by the thought that after she talked to Robert, she could turn to Dennis for advice and support.

Emily worked late. It was dark before she reached home. Robert was on the front porch when she drove into the driveway. He called to her as she opened the car door. "You're late. I was beginning to worry."

Emily hung her purse over her shoulder and lifted bags of groceries from the car seat. "I had a last-minute conference and I stopped by the deli."

Robert hurried to meet her. "Let me have your bags. We can go out to dinner, if you'd like."

"I'm too tired to go out." Emily dumped the paper bags into his arms. "I'm having deli food. You're welcome to share." She hurried up the steps and opened the front door, then held it for Robert to enter. "Take the bag into the kitchen."

Robert looked around the living room. "Where's Boo?"

"The twins have him. They take him for a walk in the afternoon and keep him until after dinner."

"Oh." Robert followed Emily into the kitchen and set the bag on the table. "I like your house."

Emily opened the bag, glad for a task that kept her hands busy and her eyes averted. "In the beginning it was a terrible mess. I called a cleaning service yesterday. They came and set the place in order." She took items from the bag. "I have baked chicken and a salad."

Robert slipped from his coat and hung it on the back of a kitchen chair. "Relax, Emily. I'm not going to make unwelcome advances, or embarrass you by baring my soul to you again."

Emily opened a package of paper plates, relaxing as she did so. "We do need to talk."

Robert dropped into a chair. "I'd offer to help, but I don't know where anything is."

Emily opened a drawer and rummaged around for a spoon. "I'm not sure I do either."

Robert's steady stare followed her every action as she moved back and forth between the cabinet and the table. "I hope you will be comfortable here." He made some inaudible comment under his breath.

They had to find a way to re-establish some common ground between them. They couldn't go on making their sons miserable. They were adults. Some compromise was in order. "I'm very comfortable here. This place has many advantages. It's smaller, easier to keep and nearer work." She opened cartons of food and set them on the table. "Did you get what you wanted from the junk in the attic?"

Robert said, "I took all of it."

Surprise halted Emily's hand in midair. "Even the baby crib and that old chest?" She dropped her hand and stared at him. "You don't have room for all that junk in your apartment. Where did you put it?"

"I don't think of memorabilia from our life together as junk. I rented a storage space."

Emily could think of no answer to that. She changed the subject. "How is George?"

"He's had to slow down, but he seems to be doing well." Robert leaned back in his chair. "He and Mom were surprised when I told them you moved. They asked me why."

"The other house was too big and too far from my work."

"Why did you choose this particular house?" Robert asked, "Was it because it was so near the Morrisons?"

There was just enough scorn in his voice to make Emily stiffen, "Certainly not!" Her words rang hollow in her own ears. Subconsciously, did she see in the Morrisons a substitute for the extended family she lost and the daughters she would never have? "I do enjoy being with the twins and they help me with Boo." She motioned for Robert to move his chair to the table.

They ate in uncomfortable silence. Once or twice, Emily stole a glance in Robert's direction. He seemed completely absorbed in eating his meal. Finally, she found the courage to say, "I'm going to ask you a personal question. I'll understand if you choose not to answer."

Robert's fork made a clattering sound as it hit the table. "About what?" he asked defensively.

Emily drew a deep breath. "I want to know what you said to Kevin when the two of you talked on Sunday."

Robert took a quick sip of water. "Why do you ask?"

Emily pushed her plate away. "Kevin was very upset afterwards."

"If he came crying to Mama, why didn't you ask *him* what happened?"

"It wasn't just what you said. Kevin, or more to the point, Stacy, picked up on the fact that you and I were ... Stacy thought we were..." She faltered, not knowing how to delicately word an indelicate assumption. "Stacy felt the tension in the room. So did Larry. They said as much to Kevin."

Robert wadded his paper napkin into a ball and dropped it in his cup. "Is this about what Stacy felt, what Larry assumed, or what I said to Kevin?"

"A little of all three," Emily admitted.

"What about me and how I felt?" Doesn't that matter to you at all?"

"I'm concerned about everyone involved in this messy situation." Tension tightened in Emily's stomach.

A sarcastic smile twisted Robert's lips. "Let it go, Emily. Some things can't be fixed."

Emily asked point blank, "Did you quarrel with Kevin?"

"We traded a few insults and then I told Kevin to mind his own business." Robert vaulted to his feet. "Is that what you wanted us to talk about?"

Emily was reluctant to admit that it was. "I want Kevin and Larry to accept our divorce without losing their father."

Robert put both hands in his pockets and raised his head to stare at the ceiling. "Is that out of concern for me or for Kevin and Larry?"

Emily replied, "For all of you."

Robert sat back down in his chair. "But mostly for Kevin and Larry." He closed his eyes and grimaced, as if in pain. "This is between you and me. We can't live our lives to please our adult sons."

"This animosity between you and your sons is tearing us all apart. We--" Emily's response was interrupted by a knock and the sound of the back door opening.

Chapter Twenty-Four

Kim burst through the kitchen entrance. "We brought Boo home. He's in the backyard."

Amy peeped over her sister's shoulder. "We gave him his dinner."

Emily motioned with one hand. "Come in. Would you like something to eat?"

"We've had dinner." Kim entered slowly, with Amy following close behind. Kim stopped when she saw Robert and inclined her head in his direction. "What is he doing here?"

Emily chuckled. Kim had all the finesse of a steamroller. "He's having dinner. Can't you say hello?"

Before Kim could answer, Amy put her hand on her sister's shoulder. "We have to go." It was obvious that neither of the twins was happy about Robert being at Emily's house.

Emily stood. "Thanks again for looking after Boo."

"We love taking care of him, and we are proving to Daddy that we are responsible enough to care of a pet of our own." Kim turned to go. "Don't forget, you're going to the museum with us tomorrow. The bus leaves at nine o'clock."

"I'll be ready." Emily closed the door behind the departing girls and turning, leaned against it.

She was surprised to see Robert putting on his coat. "Are you leaving?"

"I don't see any reason to stay." Robert buttoned his coat and turned up his collar. "Thanks for the dinner." Turning his back to her, he walked away.

She followed him into the living room. "Don't go away angry. We can talk about this."

"For how long, until the next phone call, or the next unannounced visitor shows up, or you remember some chore that can't wait?"

Was there any hope of ever making peace and bringing healing to her family? "There won't be any interruptions. If someone calls, they will leave a message. If someone knocks, I won't answer. I won't even bring Boo inside."

Robert sat down on the couch and patted the space beside him. "Come sit beside me."

Emily opted for the chair across from him instead. "Where do we start?"

"You tell me, Emily. Tell me what I have to do to mend the breach between us."

"I really don't know how to answer that."

Robert turned pale. "Do you want me to tell you about Susan?"

She didn't. "No." She didn't want to live through that hurt again.

Robert removed his coat, and tossed it across a footstool. "I could say it just happened, or blame Susan, but the truth is I was attracted to her first and I made the first overtures."

Emily lifted one hand. "I said no."

Heedless of her request, he went on. "I thought I loved her, at first. By the time I realized it was nothing more than a need for the attention of a desirable woman, it was too late. I had asked you for a divorce."

She wanted to believe what he said. That nagging little doubt wouldn't go away. "It's over now. Forget it."

"I've wanted to tell you this for a long time. I didn't think it would do any good. You had made a new life for yourself, right down to finding another man to take my place."

It took a while for Emily to absorb those words. "Do you still believe Thad and I--"

"I'm not blaming you. I let you go, but knowing you were with another man almost killed me."

Robert didn't trust her any more than she trusted him. "How many times do I have to tell you he was never more than a good friend?"

Skepticism raised Robert's brows. "I'd ask how good a friend, but I don't want to know. I blame myself for pushing you into the arms of another man."

"I blame myself partially, for your affair with Susan." Emily never had the courage to admit that to him before. "If I hadn't been so blind--"

"No!" Robert's cry rent the air. "Don't blame yourself for my stupid mistakes. If I had known, if I could have foreseen the far-reaching effects, it never would have happened. It's like throwing stones into a pool. The ripples you warned me about keep expanding. I've lost your love and my parents' respect, I've alienated my children, and still the circle widens." His jaw clenched. "I've sold my share in the real estate firm."

"Why?" The word stuck in Emily's throat

"Self-preservation. Susan is a partner in that business. She treated me with utter contempt. The tension was killing business, not to mention how long our property settlement would have dragged on in court if I hadn't agreed to let her take over."

This put a different slant on everything. "If you need money, I made a nice profit from the house. I'll give you an interest-free loan and you can pay it back whenever you're able."

"It's not that. Financially, this is a canny move. Emotionally, though, it's wrenching. I built that business from the ground up."

How bad, she wondered, was his rift with his parents? Was he making this effort to reconcile for their sake? Or was he reaching out for emotional support to see him through a difficult time. When he felt better, would he start looking for a younger woman to take her place again? "What will you do now?"

"I've opened an office downtown."

"How did Susan feel about your leaving?"

"Emily, you amaze me." Robert's fingers gripped the arm of the couch. "Why would you care about Susan's feelings?"

"If she misses you, she may want you back. And you may change your mind about her. And me. "

"So. I have to prove myself?"

"No." Emily replied, "This is not your issue. It's mine. You are asking me to trust you, and I don't know if I can."

His troubled gaze reflected her distress. "I won't betray you again."

The roots of her doubts ran deep. She might never be able to uproot them. A question she'd never had the courage to ask played through her mind. Was Susan the only one, or had there been others? "I trust you enough for us to be on friendly terms. Remarriage is out of the question."

"How can you be so sure?" Robert's voice faltered. "Relationships based solely on physical pleasure and sexual excitement seldom last. Relationships grounded in mutual friendship and respect can endure if--" His sentence halted.

Emily found no comfort in his words. It reinforced what she already feared. Susan was new and exciting, while she was like a comfortable old shoe.

Robert's lips thinned. "With Susan there was never any depth of emotion."

"There was something that motivated you to throw me away and marry her. You're telling me now it was just a fling?"

"Can't you ever forgive me?" Robert asked on a caught breath. "

She searched within herself, wanting to do the right thing, but needing to protect herself. His infidelity was something she might completely forgive, but she had come to realize she could never forget. "I can't dismiss what happened. I'd be dishonest if I told you I could."

"I don't expect you to forget. God knows, I never will." The sudden jarring ring of a telephone rent the air. Robert asked, "Do you need to answer?"

"No," Emily said without checking to identify her caller. "This is more important."

As the last clanging note died away, Robert asked, "Where do we go from here?"

"My main concern now is for my sons and how I can set their world right again. Don't tell me our reconciling would do that because that's not on the table. I've changed. My life is different now. *I'm* different."

Robert smiled, ruefully. "I could argue that basically people don't change. I don't suppose that would be to my advantage."

His self-effacing comment made her smile. "Maybe I haven't so much changed as shifted my priorities."

His brooding gaze rested on her face. "Why don't we take things slow and easy and see how it goes?" He stood and reached for his coat. "It's late. I should be going."

With the slightest provocation on her part, she knew he would take her in his arms and hold her against his heart. A part of her wanted him to do just that. Doubt whispered. *He left you for Susan. Now he's leaving Susan and wants to be with you. For how long, Emily? Until your hair turns gray? What happens if another sweet young thing catches his eye?* "I'm glad we talked."

She felt the tenseness in his body as he dropped an impersonal peck on her cheek. "Good-bye."

"Good-bye, Robert." She could have been speaking to a stranger.

Robert opened the door. Without looking back, he walked away and was swallowed up into the darkness of the night.

Emily sat staring at the open door for a long time before she rose from her chair to lock the door. She numbly walked to the kitchen. What did Robert really want from her? A temporary shoulder to cry on or a lifelong partnership? What could she expect from him in return? Or was he challenged by pursuing her, needing a new conquest? She didn't know. She wondered if he knew. A melancholy sadness smothered all other emotions. She called Boo inside and locked the back door.

Chapter Twenty-Five

Emily stood on the church steps and watched the last teenager descend from the bus and hurry toward a waiting car. She smiled at the man beside her. "That was a wonderful outing."

Dennis took Emily's arm. "I appreciate you chaperoning. So do the twins, even if they forgot to say the proper thank you." He guided her toward the street. "I'll walk you home."

"They were too excited about going home with friends." Emily stopped and blurted out, "May I take you to lunch?"

Dennis's eyes widened. "Are you asking me out?" His voice held a note of ironic amusement.

"You have to eat.

Dennis smiled. "Where am I taking you?"

"I'm taking you." Emily veered to the right. "My car is in the church parking lot."

Dennis's hand tightened on her arm. "You knew I'd say yes?"

Mischief lit Emily's eyes. "Are you?"

"I am, but don't get the idea that I'm a pushover." His smile was positively wicked. "Sometimes you modern women overwhelm this simple man of the cloth."

She doubted he had ever been overwhelmed by anything, least of all a woman. "Where would you like to go?"

The white of his teeth glistened against his tan skin as he smiled down at her. "There's a health food restaurant over on Grant Avenue."

Ten minutes later, Emily pulled her car into a parking space in front of The Healthy Habit Restaurant. "I've never eaten here."

Dennis unfastened his seat belt. "Then I think you are in for a pleasant surprise."

They found a secluded booth near the back of the dining room and sat down. A pretty waitress greeted Dennis with a smile of recognition. "Hello, Reverend Morrison. Do you need a menu?"

"I'll have the special of the day." Dennis raised an eyebrow in Emily's direction. "Ms. Franklin?"

Emily asked, "What is the special of the day?"

The waitress took a pad from her pocket and a pencil from behind her ear, "Eggplant omelet."

It didn't sound like anything she would enjoy; nevertheless, Emily said, "I'll have the special of the day, too."

The moment the waitress was out of earshot, Emily asked, "What is an eggplant omelet?"

"It's an omelet with lots of egg whites, lots of eggplant, and some fantastic seasonings."

Despite the name, the omelet, if it could be called that, was surprisingly good. Emily asked between bites, "Do you come here often?"

"Yes. The food is good and good for you."

Emily took a deep breath. "Kevin says you're a counselor."

Without missing a bite Dennis said, "You knew that before he told you."

"What we talk about here must be in strictest confidence." Emily felt a little ridiculous making such a statement, but she needed assurance.

Dennis reached for a breadstick. "It would be even if I weren't a counselor. I'm a minister of the gospel. Not even the law of the land can force me to divulge what is confessed to me in confidence."

She hadn't thought of what she wanted to say as a confession. "It's about Kevin and Larry."

"What about them?" Dennis snapped the breadstick. Crumbs flew on the table and into his lap.

"I know they talked to you about their father and me." Emily took a sip of water to ease the catch in her throat. "As you can see, this is a little difficult for me."

"Yes. I noticed." Dennis's fork halted halfway to his mouth.

Emily's patience snapped. "Come on, Dennis, you know what I'm asking you."

He laid his fork across his plate and dusted crumbs from his lap. "You haven't asked anything yet, except if I'm a counselor, and I answered in the affirmative." He popped a piece of bread stick into his mouth, and chewed thoughtfully. "Are you often at a loss for words when you're upset?"

"I'm not..." Emily sighed. "Sometimes. Often might be more honest."

" I don't have a clue what you want from me."

Emily put her elbows on the table and rested her chin in her hands. "Robert wants us to try mending our relationship." She blurted the words out before stopping to catch her breath. "Kevin objects to that, even though it's none of his business." Her strident tones died to a mere whisper. "I don't know what Larry thinks."

Dennis pressed his napkin to his lips before laying it on the table. "Has your ex-husband asked you to marry him again?"

It hit her with the force of a physical blow that Robert had not mentioned marriage. "Not exactly. It hasn't gone that far."

"How far has it gone?"

She wanted to tell him that was none of his business. How could she when she sought him out and was asking for his advice? "I haven't slept with him if that's what you're asking."

Dennis chuckled low in his throat. "You do have a way of coming to the point. Why not?"

He was being aggravating and purposefully so, she suspected. "I didn't ask you here to talk about me. I need your advice about Kevin and Larry."

Dennis signaled for the waitress. "Would you like dessert, some cheese and fruit maybe?"

"I would like to know," Emily emphasized each word, "what Kevin and Larry said when they talked to you about their father and me."

"Emily--" The arrival of the waitress cut Dennis's reply short. He took his time deciding on dessert.

As the waitress hurried away, Emily leaned across the table. "Were they upset? Larry seems indifferent. Kevin is so angry." She drummed her fingers on the table. "For heaven's sake, Dennis, say something."

"I can't reveal something told to me in confidence to anyone."

"I'm not just anyone," Emily argued. "I'm their mother."

Dennis's voice lost its bantering tone. "Would how they feel make a difference in whether or not you take your husband back?"

Emily corrected him, "My ex-husband. I don't like to see my children hurt."

"What if you are hurt again?" Dennis peeled an orange, giving it his utmost attention. "That's really what you're afraid of, isn't it?" He broke the orange into pieces and laid each section on his plate. "You are afraid Robert will hurt you again."

He spoke a truth Emily was reluctant to admit, even to herself. "He says he made a mistake."

Dennis wiped his fingers on the napkin beside his plate. "Can you believe that he won't make the same mistake again?"

"He assures me he wouldn't."

"That's not what I asked." Dennis plopped an orange section into his mouth.

Emily struggled to hold onto her temper. "What happened wasn't all Robert's fault. I was an inattentive wife. I didn't mean to be, but he says I neglected him, and I can see now why he felt that way." Her fingers pleated a paper napkin. "He took me for granted, too. In the end he turned to someone else."

Dennis swallowed his last orange slice. "Was it the end?"

She thought for a while before answering. "It was, because Robert wanted it to be."

"What did you want? More to the point what *do* you want now?" Dennis wiped orange juice from his fingers with his napkin. "I suspect you've spent most of your life trying to please the people around you. Why not try pleasing yourself for a change?"

"That's your advice? That I should be selfish?" Emily picked up the check. She half-expected Dennis to argue about her paying for his lunch. He didn't.

"Not exactly. It appears to me that during your marriage, your husband did most of the taking and you did most of the giving."

He was making her sound like a doormat. Maybe he was right. "Does Kevin hate his father?"

"Why don't you ask Kevin?" Dennis glanced at his watch. "I should be going. In less than an hour the singles group is having its monthly social at the church." He slid from the booth and stood. "You're coming, aren't you?"

She didn't want to return to a strange, empty house. Emily stood and dusted her skirt. "Sure, why not?"

Later, sitting in a circle with other separated or divorced men and women, Emily listened as a portly middle-aged man related how his wife of nearly thirty years had, "up and took off with the TV repair man." The man sighed. "I don't know what to think anymore." The situation would have been amusing if it hadn't been so pathetic.

Dennis, with his usual charm and composure, offered comfort and consolation without giving any great measure of hope or assurance. "Maybe you should think less, and set your course on some decisive plan of action, Amos. Truth reveals itself to the diligent doer." The Reverend did have an amazing ability to read people and anticipate events. He avoided giving concrete advice to anyone on any issue.

Eventually the group dispersed and Emily wandered into the kitchen for a second cup of coffee and another slice of cake. She leaned against the counter, sipped coffee, nibbled cake, and pondered the events of the past few days. Maybe Dennis's advice to Amos was not as abstract and evasive as she first thought. She stirred more sugar into her coffee and laid the spoon on the counter. "Maybe I should decide on a course of action and pursue it regardless of the consequences."

"Talking to yourself, Emily?"

Emily turned to see Dennis standing behind her. "Where is everyone?"

Dennis looked around the room. "They've gone home."

Emily put her cup on the counter and glanced at the clock on the wall. "Good heavens, it's four forty-five. I have to go, too."

"I was hoping you'd stay for a while." Dennis followed as she hurried across the room. "The twins will be home soon. Stacy and Kevin are at the parsonage."

"I can't." She was in no condition emotionally to be with the Morrisons and Kevin in a cozy family atmosphere. Emily hurried out the door, and jumped into her car. Her talk with Dennis disturbed her, and she didn't know why. Like a bolt of chained lightening the answer danced through her head. She was attracted to Dennis Morison. Was it possible to be attracted to one man and in doubt about your feelings about another? She drove the short distance to her house in a totally confused state.

As she came through the front door her phone vibrated. Emily took it from her handbag, and held it to her ear. "Yes. Hello."

"Emily?" Robert's deep voice sounded across the wire. "I called a few moments ago and you didn't answer."

She wanted to ask why he was calling. She didn't. Emily pitched her handbag on the couch. "I was driving home.

Robert waited, hoping, she suspected, that she would offer further explanation. After a short silence he said, "Tomorrow is Sunday."

"Yes, I know." *Where was all this leading?*

"Would you like to go with me to visit Mom and Dad?"

Emily hesitated, "I don't know if that's a good idea." George and Clara would ask prying questions she wasn't ready to answer, not yet anyway.

"They would love to see you. Why don't I come by and take you to lunch? We can talk about it then."

Robert and his sons making peace did not require Emily to visit Clara and George. She grimaced into the telephone. "Thank you, Robert, but no."

Robert hung on. "Why not?"

Emily broke the connection, dropped her phone back into her handbag, and walked to the kitchen. How long would it be before she felt at home in this house? She was so sure moving was a wise decision. Now second thoughts moved in to whisper through her mind. She shook her head to clear her brain. Only hours ago, she decided to set a course of action and pursue it. Now she was worrying about the wisdom of a decision she had previously made. Maybe *I'll feel better tomorrow. More certain about things.*

Chapter Twenty-Six

Doubts popped into Emily's head the next morning as she opened her eyes in a strange bedroom. She made Boo's breakfast. *I must stop worrying about the past and start making positive plans for the future.* She patted Boo's head. "Don't you agree?"

Boo wagged his tail.

"Is that your studied opinion?" Emily put a plate of food on the floor and watched as Boo wolfed it down. Her mind drifted back to yesterday's conversation with Dennis. He advised her, without actually saying it in so many words, to put her own needs and desires first. Or had she read the wrong meaning into his equivocal advice? She went to Dennis expecting him to give her some clue about how to bridge the gap between Robert and his sons. He raised even more questions, and offered no answers.

She thought, too, he would tell her something about his session with Kevin and Larry. He not only refused to do that, he refrained from giving any indication as to how either of them felt about reconciliation between her and Robert.

Dennis was a remarkable man, intelligent, gifted, and kind. Emily pushed those thoughts from her mind and decided to cook lunch instead of settling for cold cuts. That should keep her hands busy and her mind occupied.

She was only half right. Her hands were busy through the remainder of the morning. She made a pot roast and baked a lemon pie, as thoughts shifted through her mind like patterns in a turning kaleidoscope.

As she chopped lettuce and sliced tomatoes, she remembered the question Dennis put to her yesterday. *What do **you** want, Emily?* She would be happy to reply, if only she knew the answer.

She was putting the final touches to her dining room table centerpiece when the doorbell rang. She rushed to answer.

Robert stood on the other side, with a bouquet of flowers. "Please don't throw me out."

"You have some nerve."

"May I come in?"

She stepped back and motioned with her hand.

Robert stepped inside, but not before giving Emily the bouquet of carnations and babies' breath. "These are for you."

"Thank you." Emily started for the kitchen.

Robert followed. "I remembered you like pink carnations."

"They're very pretty." She rummaged around under the sink, found an empty vase, and filled it with water. "I'll put them on the table." She nodded toward the dining room. "I was about to sit down to lunch."

"Is that an invitation?"

Emily set Robert's bouquet in the center of the table and put her own arrangement of spring flowers on the sideboard. "I'll set another place."

Robert put the bottle of wine beside the flowers. "I smelled your pot roast when I came through the door. It brought back a host of good memories." He hung his hat on the back of a chair. "Is it too much to hope that you also made a lemon pie?"

"I did," Emily replied. "There's a fresh vegetable salad, too, with French dressing."

Robert gazed at the table. "Are you expecting someone else?"

"No." Emily nodded toward the table. "Sit down. I'll bring the food."

Robert ladled gravy over his pot roast. "Aunt Beth says you came to see her last week. That was nice of you."

Emily was genuinely fond of Robert's great-aunt. "I always enjoy visiting with Aunt Beth."

They ate in silence. As Robert helped himself to a generous slice of lemon pie he asked, "Would you like to stop by and see Aunt Beth this afternoon after we visit with Mom and Dad?"

Emily set her glass on the table. "I've already told you I'm not going to your parents' with you."

A frown knitted Robert's brow, "Why not? Don't you want to see them?"

"I do see them at least once a week. I don't want to go there today."

Robert laid his napkin beside his plate. "What you mean is, you don't want to go there with me. Why not, Emily?"

"Don't pressure me."

Robert closed his eyes and tilted his head back. "I'm not pressuring you; I am trying to understand you. I think that's something I failed to do for several years." He opened his eyes and stared at her. "You tried to tell me how you felt, and I didn't listen. I'm ready to do that now. Tell me, please, why you don't want to go with me to visit my parents."

Emily pushed her plate aside, put her elbows on the table and set her chin in her hands. "If I go with you, George and Clara will think we're back together again."

"Would that be so terrible? That's what they hope will happen."

"I don't want them to put their hopes in something that can never be. They would be disappointed all over again."

Robert came around the table, took her hand, and led her into the living room, where he pushed her down on the couch and sat beside her. "We can talk much better here, without a table between us." He took both of her hands in his. "You are not sure we can work through our problems." When she tried to pull her hands from his, he held them even tighter, "Why not, Emily?"

They had been over this so many times before. "We want different things. You want us to be together again. I want us to find some closure and be friends, nothing more." This time Emily succeeded in pulling her hands free. She folded them in her lap. "Things change. People change."

"I know I hurt you." He ran his fingers through his hair. "That's it, isn't it? You're afraid somewhere down the line I would walk out on you again."

"It could happen." Emily tried to retreat and found her back pressing into the couch arm.

Robert touched her face with the tips of his fingers before letting them slide gently through her hair. "You're not going to lose me, not ever again."

"I've already lost you. We're divorced. You're married to someone else, or have been. I keep asking myself, what did she offer that I couldn't give you?" She pushed his hand away. "It must have been strong and very real for you to trash your marriage and alienate your sons to have it."

He moved back as if she had struck him. "I've told you it was a mistake. Can't we leave it at that, instead of dragging out all those painful old memories?"

If they ever hoped to get past that traumatic episode in their lives, they had to talk about Robert's infidelity. "If it happened once, what assurance is there that it won't happen again?"

He stood and paced restlessly across the floor. With his back to her he said, "It won't happen again for the same reason a kid doesn't touch a hot stove the second time. I've been burned. I know the pain it brings. I also know that pain is all I would get, that and an aching wound that won't heal." He turned to face her. "I was too proud to admit that I, the great Robert Franklin, could suffer from so common a malady as middle-aged crazies. I decided I must be in love. A part of me actually believed I was. I convinced myself that what was wrong with our marriage was your fault. Susan was there, offering me solace and comfort."

"And sex," Emily added.

"That, too." Robert dropped into a chair.

A fear Emily avoided all these months suddenly surfaced. "How experienced is Susan?"

"I had the good sense to get myself tested, if that's what you're driving at. I don't have any sexually transmitted diseases."

That thought that never crossed Emily's mind. "Good move, but that's not what I'm talking about."

Robert tilted his head to one side. "What *are* you talking about?"

Emily searched for words that would get her point across and still leave her pride intact. "Has Susan slept with many men?"

Robert exploded, "Good grief, Emily. Why would you want to know that?"

"Because I'm lacking in experience. In a blushing young bride, that's excusable, maybe even commendable. She spoke aloud a fear that had tormented her for months. "What if after being with Susan you find me inadequate and boring?"

Robert gritted, "That would never happen."

Without an ounce of malice, Emily said "It already has. The last few years of our marriage, for you, sex with me was no more than a habit." It was not an accusation, but a calm statement of fact.

His voice dropped. "I've been thinking you wouldn't let me near you because you suspected I might have some social disease and I discover you're afraid of your own imagined inadequacies."

"They're not imagined They're very real."

Robert put his hand under her chin and lifted her face. "May I kiss you?"

"I'm not a child, Robert. You can't kiss me and make it better."

"How do you know until we try?" He edged a little closer.

"Do you remember the first time I kissed you?" He moved again shifting his weight. "I mean really kissed you, and not just a hello or a good-bye peck on the cheek?"

She did remember. They were standing in the backyard of her parents' home. It was her sixteenth birthday. Robert lingered after the party was over, her giggling friends went home and both sets of parents retired to the house. The cloying scent of honeysuckle hung in the warm twilight air. "You told me to close my eyes, that you had something for me."

"Close your eyes," Robert whispered. "I have something for you."

Emily closed her eyes and waited.

His lips claimed hers in a sweetly seductive kiss.

After a few blissful moments, Robert broke the embrace and moved back. "Do you remember what you said to me then?"

It had been years since she thought about that incident. "Something stupid, I imagine."

"It wasn't stupid." He still held onto her chin. "It was sweet and innocent, and very honest. You rubbed your hand across your lips and said, 'You stuck your tongue in my mouth.' Then you asked me to do it again."

"And you refused," Emily said, as that old memory sharpened and came into focus in her mind. "I thought you were completely turned off."

Robert guffawed, "Turned off? I was turned on, so turned on that I knew I had to get out of there before I did something really foolish, like try to seduce you." Remembering made him smile. "I worried for weeks that you would tell your father and he'd come after me with a shotgun."

"I never told anyone." Emily touched her mouth with her fingers. "It was too special."

"We have so many special moments to remember. You and I belong together. Don't let my momentary lapse of good sense destroy what it's taken us a lifetime to build."

It may have been a momentary lapse for Robert, but for Emily it was a life-altering event. "It's already destroyed and I'm not sure we can ever repair it."

"Don't say that. I won't hurt you again, Emily, I swear I won't."

The silence in the room was shattered by the slamming of the front door and Kevin's voice calling, "Mom? Where are you?"

Chapter Twenty-Seven

Emily pulled herself from Robert's embrace. She was smoothing her hair and straightening her blouse when Kevin and Stacy came into the room, followed by Amy, Kim, and Boo. "Good heavens, Kevin," she scolded, "Don't you know how to knock on a door?"

"I did knock." Kevin was obviously assessing the scene before him. "I banged and no one answered. I thought you must be asleep." His gaze shifted to Robert. "Hi, Dad, I didn't know you were here."

"How did you think my car got in the drive?" Robert asked caustically.

For once Kevin didn't pick up on Robert's angry retort. "I'm not my usual sharp self today." He smiled down at Stacy, his face alight with adoration. "Stacy and I have something to tell you."

Boo bounded across the room and put his paws in Emily's lap. She stroked his head. "Would you like to sit down?"

Kim asked from the doorway. "Is it okay if Amy and I take Boo outside to play?"

"Of course." Emily gave Boo a final pat. "There are some doggie treats on the shelf in the utility room."

Kim whistled for Boo. He scampered across the room, his claws making screeching sounds across the hardwood floor as he ran. "See you later," Kim called, as she and Amy ushered Boo from the room.

As the commotion created by their departure died away, Emily asked again, "Would you like to sit down?"

Kevin sat in the overstuffed chair and Stacy perched on the arm beside him. "Guess what?" Kevin took Stacy's hand in his. "Stacy and I have set the date. We're going to be married in the church sanctuary the third Sunday in June. Dennis is going to perform the ceremony."

Stacy put her free arm around Kevin's shoulder and beamed. "Kim and Amy will be my bride's maids--"

Kevin interrupted, excitement spilling into his every word. "There will be a reception in the church recreation hall after the ceremony."

"Are we invited?" Emily stole a glance in Robert's direction. He sat straight and still, his expression as unreadable as a closed book.

Kevin's eyes cut in Robert's direction, "Only if you want to come."

Emily saw Dennis's fine hand in Kevin's rather awkward move toward reconciliation and she was grateful to him. "I do."

Robert asked, "Are you inviting me to your wedding?"

Kevin shot back, "Do you want an engraved invitation?"

"If you're sending them out, that would be nice." Robert's face creased into a droll smile.

"We will have invitations printed." Stacy's fingers dug into Kevin's shoulders. "We will see that you get one." She gave Kevin another warning nudge. "Won't we, Kevin?"

Emily sent Robert what she hoped was a warning glance. "When did you decide all this?"

"Just today." The tension in the room eased as Stacy explained, "Kevin and I have wanted to set the date for months, but Dad kept insisting I was too young to make a permanent commitment. Now he's changed his mind."

Emily couldn't believe that Dennis had done such an abrupt and complete about face. "Dennis has agreed to your getting married?"

Kevin laughed. "Maybe the age of miracles hasn't passed after all."

Stacy bubbled with excitement. "Out of the blue, he agreed. Oh, there's so much to do and such a short time to do it in. You will help me, won't you, Emily?"

"Of course, I will," Emily answered, caught up in the excitement of the moment. "Will it be a large wedding?"

"Not really," Stacy answered, "Just family and friends."

Robert glanced at his watch. "I have to go. Mom and Dad are expecting me." He stood before asking Emily, "Are you sure you don't want to come with me?"

"We can talk about the wedding later," Kevin offered, "If you have other plans."

"No. Stay." Emily put her hand on Robert's arm. "I'll see you to the door." She detoured through the dining room to retrieve Robert's hat before following him onto the front porch and closing the front door behind her. "I'm sorry we were interrupted."

"We can pick up where we left off later, I hope." Robert put his hat on his head and gave it a little tap. "Have you been talking to Kevin?"

Emily shook her head. "No. But someone has, apparently."

"The Reverend?" Robert questioned.

Emily pursed her lips. "Probably."

"Maybe I shouldn't question my sudden good fortune."

"But you do?" Emily wondered why he would.

Robert asked, "Will you have lunch with me one day this week?"

Emily hesitated before saying, "I'll be too busy." She opened the door and went inside, before closing it behind her.

*****

The next several weeks passed in a whirl of activity. Lee Morgan hired an assistant to help Emily at the library. "You will be tied up from time to time with your videos," he told her, as he flashed his most winning smile. "We don't want to lose you, therefore the new assistant and the raise. Oh, and Mac Evans wants you to call him."

Emily's first meeting with Mac -was a nerve-wracking experience. "I know nothing about making videos. Please be patient with me."

Mac wore boots, blue jeans, and a tee shirt with, *this ain't my first rodeo* printed across the front. "Relax." He studied her as he rubbed his chin with his thumb and forefinger. "Yes, indeed, a photographer's dream." He pointed to a small table in one corner of his studio. "Have a seat and we'll get the show on the road."

Emily sat, wondering as she did so how she ended up in such an awkward situation.

Mac turned his chair with its back facing the table and sat straddle-legged across it. The first words out of his mouth made her consider running for the nearest exit. "You are exquisite. If sex sells, this city is on a roll."

Emily gasped. "I am here to make public service videos for the library system, not--"

Mac had the audacity to laugh, not a snicker, or a chortle, but a loud, good-humored, belly-laugh. After a few moments he brought his hilarity under control. "Excuse me if I offended you." He breathed and swallowed. "It was meant as a compliment. I got carried away. I am so pleased about having the opportunity to film you."

She had never met anyone like him before. She doubted she ever would again. "I have no idea why."

He narrowed his eyes, leaned across the table, and studied her face with unconcealed interest. "You are beautiful, not because of makeup or plastic surgery, or diet, but because you were born with fine bone structure, flawless skin, and an inner glow that I hope I can capture on film. The rinse on your hair is unnecessary."

Emily didn't know if she should thank him, or tell him to mind his own business. "This is my natural hair color. Are you always so outspoken?"

Mac smiled as he stood. "You will get used to it."

He had some gall. "What if I don't?"

"Beautiful lady, don't give me grief." He moved to the other side of the room. "Come and sit here. I want to get the lighting exactly right."

Emily came, sat down, and endured Mac having a young, very attractive woman redo her makeup and remove the pins and clasp that held her hairdo in place. It fell in waves down her back.

Mac stood a distance away, reviewing the woman's handiwork. "Good job, Nancy." He came to face Emily, borrowed Nancy's comb, and arranged a curl of hair to fall toward the front over each shoulder. "Perfect, almost." He unbuttoned the top button of her blouse and grasped each side of her collar, exposing a narrow expanse of cleavage.

Emily slapped his hands, and pulled her collar back in place. "This is not a glamour shot."

Mac grinned. "How could it be anything else?"

No one ever told Emily she was beautiful before. She didn't think of herself as pretty or glamorous. Mac insisted she was all three. She adjusted her collar. I am due back at my office in half an hour."

An hour and a half passed before the filming was completed to Mac's satisfaction. "All done. How about dinner tonight?"

"Certainly not." Emily grabbed her handbag, and made for the door. Not until she was in her car and driving toward her office, did she breathe a sigh of relief.

Little by little Emily's new house became her new home. She was starting her second year as a divorced woman. Looking back over the wide chasm of days and doubts that separated the present from the past, she realized how much she had changed. It was a slow and subtle process and one of degree more than kind. How imperceptible were the alterations of time.

Plans for Kevin and Stacy's wedding consumed much of Emily's spare time. As she helped Stacy make plans for the big event, she was pulled more and more into the Morrison family circle. She kept reminding herself to keep a discreet emotional distance. Was it caution or cowardice that warned her against becoming too intimately involved with Kevin's soon-to-be in-laws?

One Saturday morning only weeks before the wedding, Stacy called and invited Emily to join the Morrison family for a picnic in the country. "Dad thinks we all need to relax and unwind."

Emily was pleased that she was included. "Tell me where and when."

"It's a private picnic area that belongs to one of our church members. Kevin and I are going out early this morning." Without asking Emily's consent for such an arrangement, she added, "You can ride out with Dad and the twins later."

Emily didn't argue. If Kevin wanted her along on a family picnic, she would go, and not complain.

The outing was pleasant but it lasted much longer than Emily had imagined it would. It was almost nine o'clock in the evening when Dennis pulled his van into her driveway. "I'll walk you to the door."

"That's not necessary." Emily got out and shut the door. "I'll see all of you tomorrow, and thank you for a lovely time."

As the car pulled from the drive, Amy poked her head out the back window. "We'll come for Boo early in the morning."

Emily hummed under her breath as she rummaged in her bag for her door key. She had put the key in the lock when a voice from the shadows said, "I've been waiting for you since six-thirty."

Emily narrowed her eyes against the darkness. "Robert? Is that you?"

He emerged from the shadows. "It's me. I called Kevin on his cell phone about seven. He didn't tell you?" The dim light from the street lamp cast eerie shadows across his face. "You have hay in your hair."

Kevin didn't tell her, and she thought she knew why. Emily unlocked the door. "Actually, it's grass. I wasn't expecting you."

Robert followed her into the house. "I wasn't expecting to be here either. But this is an emergency."

"George?" Emily hit the switch on the wall, flooding the room with light.

Stubble of beard grew on Robert's face. "No, it's Aunt Beth. She's had a stroke. She's asking for you."

Emily dropped her keys into her handbag, "Which hospital?"

"She's at Southwest General." Robert's eyes scanned Emily's face. "Your nose is sunburned."

"I'll be there as soon as I can." Emily rubbed her fingers across the rough surface of her nose. "I have to feed Boo first."

"Go change," Robert told her. "I'll look after Boo. Then I'll drive you to the hospital."

"How am I supposed to get back home?" A dull ache began in Emily's shoulders. She rubbed her hands across the back of her neck. It was sunburned and stiff.

"This is Saturday night," Robert reminded her. "The area around the hospital is jammed with teenagers. They will be cruising up and down Main Street most of the night. It's not safe for you to go into that area alone."

Emily took a hasty shower and was dressed and ready to go in twenty minutes. When she came into the living room, Robert leaned against the door holding her handbag. "Ready?"

Emily nodded. "Yes." She hung her bag over her shoulder and followed him outside. Once in the darkened drive, she squinted and looked around. "Where's your car?"

"This way." He took her arm and hurried toward the street.

"Why did you park out here?" Emily trotted to stay up with his long strides.

"I knew you were with the Morrison family. If they saw my car, they would find some reason to stay." Robert quickened his pace.

It was after eleven when Robert stopped his car into the parking lot of the hospital. As they hurried through the emergency entrance, he took Emily's arm. "I wouldn't insist you come here at this hour of the night if Aunt Beth wasn't asking for you." He guided her toward the elevators. "She's in intensive care on the fourth floor."

The hospital corridors were deserted except for an occasional nurse and a few night custodians. They got into the elevator and Robert jabbed his finger into the button labeled four. The cage climbed upward.

Emily leaned against a side rail and watched the numbers over the door flash as they zoomed upward. Thoughts and memories of Aunt Beth crowded all other concerns from her mind. Aunt Beth never had a husband or children. She missed so many of the joys of life. Maybe she missed a good portion of the heartaches, too.

The elevator coming to a sudden stop brought Emily back to the present with a jolt. As the doors clanged open, she drew a deep breath and prepared herself for what lay ahead, "Which way?"

Robert's hand was on her elbow. "Down the hall and to the right."

They entered a small waiting room where George and Clara huddled on a couch in the corner. They jumped to their feet when Emily and Robert came into the room. George patted Emily's shoulder. "Mama and I were afraid you weren't coming."

"I was out with Kevin when Robert came." Why did Emily feel it necessary to say she was with Kevin and skip the fact that she had been with the Morrisons, too? "Robert waited for me and I'm glad he did." She urged George to sit down. "Try to get some rest. I'm going in to see Aunt Beth."

Clara settled on the cushion beside George. "Aunt Beth is asleep, dear. About an hour after Robert left, she took a turn for the better. The doctor was amazed. Dad and I would have gone home hours ago except we thought we should wait for you and Robert."

Emily perched on the edge of an overstuffed chair and breathed a sigh of relief. "Aunt Beth's recovery is good news."

George frowned. "It's not a recovery, just a reprieve. The doctor says we can see her tomorrow afternoon." With an effort, he stood to his feet. "Can you come back then, Emily?"

Clara consulted her watch. "Except tomorrow's today now. It's five minutes past twelve."

"I'll be here this afternoon. I'll call a cab." She reached inside her handbag

George and Clara, in unison, objected. "No, it's not safe out there." George said.

Clara jumped to her feet. "I would be worried sick if I thought you were out in that mess of teenagers in a cab with a stranger driving."

George took his wife's arm. "Mama. Don't go looking for something else to worry about. Robert will take Emily home." He turned to Robert. "Won't you, son?"

Robert nodded. "I will."

George and Clara disappeared down the wide corridor and still Robert sat on the edge of the low couch. "It's very quiet here."

Emily stirred to her feet. "I'll call that cab now."

Robert said, "I'll take you. If, by some outside chance, something happened to you, Mom and Dad would never forgive me.

"By the time you get back to your apartment it will be time to get up." Emily was bone-weary. "If you'd like you can take me home and stay at my house for the remainder of the night." The surprised look that flitted across his face made her add, "You can sleep in the spare bedroom."

"I'm surprised you would agree to spend even a part of a night under the same roof with me."

Emily didn't care where she slept, so long as she did. "I don't mind."

Robert pulled himself to a standing position. "We can go to my apartment. It's only ten minutes away. I'll sleep on the couch. You can have my bed."

Their footsteps echoed down the deserted hall. Emily was so weary her boned hummed. "I can sleep on the couch."

Robert took her arm. "Did you enjoy your outing with the Morrison family?"

His question told her he was itching for a fight. Emily was not up to verbal sparring with Robert, or anyone else. "Not tonight, Robert. I'm too tired."

Robert pulled her around to face him. "I am losing you and Kevin to another man."

He had no right to jump to such unfair conclusions. "Dennis is the person who persuaded Kevin he should forgive you."

"Forgive me?" Robert echoed incredulously. "For what, I've never done anything to Kevin."

"Kevin thought you had, until Dennis convinced him otherwise."

"I should thank the man who is trying to steal my wife and sons away from me?" Robert asked caustically.

As they walked down the hall toward the elevator, Emily reminded him, not unkindly, "I'm not your wife."

Robert ignored her. "Don't you know what Dennis Morrison is trying to do?" He held the elevator door open.

Emily stepped into the cage and Robert followed her. "Reverend Morrison isn't 'trying to do' anything. I'd like to think he and his daughters think of me as family."

Over the clang of the closing door, Robert murmured, "Little by little the man is seducing you away from me."

If he only knew how platonic her friendship with Dennis was. "If you think Dennis has some ulterior motive in being kind to us, you're wrong." The elevator sped downward and stopped. "I am fond of Kim and Amy. They are almost like my own children."

"The daughters you never had?" Robert followed Emily into the hallway. "How very nice."

A nurse came from behind the lobby desk and walked toward them. "Unless you have some reason to be here, you should go."

Robert assured her, "We're leaving." He took Emily's arm. "Tomorrow you and I are going to have a long talk."

Emily stepped through the lobby door. "I have nothing more to say to you." The cool night air blew across her burned face and penetrated her thin blouse, making her shiver.

"Maybe, for a change, you'll listen to what I have to say." Robert guided her across the parking lot and to his car.

Chapter Twenty-Eight

Muscles Emily didn't know she had twenty-four hours ago, ached unmercifully. She tossed her handbag on Robert's couch, kicked off her shoes, and sank into the nearest chair. "I'll sleep on the couch. It's too small for you."

Robert closed the door and secured the lock. "It makes into a bed." He nodded toward a door at the other end of the room. "The bathroom's that way, through the bedroom."

Emily was too tired to move. "You go first." It occurred to her that she had nothing to sleep in. "Do you have an old shirt I can borrow?"

Robert strode toward the bedroom. "I'll find something." He returned carrying sheets, a pillow, a blanket, and a frayed-at-the-cuffs denim shirt. He pitched the shirt in Emily's direction and dumped the bedding on the floor beside the couch.

Emily caught the shirt. "Thanks." She laid it across her lap.

Robert pulled a handle at the base of the couch. "Go on to bed." A mattress unrolled and stretched into full view. "Put something on your face. It looks like it's going to peel."

Emily ran her fingers across the bridge of her sore nose. The skin was rough and hot. "It's been a long time since I was this sunburned."

Robert made the bed. "You should know to put on sun screen and wear a hat when you go out in the sun."

"My sunburn's not the worst of my problems." Emily rolled her head around on the back of her chair. "I played baseball today. My back hurts, my shoulders ache, and my legs are sore."

Robert scoffed, "At your age you played baseball?"

Anger brought Emily's head up. "What do you mean, at my age?"

"You're no longer a teenager, even though sometimes you insist on acting like one." Robert sat on the edge of the bed he had made. "Take a shower. That will help."

Emily began the painful process of standing. " Go to bed. I'll see you in the morning."

"Why must you argue about everything?" Robert stretched out on the bed. "It's almost three in the morning. Good night, Emily."

Emily pointed to the couch. "I am sleeping here!"

He snorted, "No way."

It occurred to her, as she let the cool spray from the shower wash over her weary, aching body, that arguing was unnecessary and stupid. What difference did it make who slept where? She dried carefully because of her sunburn, wrapped the towel around her wet hair, and slipped into Robert's shirt. It was too big. She rolled up the sleeves, and rummaged around in the medicine cabinet, looking for something to put on her sunburned face.

"Need some help?" Robert stood in the doorway, barefoot and wearing nothing but a pair of tight jeans.

Emily snapped, "You could have knocked."

"You wouldn't have heard me. You were in the shower." He came to stand beside her. "Let me look."

He nudged her aside, and searched until he found a tube of ointment. "Aha, just the thing for sore muscles."

How long had he been standing there? "I was looking for something for my sunburn." She backed toward the door.

"Would you like me to massage your back and your legs?" His chest rose and fell in rhythm with his shallow breathing.

"No, thank you." Emily shook her head, slinging beads of moisture across Robert's face and bare chest.

"Come here." He pulled her to him, and rubbed her hair with the towel. "I can remember when you loved having me shampoo your hair and give you a body rub."

Emily braced herself against the onslaught of emotions those memories evoked. "I can remember when you loved doing it."

His fingers rubbed across the tightness of her neck. "These muscles are rigid."

"Maybe I did overdo." Emily turned her head from side to side.

Robert's fingers massaged gently. "You need to relax. Let me give you a good rub down."

Emily didn't object when he led her to the next room and pushed her down on the side of the bed. A little voice in the back of her mind whispered she was playing with fire. She paid no heed. What would have been cause for concern in the logical light of day seemed relatively unimportant in the weary hours of early morning.

He massaged her calf. "I can feel the tension here and here and here." His hands moved up and down her leg, kneading, stroking, and caressing. As he rubbed along her calf, he kissed her toes, a soft feathery, wisp of a kiss that sent a tingle up her backbone. "Now your back." He sat beside her and unbuttoned her shirt.

Emily let him slide the shirt off her shoulders. His fingers felt cool against her skin. She lay down and turned on her stomach.

His fingers massaged her neck and then her shoulders. "You always had the softest skin."

The thought that he might be comparing her to Susan brought Emily back to reality with a jolt. She rolled over and sat up. "That's enough."

Robert's arms fell to his side. Passion was etched into every line of his face. "I've missed you, Emily, so much. Let me hold you in my arms. Let me show you how much I care, how much I've always cared."

The memory of that terrible night in Cedar Creek rose like a specter to taunt her. She pulled herself from his embrace. "I can't." She twisted away from him.

Robert reached for her. "I love you, Emily, only you. You're my world, my life, the heartbeat of my existence."

He had never before spoken such tender words of love, not even when he was caught in the throes of intense passion. Had Susan taught him the art of gentle wooing? "I can't do this."

A shudder ran the length of his body. "You are right. This is neither the time nor the place for love making. He stepped back and turned from her. "I'll sleep on the couch."

Emily crawled into Robert's bed and covered herself with a sheet. What he sought was not love, but sex. *I shouldn't have come here.* She doubled into a fetal position and surrendered to sleep.

She awoke the next morning to see the sun beaming through the bedroom windows. Emily rolled over, and sat on the side of the bed.

She was dressed when Robert came through the door carrying two cups of coffee.

He sat beside her on the bed and offered her one of the cups. "Drink this."

Emily wrapped her hand around its warmth. "Thanks." She took a quick sip of the warm coffee. Robert didn't appear to be angry. She had expected him to be furious.

He set his cup on the table beside the bed. "After we see Aunt Beth we can decide where we go from here."

Emily tightened her grip on her coffee cup. "There is no need for you to tag along with me to see Aunt Beth, and there is nothing to decide." She put her hand over the top of her cup and scooted to the other side of the bed. "I must call Dennis and the twins." Robert's scowl made her add, "Somebody has to look after Boo until I can get home."

She set the cup on the table beside the bed and searched in her handbag for her phone. As she pushed the call button, a collage of photos and snapshots hanging on the wall, caught her attention. The phone slid from her fingers. "All those pictures are of me." She pointed. "That one was taken when I was barely six-years-old. Where did you get that snapshot?"

Robert sat beside her. "I went through the pictures that were in the attic. I hope you don't mind. I need your presence. Your pictures were as near as I could get to you."

Emily pointed to a snapshot on the far end of the collage. "That was taken at my high school graduation."

"I had a studio mount each picture and then put them together." He took her hand in his. "My favorite is you standing by the big oak tree in our backyard. Do you remember the day I snapped it?"

Emily remembered all too well. "You took it on our fifteenth wedding anniversary." *Before our world fell apart.* "I'm not that woman in the picture anymore."

Robert shifted to stare at her. "We have so many wonderful memories. Can you see now why I didn't want you to throw our past away?"

Emily scooted away from him. "I know we have a past. I'm not sure we have a future."

Nothing she said dampened Robert's high spirits. "After last night, I think you're wrong."

Emily raised an eyebrow. "Nothing happened last night."

Robert disagreed, "Enough happened to make me know you still care for me."

The man was either crazy or an egomaniac, maybe both. "I have to get home. I'll call a cab." He made her uncomfortable as only he could. She clasped her hands in front of her as she stood. "Thanks for letting me crash here last night."

A sudden anger sent Robert catapulting to his feet. "Don't make light of what happened between us last night. You wanted me as badly as I wanted you."

His fury sparked an answering rage. Emily battled to bring it under control. "Lust is a powerful emotion."

"You still want to punish me." Robert dropped to the side of the bed. "Go ahead, I deserve it, but I know now you still love me."

The anger she had so far controlled blazed forth. "Like you loved me that night at Cedar Creek? The next week you filed for divorce."

"We can work through all of that, if we're both willing to try."

"Can we?" Emily asked.

Robert's mouth was a thin contemptuous line. "Is it Dennis Morrison?"

"No." Emily paused, sorting through her thoughts. "At least not in the way you think." To some extent, Dennis was responsible for so many of her questions, not necessarily about Robert, but about herself. "I've learned a lot from him.

"Maybe he should be called Saint Dennis instead of Reverend Morrison," Robert remarked caustically.

Emily thought of Dennis's almost uncanny ability to direct people gently. She doubted that either of those qualities could be characterized as saintly. "Dennis is far from being a saint."

Robert shot back, "Is that the voice of experience speaking? Just how well are you acquainted with this man?" He laughed -- a low ugly growl that began deep in his throat. "Do you know him in the Biblical sense?"

"Keep your insults to yourself." Emily rubbed her forehead with her hand. "Dennis listens to me when I talk to him. He's kind and considerate. I enjoy his company." She was beginning to realize what an extraordinary person Dennis was.

Robert's anger drained from him, to be replaced by a visible sadness. "Those are things you haven't had with me for a long time."

"I'm not comparing you to Dennis." *Or was she?* "I don't want what happened last night to destroy our friendship."

"I can no longer settle for friendship." Robert moved nearer and lifted her chin until she was looking into his eyes. "I can't go on this way. I want an answer, now, today. Will you give me another chance?"

His demand aroused of old fears and uncertainties. "Leave it, Robert, please."

"Will you trust me enough to let me try to rebuild your faith in me?" He extended one hand in mute supplication. "Will you let me show you that I can learn to listen to you, that you can find joy and happiness in being with me, too?"

Did she owe him that concession? "I wouldn't know where to start."

"Would you go out with me this evening?"

Hadn't experience taught her the futility of trusting this man? "I don't think..."

"Please."

With a sigh, she refused. "No."

"Why not?" Robert asked.

Didn't he ever give up? "I have to call Dennis."

"I'll change." Robert started for the bathroom. "We can go to the hospital and then I'll take you to your house."

"Robert, please..."

"Please what?" His smile was tender. "Tell me what's on your mind."

"I don't want George and Clara or Kevin and Larry to get the wrong idea."

Robert raised an eyebrow. "About what happened last night?"

"*Nothing* happened last night. I don't want you telling George and Clara things that will make them think something did. I have no idea how Larry and Kevin would react to some exaggerated tale." Emily drew in her breath and waited, sure Robert would disagree or object.

Instead, he asked, "Why don't you want anyone to know that we're together again? Tell me and be honest. Why?"

Emily exploded. "Merciful heavens, Robert. Can't you get it through your thick skull? We are *not* together, and we never will be again."

His breath expelled in a long sigh, "I'm willing to wait."

"All I can think about now is Kevin's wedding."

"Meanwhile will you continue to let me see you?" He leaned against the wall. "I need you, Emily. I need you in my life every day and in my arms every night."

For how long? "Don't push me."

"Come off it, Emily. I..." The sentence levitated in mid-air and hung there for several seconds. He shrugged.

Emily reached for the telephone. As she called, Robert disappeared through the door.

Chapter Twenty-Nine

Through breakfast and during the short ride to the hospital, Emily thought Robert would bring up the subject of seeing her again. She was surprised and relieved when instead he was content to hash over old memories or discuss trivial events and happenings.

When they arrived at the hospital, Aunt Beth was sitting up in bed, complaining to the young nurse's aide that she could never rest in any room except her own, and demanding to know when she could, "Get out of this place."

"She's better," Robert said with a sly wink.

They stayed until a nurse came and suggested that it was time her patient got some rest. Emily gave Aunt Beth a good-bye kiss on the cheek. "You have to hurry and get well. Kevin's wedding is next week."

"I wouldn't miss it for the world," Aunt Beth answered.

As they walked down the hall toward the elevator, Emily questioned, "She is going to be all right, isn't she? She looks so fragile."

Robert nodded, "Temporarily, at least. The doctor says she's in remarkably good condition for someone her age, but she has a weak heart."

The elevator door opened and they stepped inside. A pall of sadness washed over Emily. "How old is she?"

Robert pushed the down button. "She was ninety-four last March."

As they made their silent descent, a web of melancholy spun itself around Emily's gloomy thoughts. Life was so uncertain and death so sure. She gave herself a mental shake and hurried from the elevator and out into the waiting room.

Robert took her arm as they walked through the front door. "Don't look so sad. Aunt Beth is fine for now."

They stepped out into the bright sunlight and were greeted by the sounds of a sleepy Sunday morning hovering over the city.

"Would you like to stop somewhere for an early lunch?" Robert asked as he wheeled his car out of the hospital parking lot.

Emily declined. "I have too many things to do."

He glanced briefly in her direction. "We just passed the Crystal Ballroom, remember how we used to go there on Sunday evenings with Mike and Debra?"

Emily remembered. "They always had such a crowd."

"No more." Robert kept his eyes straight ahead. "The Crystal Ballroom has been closed for more than five years."

That revelation reinforced how out of touch she was with her old world. "I didn't know."

Robert deposited her at her front door and drove away.

Emily entered her empty house. She couldn't shake her depression. *It will pass.* She knew it wouldn't.

A half-hour later, the doorbell's chiming made her hurry to open the front door. Mac Evans stood on the other side. Emily gulped. "This is a surprise."

Mac's handsome face creased into a beguiling smile. "I'm a little surprised myself." Sobering, he asked, "Do you believe in psychic nudges?"

Emily held the door open, thinking as she did so, how he had asked her out repeatedly through three sittings for public service announcements. Each time she refused. Emily's spirits lifted. "Do you?"

"Always," Mac said. "I follow my heart and my hunches." Uninvited, he stepped inside.

Emily led the way to the living room. "Would you like to sit down?"

"I would like to take you to lunch." He sat on the couch. "I have a strong hunch you need some time away from your problems."

Emily searched for excuses. Not because she didn't want to go, but because she did. She didn't need another complication in her life. *Mac could be such an exciting complication.* "My aunt has been ill." She corrected herself. "She's my ex-husband's aunt, but I love her dearly. I've just come from the hospital."

"That must be why I had a strange premonition that you needed me." Mac leaned back and crossed his legs. "Do you feel up to going out to lunch after spending the night at the hospital?"

She didn't want to tell a lie, but she couldn't tell Mac she spent last night in the apartment of her ex-husband. "Aunt Beth is much improved. She's going home soon."

"I'm glad." Mac said. "You look tired."

"I am, a little." Emily perched on a chair arm and blurted out, "I'm also a little depressed."

"Aha!" Mac's face wreathed in a smile. "My hunch was correct, let's go."

This was a chance to get away from problems that were smothering her. Mac was an outsider who didn't know or care about her self-made dilemma. She stood and grabbed her handbag. "I'm ready."

Mac jumped to his feet. "I know the perfect place."

He took her to a charming little Italian restaurant with checkered table cloths and candles on the tables.

They sat at a table in a dimly-lit corner. When a waiter appeared, Mac conversed with him in Italian, even though the waiter spoke fluent English. They chatted for several minutes before Mac ordered clams with linguini. Emily opted for a salad.

As the waiter walked away, laughter rippled from Emily's lips. "Where did you learn to speak Italian?"

"I lived in Italy several years," Mac said. "When my parents passed away, I came home." He unfolded his napkin. "Have you been to Italy?"

"I've never been out of Texas," Emily admitted, reluctantly.

"Would you like to travel abroad?"

"I used to dream of bicycling through Europe, but that was a lot of years ago."

The food arrived along with a bottle of Chianti. The waiter lifted the container from its basket and poured two glasses of the fruity liquid, chatting all the while in Italian. He waved as he walked away

Mac spread his napkin across his lap. "Tony approves of you. He thinks you are beautiful. But then, who doesn't?"

His flattery made her uncomfortable. "I could name quite a few people who don't."

"You look lovely to me."

She didn't believe him, but what woman didn't like being told she was beautiful? "How long did you live in Italy?"

"Off and on for five years."

"I see."

Mac grinned. "No, you don't.

If he could be bluntly honest, so could she. "No, I don't, but I'm not going to ask."

That stupid grin was glued to his face. "Why not?"

"I don't care."

Mac's grin blossomed into a laugh. "You do have a way of putting me in my place. I'm going to tell you anyway. I was living with an Italian woman. We had three good years together before the fire went out. She stayed in Rome, and I moved to Barcelona. Later to Paris and Brussels, then back to Rome. When Mom and Dad died in a plane crash, I returned to the States."

They chatted amiably through the meal. Emily declined dessert. "I've had a lovely time." It was true, she had. "I must go home. I have a meeting tonight."

Mac tossed his napkin on the table. "You have a Sunday night meeting?"

"It's a church meeting."

Mac offered his arm. "Church? You never cease to surprise me. We must do this again."

Emily hooked her hand through his arm. She should say no. "I'd like that."

Chapter Thirty

Emily enjoyed the speaker Dennis brought to the meeting. The question-and-answer session that followed was informal and lively. After the meeting came to an end, the church deacons and elders prepared and served dinner to the participants. It lasted into early evening. Dennis insisted that she stay until everyone else was gone. "I want to see you home."

"You have evening services in little more than an hour." Emily pointed out. "I can find my way."

Dennis didn't intend to take no for an answer. "I'd like to talk to you, if you have time."

He sounded serious. What did he want to talk about? Emily didn't ask. "I have time." She guessed it was something about the twins or the wedding, or both.

As they walked down the sidewalk, Dennis caught her hand in his. "You fit well into the singles' group. The other participants like and respect you."

"I like them, too. They're all very kind and accepting."

"You bring out the best in people." He smiled down into her eyes.

A touch of caution edged in around Emily's elation. "Are you trying to flatter me?"

His hand tightened around hers. "I don't flatter people. I tell them the truth as I see it."

Had she had offended him? "I thought you were feeling sorry for me." Emily wanted to ease the moment. "Maybe flattery, like selfishness, is not always a bad thing."

"You're using my own words against me." Dennis's frown transformed into a bright smile. "I'm being hoisted on my own petard."

Emily squeezed his hand. "I don't want you to pity me."

"Why should I?" They turned onto Emily's walk.

"You shouldn't, not now." Emily smiled up at him. "When I met you over a year ago, I was a basket case. You have helped me so much."

As Dennis stepped onto the porch, his smile broadened. "I have? How?" He held the screen open for her.

Emily stepped inside. "You have dispelled forever my belief that all ministers are stuffed shirts."

Dennis followed her inside and shut the door behind him. "You've taught me some things, too." He extended one hand toward the living room. "Let's sit down, shall we?"

Emily nodded, found a chair and sank down into it. "Is this about the twins or the wedding?"

"Neither really. It's about us, you and me." Dennis sat down on the edge of the couch and tented his fingers. "Let's talk about this past year."

Emily wondered where this was headed. "You're doing that thing with your fingers again."

"You're erecting barriers again," Dennis accused gently and then asked, "Do you ever let your defenses down?"

Was she that unapproachable? "I'm sorry. I'm trying to be less guarded with people, but it isn't easy. So, what about this last year?"

"It's been a benchmark in my life. Knowing you has caused me to reassess one of my most basic beliefs."

"Knowing you has had a tremendous influence on me." She felt as if she were undressing, emotionally. "I hope I don't sound melodramatic, but you've restored my faith in human nature."

Dennis looked down at his tented his fingers before placing his hands in his lap. "And you have shown me that life is for the living." For an assessing moment, he studied her face. "You've brought me out of the shadows and into the light again." He rubbed his hands along his pants legs, and exhaled slowly. "I enjoy being with you, Emily. You're like a bright ray of sunshine."

"That's partly because I'm with you," Emily confessed. How easily she slipped into confiding in him, "and your family," she added, realizing how hungry she was to have someone she could trust to confide in. "I like Stacy very much, and Kim and Amy are such wonderful girls." She reflected for a moment before saying. "I always wanted a daughter."

"I always wanted a son," Dennis admitted. "Ellen had such a difficult time with the twins that we decided it was best not to try again." After a space of time that heard only the ticking of the clock, he questioned, "Why didn't you and Robert have more children?"

"I wanted more, but Robert didn't." Why should that admission lift a burden from her heart?

Dennis leaned forward with his hands resting on his knees. "Did he always make your decisions for you?"

"Looking back, it seems he did." Emily felt at once vulnerable and foolish. "Robert has known me all my life. It just seemed natural to let him make choices for us when we were children. I suppose it became a habit. But he didn't mean any harm to me."

Dennis sat up and leaned back. "He betrayed you and divorced you."

She had never come to grips with that truth before. "I was far from a perfect wife."

"I'm not judging him, or you. I can't be objective because I'm prejudiced in your favor, but that's all in the past." His eyes narrowed as he questioned, "Isn't it?"

"Yes." If that was true, why was she still seeing Robert's family? "The past always affects the present." She pushed down old memories that rippled across her mind like wind over water. "Robert and I have resolved most of our differences."

From out of the blue, Dennis asked, "Do you still love him?"

That question deserved careful consideration. Did she? After an introspective moment, Emily answered, "I don't know that I can ever trust Robert again. And the odd thing is, he doesn't trust me either. He insists I've been having affairs since our divorce. No matter what I say, he refuses to accept the truth from me. I suppose a part of me will always love him in a sense, if for no other reason than he's the father of my children. Perhaps you can understand how I feel. You once told me that you would always be in love with Ellen."

"Ellen will always have a special place in my heart." Dennis tented his fingers again and looked over them into Emily's eyes. "Over the last year I've come to realize that doesn't mean I can't care for someone else. What about you, Emily, could you learn to care for someone other than your ex-husband?"

Emily hesitated. The thought never crossed her mind before. She'd assumed if Robert didn't want her, no one else would either. "I never considered it."

"Perhaps you should." Once again, Dennis leaned forward in his chair. "Will you?"

Emily's first inclination was to say no. She reconsidered. Why should she shut the door on the future because of what happened in the past? "Would that be fair?"

"To whom?" Dennis asked, "Have you made any commitment to your ex-husband?"

"No, we are trying to find a way not to hurt our sons again by snarling at each other each time we meet." She shouldn't ask, but she wanted very badly to know. "Why do you want to know?"

"Can't you guess?" A touch of color stained Dennis's cheeks and splotched across his neck. "Don't you have any idea?"

She was beginning to. With realization came a strange mixture of excitement and peace. She was safe with Dennis. She liked him. Could she ever love him? Maybe she already did. "When you say you and me, you mean you and me, as in a couple?"

A gentle smile creased Dennis's face as the color receded. "Given time I'd like to hope you and I could become a couple." He sat perfectly still, obviously waiting for her to speak.

"This is so...unexpected." She giggled like a teenager, trying to cover her confusion. "I don't know what to say."

Dennis reached across the space between them and took her hand in his. "You don't have to say anything. Just think about what I've said."

"I need to tell you about Robert and me. I..."

Dennis lifted one hand. "Don't, please. I don't want to hear about you and Robert. That's in the past."

Emily wasn't sure that was true. "I'm connected to Robert through our sons. My parents and his were best friends. Debra, Robert's sister, and I were very close."

"I can understand all that." Dennis dropped her hand. "You wouldn't be the Emily I have grown to admire and respect if you could put Robert's family out of your life completely." He stood slowly, as if rising took an effort. "I have to go. I am expected in my pulpit in less than thirty minutes." He backed toward the door. "Think about what I've said." He turned on his heel and was gone.

With a dazed shake of her head, Emily moved toward the bedroom.

Chapter Thirty-One

Sometimes Emily doubted her sanity. After her last luncheon date with Mac, she vowed she would not go out with him again. Yet here she sat, less than a week later, waiting for him to arrive and take her to dinner. She justified her about-face by reasoning there could never be anything serious between them, and she enjoyed his company. *Snap out of it, woman, you are single with no ties. There is no need to feel guilty about enjoying the company of a male friend.*

By the time Mac arrived, much of Emily's confidence had returned. She decided to sift through her ambivalent thoughts later.

Mac took her to an elegant supper club. The ambience was perfect and the food delicious, but Mac sat pensive and silent.

"Aren't you enjoying your meal?" she asked as he used his fork to push food around on his plate.

Mac never approached a subject tactfully. He said what was on his mind. "We have completed our last video shot. I will be using your cameos over and over to insert in ads for tourists' attractions in the city."

Emily was both pleased and annoyed. "Whose idea was that?" Her mind kept hopping back to her recent conversation with Dennis. *He wants us to be more than friends, much more than friends.*

Mac took a quick sip of wine. "Not mine, I assure you. The city fathers are always out to save a buck." Before she could answer, he added. "I think what they really want is your picture on their ads."

"That's flattering, I guess..." *In the year or so Emily had known Dennis, he had never hinted that he felt anything for her but friendship. True, that friendship had grown.*

"Emily?" Mac leaned across the table. "Is something troubling you? You are a million miles away."

"Sorry." Emily shook her head, trying to clear her mind. "I have a lot to think about, what with Kevin's wedding so near." She popped a green bean into her mouth and chewed thoughtfully. "And there's Aunt Beth."

Mac sighed. "Can you put all that from your mind long enough to listen to what I have to say?"

He almost sounded like Robert. "Of course." Emily pushed the remainder of her green beans into her mashed potatoes. *Why would Dennis, or any other man for that matter, contemplate a lasting relationship with her?*

From what seemed a long way off, Mac said, "Is this a private joke or can anyone get in on it?"

Emily wiped the smile from her face. "You were saying our video shoots are done."

"Does that bother you?" Mac laid his hand over hers, and waited for an answer.

She could think of no reason why it should. "I have enjoyed working with you." Again, Emily's thoughts strayed. *Maybe Dennis didn't expect undying love.* The more she pondered his strange proposal, the more tangled her thoughts became.

Again, Mac's voice intruded into her thoughts. "Can you forget about Kevin's wedding and Aunt Beth's illness for tonight?"

Emily pulled her hand from his grasp and her mind back to the present. She pasted a smile on her face. "You were saying?"

As Mac told of his plans to sell his studio and travel for a few years, her mind wandered, once more, back to her strange conversation with Dennis. *It was not his suggestion, but her response that troubled her. She liked the idea of them being a pair and a couple. Dennis was warm and caring and handsome. Most of all, she trusted him. He was someone she could depend on.*

Mac's caustic voice cut through her preoccupation. "Am I boring you?"

"No. I'm sorry." Emily brought her mind back to the here and now. "What were you saying?"

"I was saying," Mac laid his napkin on the table. "I would like to have you for a traveling companion. We can see Europe together."

She had been too occupied with a past conversation to pay attention to the present one. "What would my job as your traveling companion entail?" she asked, and then felt like a fool for having done so.

Mac laughed. "I want you, Emily. You are different from anyone I have ever known. You intrigue me."

She asked because she had to be sure, "Are you asking me to marry you?"

"Me, get married, Darling?" Mac rammed his forefinger into his chest. "No way. I am one of a dying breed, a confirmed bachelor. But I do promise to make you happy."

"Can you afford to sell your business and go on an extended vacation?"

Mac dropped his head and smiled before lifting it again. "My sweet, practical Emily. Yes, I can. I am one of those fortunate trust fund recipients. I work because I like to, not because I have to." He turned the full force of his smile on her. "Let's dance"

Emily returned his smile. "I'd love to."

Once on the dance floor, she slid into his arms with practiced ease, even though it had been years since she had danced. She felt the heat from his hands on her back, penetrating the flimsy fabric of her dress. This man oozed charisma and sexual magnetism.

Mac pulled her very close, and whispered in her ear, "Come live with me and be my love."

The music was soft and seductive. Lights moved in ever changing colors across the dance floor. Emily lost herself in a setting made for romance. As the last strains of the orchestra faded away, Mac took her hand and led her toward their table. "You dance divinely." He held her chair for her.

Emily sat down and watched as Mac sat across from her. He settled in his chair before saying, "You'll need a passport. You'll have to pay extra for expedited processing."

He also possessed an abundance of self-assurance, and an added sprinkling of arrogance. Those traits should have angered her, or at least annoyed her. How could she be angry with a charmer like Mac Evans? "'Aren't you taking a lot for granted?"

Mac lifted her hand and kissed her fingertips. "Time is short. I'm leaving in a week." He released her hand. "I could awaken the slumbering passion in you, Sleeping Beauty. Do you want to dance again?"

Her body heated at the thought of being in Mac's arms and having him hold her close. "Yes."

The band played a slow waltz, as Mac led her onto the dance floor and took her in his arms. Her pulse quickened with physical need. All too soon the dance ended.

As they sat down at their table, Mac signaled for the waiter. "Would you like to go to my apartment?" Even with a frown creasing his brow, he was more than sexy.

Emily reached for her handbag. If he was trying to shock her, he'd succeeded royally. She put her hand over her mouth to stifle a yawn. "No, thanks. In case you haven't figured this out yet, I don't sleep around. You can take me home."

The waiter appeared. Mac dispensed with him in record time.

Later, as he helped Emily into his car, he asked, "Have you decided to come to Europe with me?" Before she could reply, he hurried to the other side, slid behind the wheel, and put his keys in the ignition. "I had a great time tonight." He looked over his shoulder, and backed the car from its parking slot.

Emily fastened her seat belt. "So did I." All around them night sounds of the city converged, the rumble of traffic, the shrill scream of a siren and the distant resounding blare of a car horn echoing down the canyon of a busy street

Mac pulled the car into the steady flow of traffic. He squinted his eyes against the lights of oncoming cars. "A friend of mine owns a Greek Island. There's a little beach cottage there where I'm planning to spend a few weeks unwinding. It's just a short ferry ride from Athens. I'd love to take you there."

"This may be hard for you to understand, Mac, but I have some unshakable beliefs, based on the Bible. One of them says sex belongs in marriage and nowhere else. You're one of the most exciting men I've ever been around. We might have a grand time together, for a while. But when the physical attraction cooled--and it will--we would both have regrets."

"You're not kidding me, are you?"

"No," Emily replied. "I've lived long enough to realize instant satisfaction isn't worth the long-term consequences it usually brings. Said my old-fashioned way, sin doesn't pay."

220

"Sin?" Mac guffawed. "I didn't know anyone used that word anymore. I don't think I've heard it since my grandma took me to a revival meeting in a brush arbor."

They left the city with its array of lights and noises, and drove down a tree lined street in Emily's quiet neighborhood. Mac slapped his steering wheel with the palm of his hand. "Just my luck to get hung up on a lady with principles."

Emily stared out the window at the blur of passing houses as a dozen dissenting thoughts chased themselves around inside her head.

Mac pulled into Emily's drive and stopped his car. "When can I see you again?"

"I didn't think you'd want to." Emily reached for the door handle. "You can call me tomorrow if you like."

Mac unfastened his seat belt, turned, and pulled Emily into his arms. He kissed her as she had never been kissed before. She reacted as she never had before, melting into his embrace and reveling in the passion that blazed between them.

After what seemed too short a time, he released her. The slanting moonlight gave him an ethereal appearance. "You fascinate me, Emily. You're not like any woman I've ever known."

Emily dug for her house key. "I have to go inside. Thank you for an interesting evening"

The following day, Mac called and asked her to lunch. "I'm sorry, Mac. There's a luncheon I can't wiggle out of."

"How about dinner?" he persisted. "I'll only be in town a few more days, and I need a dose of your wisdom."

"Okay, but I may have to work late. Why don't I meet you?"

"Seven o'clock at the Italian Trattoria?"

"That works. See you then." What a different kind of guy Mac was. Emily never expected to hear from him again after refusing to go to Europe with him.

Mac's red sports car was already parked at the restaurant when Emily arrived. It was the first time she could remember him being on time.

Mac met her at the entrance, kissed her cheek, and led her to a table where he had an open bottle of Chianti. "You look fabulous. Would you like a glass of wine?"

"No, thank you," Emily replied.

"Oh, I forgot." He grinned. "You don't drink."

"Yes, I do." Emily returned his smile. "I drink coffee, every morning, and water all day long on top of that."

Although she was curious to know what Mac wanted to discuss with her, she waited for him to introduce the topic. Meanwhile, they engaged in chit chat and enjoyed their salads.

After the waiter delivered steaming plates of ravioli, Mac said, "I didn't sleep much last night."

"Why not?"

"You." His eyes searched her face. "Not to be egotistical, although I am, I really thought you'd be excited about me whisking you away to travel the world."

So, she'd wounded his male pride. "Mac," she began.

He held up a hand. "Let me finish. I did a lot of thinking after I dropped you off. I realized your integrity is what draws me to you. Well, that along with your beauty, and a great sense of humor. You're different, and I find that most attractive." He drew a deep breath. "And so, after a lot of soul searching, I'm asking you to marry me."

Emily sat stunned for a moment. "Mac, we hardly know each other."

"That will be part of the adventure." He smiled and grasped her hand. "I want to take you places you've never been, and introduce you to a big, wide world of adventure. I want to take you to the opera at La Scala and show you Paris at night. I'll buy you a diamond wedding ring that'll knock your eye out and anything else your heart desires. I'm in love with you, Emily. The thought of being with you makes me positively giddy."

"Let me ask you something. Are you a Christian?"

"I believe in God, if that's what you mean."

"Not exactly." Despite her discomfort, Emily had to know more. "I am a follower of Jesus. Are you?"

"I'm a free spirit." Mac's engaging smile made her heart flutter. "But I respect your beliefs and I'll never try to get you to change them."

"You excite me, Mac, more than any man I've ever known, but a successful marriage is built on love. And love means commitment, the 'till death shall us part' kind that holds on through thick and thin, whether you feel like it or not. I don't know if either of us is ready to make that kind of promise to each other."

"I'm willing to give it a try." He lifted an eyebrow and flashed a wicked grin. "And I guarantee it will be a fun ride." Mac released her hand at last. He picked up his fork and pushed ravioli left and right on his plate. "You don't have to answer right away. Think it over. Meanwhile, I'll make you a passport photo from one of my ad stills."

Sleep eluded Emily that night. She'd never been popular as a teenager, but now in her forties there were three men pursuing her. What a dilemma. How she wished for a friend to talk things over with. However, the only person she could confide in was Dennis, and she could hardly discuss Mac with him. She couldn't go on dividing her attention among an ex-husband she could never again trust because of their past, an exciting rascal who lived only for today, and a steady man who offered her a secure future. She knew the time had come for her to decide what she wanted and go after it.

Chapter Thirty-Two

Sunbeams danced through the open window as a morning breeze stirred the ruffled curtains. Emily turned in bed. What a perfect day for Kevin's wedding. Memories of her own wedding day drifted across her memory. "A marriage made in heaven," her mother whispered as she helped Emily adjust her train. Mother didn't live to see how wrong she was.

Emily heard Larry stirring in the kitchen. She put on her robe, slid her feet into her slippers, and started for the kitchen. As she came through the door Larry pointed toward the table. "I made coffee. Would you like a cup?"

Emily nodded, and sat down.

Larry poured coffee into cups, set the pot on the table, and perched on the chair across from her. "This is the big day."

Emily sipped her coffee and studied the youthful face of her younger son. He had matured over the past year. The person who sat across from her now was a man. "I'm going to the church to be with Stacy."

Larry took a gulp of coffee. "Is Dad coming to the wedding?"

Emily shrugged. "I don't know. Kevin did invite him."

"I know. Kevin told me," Larry put his cup on the table. "You and Dad called it quits, didn't you?"

"Our marriage is over. We are still friends." If Dennis's invitation to explore a relationship and Mac's proposal did nothing else, they forced her to pray for guidance and think about where her life was headed.

Larry's countenance fell. "We will never be a family again. Kevin said he suspected as much."

Annoyance made Emily testy. "We've been over this a million times. Things change. You and Kevin are adults now. It's time you made a life of your own. I keep saying that and neither you nor Kevin seem to believe me."

"You're our parents. We care about you." The look on Larry's face said he intended to pursue the subject.

"Let it go, Larry."

Larry paid no heed "Dad asks about you when he sees me."

"Your father and I have been divorced for more than a year. He is no longer a part of my life."

Larry ignored her sharp reply. "Kevin says Dad is upset."

"Kevin has seen Robert?" Emily didn't know if she should be pleased or concerned. "When?"

"Dad came to see Kevin a few days ago. They had a long talk. Dad apologized to Kevin, and Kevin apologized to Dad. I think they have finally started to mend their fences."

Emily breathed a sigh of relief. "I'm glad they were able to put the past behind them."

"I wouldn't say it's gone that far, but they have made a beginning. Now maybe you and Dad can do the same."

Suspicion reared its ugly head. "Did your dad ask you to talk to me?"

Larry assured her that he hadn't, but she suspected he had. What was wrong with Robert? When she wanted him, he divorced her. Now she wanted nothing more than to have him out of her life, and he kept turning up like a bad penny.

Larry reached for a sweet roll. "Kevin and I talked to Dennis last night."

Emily's curiosity overtook her better judgment. "What did Dennis say?"

"A lot of things." Larry eased back down into his chair.

"Tell me what Dennis said."

"The good thing about talking to Dennis is that he doesn't give answers. He clarifies the problem and lets you find your own answer."

Emily tasted her coffee. It was cold and bitter. "Did you find answers?"

Larry grinned sheepishly. "Dennis sort of said without saying it, that this was between you and Dad. He suggested that we be supportive and accepting."

Dennis had diffused a potentially explosive situation. "We can talk about this later." Next year was okay with Emily, or sometime in the next decade. "You should be getting over to Kevin's apartment. I'm due at the church in less than an hour."

"I'm glad we talked. See you in church." Larry dashed out the door.

The thought came to her like an epiphany. Until this moment Emily had put the feelings of her sons above everything else. She was beginning to embrace a different perspective. Through the time it took her to dress and get to the church, she reviewed how much she had changed since her divorce.

All brides are beautiful Emily thought, as she adjusted Stacy's long train. "You look radiant."

"I'm happy," Stacy confided breathlessly, "so happy that it scares me."

Emily gave Stacy's veil a last tug and pat. "Don't be afraid to be happy. Grab every moment of joy that comes your way and savor it." She stepped back. "You are gorgeous, and so is your gown."

Color rose in Stacy's cheeks. "This was my mother's wedding dress. I wish she could see me now."

"Maybe she can," Emily whispered. She picked up her purse and gloves. "I have to go."

Stacy grabbed Emily's arm. "Thank you, Emily, for everything."

"I was glad to help you. I feel honored that you wanted me here with you today."

"I'm not thanking you just for today," Stacy said. "Or for all you've done for me and the twins. I'm most grateful to you for bringing happiness back into Dad's life."

Emily felt behind her for the doorknob. "Thank you. You are too kind." She opened the door, and backed through. She walked down the walkway toward the sanctuary. She had not known until now how Stacy felt about her friendship with Dennis. It helped to know Stacy approved.

Once inside the church and seated, Emily surveyed the people around her. George and Clara sat on the pew behind her, all smiles and anticipation. Aunt Beth, in a wheelchair and accompanied by an attendant from the nursing home, was parked at the end of the first pew. Emily nodded to George and Clara and waved to Aunt Beth. She let her gaze come to rest on the man who sat not three feet from her. "Hello, Robert."

Their eyes met. Without answering Robert dipped his head and turned away.

Emily sat erect. This was her son's wedding day, a time for joy and celebration. She was determined to push all else from her mind.

The altar was banked high with a beautiful array of flowers. Dennis, straight and tall in his formal attire, stood before the stunning couple. Larry was on his brother's right, looking handsome and impressed. Kim and Amy, beautiful in flowing chiffon gowns were to Stacy's left, their wonder-filled gazes glued to their sister's radiant face. Perfection, Emily thought. This would be a moment to treasure for a lifetime. She forgot everything except the scene unfolding before her.

A breathless hush hung over the sanctuary as the ceremony in all its simplistic grandeur began. "Dearly beloved," Dennis's sonorous voice echoed through the sanctuary. "We are gathered here in the sight of God and these witnesses..." Tears filled Emily's eyes. She brushed them away. She had promised herself, no crying. That included weeping over something as poignantly nostalgic as a lovely church wedding on a perfect June afternoon.

When the ceremony came to an end, the organ burst forth in joyous tones. The bride and groom came up the aisle, taking their first steps together as husband and wife. Silently, fervently, Emily prayed, *Please, God, let it last.*

The sanctuary cleared as the guests departed for the reception hall. Emily lingered behind. Sooner or later, she would have to face George and Clara and Robert. She wanted to postpone that moment as long as possible.

As the crowd filed out of the church, a hand touched Emily's elbow. She turned to see Dennis smiling down at her. "I was not this nervous when I performed my first wedding ceremony over twenty-five years ago." He slipped Emily's hand through his arm. "Let's get over to the reception hall before the festivities start without us."

"Wasn't Stacy beautiful?" Emily held onto Dennis's arm, glad for the comfort of his presence.

"She was." Dennis's eyes scanned Emily's slight figure. "You are nothing short of spectacular yourself. You remind me of a gorgeous topaz set in a frame of shimmering gold." His eyes held hers in an admiring stare. "Amber is definitely your color."

If she could elicit a complement such as that from Dennis, the money she'd invested in this expensive outfit was well spent. "You're rather handsome yourself." He was more than handsome. He was distinguished. "We should be in the reception line."

The line of guests entering the hall was long. That made it easy for Emily to shake the hands of her former in-laws and move onto the next guest without having to make small talk. It seemed hours before the last straggling guests made their way into the hall. As the final figure passed through the line and faded into the crowd, Emily sank into a nearby chair.

Dennis came to stand beside her. "Don't desert me now. It's time to cut the cake." He extended his hand. "Shall we?"

As they pushed through the crowd, Emily spied Robert, his parents, and Aunt Beth sitting at a table near the back of the hall. "Maybe we should ask Robert to come with us. He might like to make a toast to the bride and groom."

Dennis's hand tightened on Emily's arm. "This is Kevin and Stacy's wedding. Shouldn't they call the shots?" They came to stand beside the long buffet table that held the cake and a huge array of food and drink.

After watching the bride and groom cut the cake and listening to several toasts, Emily eased away from the crowd and sat at a table near the entrance. It provided an excellent place to view the panoramic scene before her and still be inconspicuous. She watched as Larry laughed and joked with Amy and Kim. They were hanging onto his every word. There's nothing like hero worship to feed a young man's ego, she thought, as several other young girls joined the twins to surround Larry.

A tap on her shoulder interrupted her thoughts. Emily looked up to see Aunt Beth's attendant standing beside her. "Miss Franklin is leaving," the attendant explained over the din of laughter and voices that filled the room. "She wants a word with you before she goes."

"Of course, where is she?"

The attendant pointed toward the entrance, "This way."

Emily followed the young woman to the ramp outside.

Aunt Beth sat in her wheelchair, her fingers drumming on the arms. "What took you so long?" She held out her hands. "The wedding was lovely."

Emily clasped Aunt Beth's age-splotched hands and kissed her soft wrinkled cheek. "I'm so glad you could come."

"I told you I wouldn't miss it for the world." Aunt Beth turned to the attendant. "Can you find something to do for a few minutes? I want a private word with my niece."

The attendant winked at Emily. "I can manage that." She asked, "You won't leave until I return, will you?"

"I won't leave."

Aunt Beth waited until the attendant was out of earshot before saying, "I have something for you." She reached into the beaded bag that lay in her lap, took from it a flat, oblong jewel case and laid the case in Emily's hands. "This has been in my safe deposit box for years. I had my attorney bring it to me yesterday."

The velvet was soft to Emily's touch. "What is it?" She ran her fingers along the edge of the oblong case.

A sudden breeze blew across the ramp, ruffling Aunt Beth's silvery hair. She smoothed it back with one blue-veined hand. "Open it and see."

Emily lifted the lid. An exquisite oval locket suspended from a heavy gold chain nestled inside. Her breath caught in her throat. "It's beautiful."

"I always thought so. It was given to me a long time ago by someone I loved very much. I want you to have it."

Emily stared down at jewel-encrusted locket and thought that it must be worth a small fortune. "I can't accept this."

Aunt Beth snorted indignantly. "Would you mind explaining why?"

Aunt Beth was old, but her mind was as sharp as a steel trap. She knew what Emily meant. "This should be a family heirloom. I'm not a relative."

"You are if I say you are," Aunt Beth harrumphed. "Do you know what your problem is?" She answered her own question before Emily had the opportunity to respond. "You don't know how to grab life by the throat and choke it into submission." In the strong sunlight, Aunt Beth looked every day of her ninety-four years. "I want you to have the locket."

Emily swallowed over the lump in her throat. "Are you sure you want to part with it?" She closed the lid of the box.

"I'm very sure. I never wore it. I couldn't afford to, since it was a gift from a man my father disliked. In my day if the family disapproved of someone, that was that."

In the space of a heartbeat, Aunt Beth answered a question that had mystified Emily for years. "Is he the reason you never married?"

Tears filled Aunt Beth's eyes. "He was the reason for my existence. Anything I lost, I counted but gained so long as he loved me." A tear rolled down her cheek. "He's been dead over fifty years."

"I'm sorry," Emily whispered.

"Oh, Lord, child, don't pity me." Aunt Beth's voice snapped with indignation. "I made my choice a long time ago and I never regretted it."

"Why didn't you tell me before?" All these years and Emily hadn't guessed.

"I didn't think it was any of your business." Aunt Beth's smile took the sting from her words. "Just like I didn't think I'd ever have to depart this vale of tears. Time is catching up to me. I am not much longer for this world."

Emily caught the old lady's hand. "Don't say that, please."

"It's no more than my doctors insist on pointing out to me at every opportunity. I'd be a fool not to face the inevitable and prepare."

Emily clasped the velvet box to her heart. "I'll keep it always."

"When that always is over, you might consider passing it on to Kevin's Stacy." Aunt Beth looked over her shoulder. "Where is Irene? I need to get home to my own bed."

Through a rainbow of tears, the old face before Emily distorted. "Thank you."

"You're welcome," Aunt Beth snapped. "And one other thing, Emily."

Emily wiped her eyes. "Yes?"

"All these years you have been your parents' little girl, Robert's dutiful wife, and Kevin and Larry's doting mother. Now maybe you're ready to accept the lesson that comes from surviving and overcoming heartache." She wiped a tear from her cheek. "You will never find happiness until you find yourself. It's time for you to quit worrying about what other people think and decide who you are and what you want." She put her hand to the brake of her wheelchair. "At last, Irene is here. Good-bye, Emily."

Emily called after the departing duo. "I don't understand--"

Aunt Beth called over her shoulder. "Yes, you do. All you have to do is discover Emily."

Emily watched the attendant push Aunt Beth's wheelchair down the ramp and toward a waiting van before ascending the steps that led back to the reception hall.

As she came through the door, Dennis fell in step beside her. "Is everything all right?"

Emily dropped the velvet case into her handbag. "I was saying good-bye to Aunt Beth."

Dennis guided her toward a table near the door. "Would you like to come over to the parsonage after the reception?"

Emily hesitated, "I don't know, Larry may have other plans."

"I've asked Larry. He said he'd love to come."

Again, Emily hesitated, "I'm not sure..."

Dennis hit where she was most vulnerable. "Kim and Amy are going to feel the impact of Stacy being gone, really gone, for the first time. It would take the edge off their sadness if you and Larry were there to console them."

If Kim and Amy needed her, she would be there. "All right but only for a little while. It's been a long day."

Dennis pushed his chair back. "I have to circulate. I'll see you later."

Emily looked around the hall, festive with decorations and alive with merriment. Words Aunt Beth spoke earlier came back to run around in her head. *You will never find happiness until you find Emily.* She turned to see Robert standing behind her. "Mom and Dad would like you to come to their table."

Emily pushed herself to her feet. "Lead the way."

Chapter Thirty-Three

Emily threaded her way across the crowded hall as she followed Robert. Halfway to the other side, she stopped and turned. "I just said good-bye to Aunt Beth."

Robert skidded to a halt. "Oh?" Surprise raised his eyebrows. "Did she give you a bad time?"

"Not at all," Emily replied. "Why would she?"

"She's been giving me the dickens. She called me, among other things, stupid and selfish."

Emily leaned against a post." She didn't mean it."

"She meant every word." Robert lowered his voice. "She saw you with Reverend Morrison, and told me I was a fool for letting you go. She let me have it with both barrels." He drew a deep breath and let it out slowly. "I'm beginning to see why you went to such lengths to get Kevin and me to reconcile. You wanted to make sure I was here today." His eyes narrowed. "Am I right?"

"Of course, I want you here." Emily steadied her voice "This is your son's wedding day."

A sneer curled Robert's lips, "How unselfish you are, how full of the milk of human kindness; how ready to make my life miserable with your pious help."

There was a time when his words would have brought Emily to tears. Not now. "You're the one who came to me, asking that I help you get back into your sons' good graces." How foolish she was to think Robert had put the past behind him and changed. "I didn't interfere until then."

Robert's nostrils flared. "Revenge is sweet, isn't it?" He leaned forward and put his hand on the post above her head. "It wasn't enough that you kept me dangling for months, laughing behind my back while you slept with the handsome Reverend, you brought me here today to show me how the Franklins and the Morrisons have become one big happy family."

Emily ducked under his arm and walked away. She didn't slow her pace or turn around until she reached George and Clara's table. "Hello, George, Clara. Robert said you wanted to see me?"

George said, "We were wondering if we'd done something to displease you."

Emily pulled out a chair and sat down. "No." What had Robert told them? "Why would you think that?"

George took Clara's hand in his. "You've been ignoring us. Mama was concerned."

These dear old people should be enjoying their grandson's wedding, not worrying about anything else. "I've been very busy."

Clara asked, "Could you stay and visit for a while?"

Emily settled back in her chair. "I'd love to."

Robert sat in the chair next to her and smiled at his parents.

Clara asked, "Did Aunt Beth find you before she went back to the nursing home?"

Emily relaxed, but only a little. "Yes, she did."

"Debra and Mike send their regrets." Clara said, "They were called out of town. Mike's father passed away last Thursday."

Emily avoided looking in Robert's direction. "I know. Debra called me."

"Today is like an oasis of happiness in a desert of sickness and death." Clara smiled. "Wasn't the bride beautiful? And her little sisters are adorable."

George picked up on Clara's cue. "The groom was handsome as an Adonis and the Reverend is no slouch himself. All in all, I'd say it was about as perfect as a wedding could be." He pointed. "Look."

The newlyweds appeared at the top of the stairs, dressed in travel clothes and beaming with happiness. All looks shifted to stare at them. Emily pushed her chair back. "Excuse me." She made her escape and went to stand beside the door.

From nowhere Dennis appeared to stand beside her. "If you stay here much longer, you won't get to throw rice at the bride and groom." He took her arm and guided her through the crowd. "You wouldn't want to miss that."

Emily held onto Dennis's arm. "We're tossing birdseed. It's better for the environment."

Amid the tossing of birdseed and shouts from a host of well-wishers, the bride and groom scrambled into Kevin's car and with a cheerful wave pulled away from the curb.

As soon as the car disappeared around a bend in the road, the crowd dispersed and moved off in all directions, leaving the area around the recreation hall littered with debris. Emily surveyed the scene with distaste. "Is someone coming to clean this place?"

Dennis pressed his hand to the small of his back. "The custodial service that takes care of the church will be here soon. Are you ready to go?"

"I want to have a word with my in-laws--" She caught her error before she could finish the sentence, "My ex-in-laws."

"They left when Kevin and Stacy did. You can call them when we get to the parsonage if it's important." Dennis took her arm. "Larry and the twins are waiting for us."

They walked down the steps and turned toward the parsonage with Dennis still holding Emily's arm. Without so much as a change of voice or a falter in his steps, Dennis asked, "Did you quarrel with Robert again?"

Emily grunted. "It's more like an extension of the same old fight."

"Did the two of you squabble like this when you were married?"

"Strange as it sounds, we didn't." Emily speculated, "Maybe we would have been better off if we had."

Dennis smiled down at her. "That's a strange thing to say."

She returned his smile. "Yes, it is, isn't it? When Robert and I were married we seldom disagreed. I simply gave in to his every whim. Looking back, I can see there were times when a little disagreement would have been healthy."

Dennis held the parsonage door open for her "Maybe we can talk about this at our next singles' session."

Emily went inside and laid her handbag on the table in the hall. "What good would that do now?"

Dennis closed the door. "It could help someone else, and maybe it would keep you from making the same mistake the next time around."

Emily smiled. "Next time, if there is a next time, I will choose my husband more carefully."

They were interrupted by noises from the kitchen. Kim and Larry were arguing good-naturedly.

Dennis called, "We're home."

Three voices called greetings as Amy appeared in the doorway. "The housekeeper left sandwiches and coffee."

Dennis and Emily followed Amy into the kitchen. "Only coffee for me," Emily said as she sat at the table across from Kim and Larry.

Dennis eased down in the chair beside her. "I'll have one cup of coffee, black." He removed his cleric's collar and tossed it on the sideboard.

Amy brought the coffee and sat on the other side of Emily. "Larry and Kim are having a disagreement."

Dennis chuckled. "I guessed as much."

Kim announced, "Larry thinks Kevin and Stacy should have included the word 'obey' in their wedding ceremony. I say that's old-fashioned and outmoded."

Dennis tasted his coffee before setting his cup on the table. "I think Larry is teasing you."

Kim turned to Larry and asked, "Are you?"

Larry smiled. "A little, I guess. I can't have you growing up to be a female chauvinist."

Kim struck him playfully on his arm. "You're a terrible tease."

Emily's observant stare moved from Larry to Kim and then to Dennis, who was smiling. Here in the warmth of this cheery kitchen, how right the world seemed. At last, she began to unwind.

Amy asked, "Does anyone want more coffee?"

"No more for me." Larry put his hand over his cup. "I'd like to take Kim and Amy to the movies, if that's all right with you, Dennis."

Before Dennis could answer, Kim and Amy, in unison, chanted, "Please, Dad, please."

"Sure," Dennis agreed. "Be home by ten."

Larry waved to his mother. "I'll be home early, Mom."

As the young people exited the room, Dennis called after his daughters, "Did you hang up your formals?"

Kim shouted over her shoulder, "Amy did."

Dennis leaned back in his chair and over the slam of the front door said, "Oh the problems and perils of parenthood."

"Don't knock it," Emily answered. "When they're gone, you will miss having them around." The bleak reality of how alone she was hit Emily with sudden impact.

"Are you feeling a post-wedding let down?" Dennis's hand reached to cover Emily's fingers.

"A little," she admitted, grateful for the warmth of his touch.

"Me, too." His fingers caressed the back of her hand. "It's only natural, I suppose." Out of the blue he said, "I would like us to become better acquainted."

After an interminable length of time, Emily said, "We are acquainted."

Dennis raised one eyebrow. "Not as well acquainted as I would like us to be."

Emily's heart beat a little faster. "How well is well?"

Dennis's laughter filled the room. "I'm not proposing anything improper."

Color burned in Emily's cheeks. "That didn't come out the way I meant it to." She looked Dennis squarely in the eye. "What *are* you proposing?"

Dennis countered, "I want to court you with marriage as the objective." He stood and extended his hand in her direction.

Emily swallowed. Was what she felt for Dennis love? It was nothing like what she once felt for Robert, and certainly not like the passion that drew her to Mac. She felt secure with Dennis, and she trusted him. There was no denying the deep affection she had for him. He was all the things any woman would look for in a man. Her voice was husky. "Aunt Beth offered me wise words of advice today. She told me I would never find happiness until I found Emily. I need some time to find myself."

Dennis took her hand, pulled her to her feet, and drew her into a tight embrace. "May I court you as you search for that elusive Emily?"

"Yes." Emily stood on tiptoe. "You are very dear to me." So dear that the thought of losing him frightened her more than she had realized before. She knew it was time to declare her choice. "I'm going to kiss you". She did, pushing her tongue into his mouth and sweeping around in circles.

The air ignited as Dennis became master of the situation. He kissed her with abandon. Her pulses pounded and passion ran to the tips of her fingers, knotted in her stomach and raced down her legs to the tips of her toes.

He released her and stared down into her eyes. "Come into the living room where we can be more comfortable."

Emily put her arms around his waist. "You may have to help me get there. My knees are weak, and my toes are curled. "

Dennis roared with laughter. "This relationship has many promising possibilities."

They went into the living room where Emily snuggled into a corner of the couch.

Dennis sat beside her and pulled her into his arms. "We must find Emily, and soon."

She rested safe and secure in his embrace. "I agree."

Chapter Thirty-Four

Dennis slipped out of his coat and hung it on the back of a chair. "I never thought I'd be interested in another woman. Then you came along. The first time I saw you, I was attracted to you." He smiled ruefully. "It was not the kind of attraction I felt for Ellen. Ours was young love, quivering with expectation and in some ways superficial. What I feel for you is the love of a mature man for a mature woman. It's stronger, more complete. It runs deep and true. We were friends first. For me, that friendship has blossomed into love and produced a passion such as I never felt before. I look forward to someday being your husband and curling your toes every night of my life."

His sweet declaration brought tears to Emily's eyes. He said so exactly what she was not able to put in words. Mature love was different from first love and in some ways better.

Dennis released her and moved away from her. "I believe love is the most powerful force on earth. I believe God and love are synonymous in the sense that both are eternal. I am finding there are many kinds and degrees of love." He took her hand in his. "Being in love is very unique and personal. What I feel for you is a quiet, abiding, and at the same time, a fiery and, all-consuming emotion. Youth cannot handle such a complex, and at the same time, simplistic emotion. Mature love is reserved for mature men and women."

Anything she felt for Robert or Mac paled in comparison to mature love. With Dennis it was different. She wanted that kind of love, but first she had to do some soul searching. "I have some reservations about becoming a pastor's wife. I'm not the most spiritual person and I'm certainly no Bible scholar."

"All you have to do is be yourself. We will grow spiritually together."

Dennis dropped her hand and put his arm around her shoulders. "I haven't asked that you have sex with me before you agree to marriage because I respect you, and I revere God's teachings about matrimony. It doesn't mean I don't desire you. I do. I want to be your friend and your lover." His smile was nothing short of seductive. "I'm a restrained man, but I'm also very passionate."

She believed that. No man could kiss with the toe-curling fervor he did, and not feel intense, deep-seated passions.

Dennis drew her nearer. "I wish I had more to offer you in the way of worldly possessions than a pastor's salary and a parsonage in which to live."

He was offering so much more than worldly possessions. He would be a faithful, devoted husband. As a fringe benefit, he would give her two children she loved dearly. She wasn't sure how Larry would feel. Kevin wouldn't object. He might even be pleased. "You are giving me the rarest of gifts, a husband I can respect and trust."

"What about love?" Dennis asked.

"I have to be sure this is a relationship I can commit to for a lifetime." *Dennis is too dear a man to be hurt by my self-doubts and fears.* "I need time."

Dennis dropped a kiss on her cheek. "I won't rush you. You can tell me what you decide, when you decide."

He was being more than generous. Emily kissed his cheek. "Thank you for understanding."

He chuckled. "You are worth waiting for."

Emily stood. A warm glow filled her heart. "It's time I went home."

"I'll walk you home." Dennis reached for his coat.

Emily stood by the door. "This has happened so suddenly."

Dennis slipped his arms into his coat. "It has been happening for a long time. You couldn't see it until you let go of your past."

Emily picked up her handbag. She had let her grief over her failed marriage, and then a fleeting infatuation with a live-for-the-moment man blind her to all else. "You are a wise man."

Dennis took her hand in his. "And a patient one. I couldn't speak until I was sure you were over Robert."

"When did you know? How could you tell?" A street lights came on, illuminating their way.

Dennis lifted her hand and kissed her fingers before he replied. "I saw the two of you together today, and I knew. There is no longer any love between you."

He zeroed in so succinctly on her emotions, one of them she refused, until now, to admit. "At first I wanted revenge. I don't anymore." She was only now beginning to recognize the depth of liberation Dennis's love brought to her.

They reached Emily's front door. She opened her handbag and pulled out her keys. "Good night."

Dennis stepped a little closer. "May I kiss you good night?"

"I'd like that."

Dennis drew her into his arms. She felt heat and strength emanating from his muscular body. His lips were sensuous and warm. Fire built inside her, not by degrees, but suddenly and with the force of a spontaneous combustion. Then he released her. She stepped back and placed her hand over her lips.

His voice was deep and husky, "Oh, Emily."

She swallowed, and caught her breath. "You made my toes curl again." She put her key in the lock.

"I wanted to do so much more. I'm going now before I yield to temptation." He stepped onto the walk. "Will you and Larry have dinner with us tomorrow evening?"

"Larry's going back to Austin tomorrow afternoon." The lock clicked and Emily pushed the door open.

"Then you must come," Dennis replied. "You can walk over with the twins when they bring Boo home."

His concern touched her, and having dinner with Dennis and the twins brought a surge of anticipated pleasure. "I'd love that. I'll see you then."

Dennis waved a hand. "I'll see you tomorrow." He hurried down the walkway.

Emily went inside and closed the door. Her head swirled. She refused to question the suddenness of her new-found joy. She would grab this second chance at happiness with no questions and no looking back.

Mature love. Thank God she was forty-three instead of twenty-three. A twenty-three-year-old girl might well mistake what she felt for Mac as love. As an experienced, forty-three woman, she knew better. Hearth and home appealed to her much more than a thrilling existence traveling Europe.

She took her phone from her handbag, and rang Mac's number.

He answered immediately. "Hello, beautiful lady." Before she could respond, he said, "I have a feeling your answer is no."

"You're correct. It's no."

"I am leaving at noon tomorrow. If you change your mind, call me."

If he was heartbroken, he covered it well. Emily assured him, "My mind is made up. But thank you for doing what you did, and being who you are." She heard music in the background and the babble of voices.

"My pleasure. So long, and have a good life."

Emily closed her phone and put it back in her handbag.

The sound of Boo scratching on the back door made her rush across the room. The poor dog must think he had been deserted. She opened the back door and was greeted by loud yelps and a wet tongue. She was leaning against the cabinet watching Boo devour the last of his food when Larry came through the kitchen door. Love softened Emily's smile. "Did you enjoy the movie?"

Larry shrugged. "It was okay if you're into horror movies. I'm not."

Emily was not the only one with a change of heart. "You once loved horror movies."

"Not anymore." Larry opened the refrigerator. "Would you like something to drink?"

Emily sat at the kitchen table. "I'll have a flavored water."

Larry took two drinks from the box and came to sit across from his mother. "I've grown up. Gory movies seem juvenile to me now. Amy and Kim enjoy every creepy, crawly moment." He popped the top on both cans and passed one to Emily. "I like seeing them have a good time." He took a long drink from his cola and set it on the table where it made a wet circle. "You've changed, too, Mom, since you and Dad divorced."

There was a time when Emily would have felt uncomfortable with that observation. She didn't now. "I've grown up, too." She took a sip of her water. The cool liquid soothed her dry throat.

Larry moved his cola around on the table, leaving wet circles. "When I look around me, I think that life is one long process of growing up and up and up."

Emily smiled at her son's very adult insight. "You've become very observant."

Larry turned his can around in his hand. "I observed something at Kevin's wedding today that I'd never noticed before. You're miserable around Dad and happy when you're with Dennis."

There was no point in denying an obvious truth. "Does that bother you?"

Larry thought for a moment. "No. I've reconciled myself to the divorce. All I want now is for both you and Dad to be happy."

Emily pushed her half-filled can aside. "I am happy with Dennis."

"It would appear so." Larry grinned at her. "If you are happy with him, go for it." He swallowed, awkwardly. "Kevin feels the same way."

"Does he?" Emily's eyes widened. "When did he tell you this?"

"The day we talked to Dennis, after we had a talk with Dad."

This was news to Emily. She wanted to ask for specifics but didn't. She was content to know her sons liked and accepted Dennis. "Why did you decide to talk to Dennis after you'd talked to your father?"

"Kevin and I were both still confused and unsure about some things." Larry crushed the aluminum can in his hand. "Dad made Kevin and me promise to keep what we talked about in strictest confidence."

"You told Dennis what your dad said." Was this the son she so recently assessed as being mature?

"Mom." Larry made an effort to placate. "Dennis is a counselor. What we tell him doesn't count. It's okay to confide in your counselor. Besides, Dennis is also an ordained minister."

"True," Emily conceded. She was glad her boys saw Dennis for the fine man he was. "I am very fond of Dennis." She was not being truthful, not with Larry and not with herself. "That's not true. I'm in love with Dennis." There, she'd said it.

Larry grinned. "That's good, because he loves you too."

Emily was aghast. "How could you know? Who told you?"

That silly grin still stretched across Larry's face. "I'm not blind. Nobody had to tell me."

Emily's tone softened. "Is it that obvious?"

"Not to everybody. It is to me. I'm your son, remember." Larry's grin faded. "I approve, Mom. I like Dennis. I know you don't need my permission to have another man in your life, but I want you to know that I'll respect and support any decision you and Dennis make." He stood. "I'm happy for you." He shoved his chair under the table. "I'm going out again. I'm meeting Gus and some of the guys at Tony's Pizza Shack."

Emily refrained from reminding him that it was late and he'd had a long and tiring day. "I won't see you again before you leave for Austin."

"I could get up and have breakfast with you in the morning," Larry offered.

"You don't have to do that." Emily gave him a quick hug and a peck on the cheek. "Lock the door when you leave."

Larry hurried toward the living room. "Good night, Mom. I'll call you tomorrow evening." The silent house vibrated with the slamming of the front door.

As Emily cleared the table and straightened the living room, a host of conflicting thoughts rolled around inside her head. What she needed now was a hot shower and a good night's sleep.

Chapter Thirty-Five

Emily awoke the next morning with a clear head and renewed resolve to put the past behind her and get on with her life. A busy morning in her office helped her forget the events of the day before. It was almost noon before she glanced at her watch for the first time and wondered where the morning had gone. She switched off her computer, and decided to have an early lunch.

She was scarcely seated in the diner when she looked up to see Robert striding toward her table. He sat down before Emily had time to protest. "I thought I'd find you here."

Something was wrong, she could tell by the look on his face and the tone of his voice. "Has something happened to George?"

"Dad's fine. It's Aunt Beth." He reached across the table and took both Emily's hands in his. "She passed away last night."

Emily closed her eyes. "I'm so sorry. Did she suffer?"

Robert's hold on her hands tightened. "No. She died in her sleep."

Emily opened her eyes and stared into the distraught face of the man seated across from her. "How is George?"

"Not well, I'm afraid. Aunt Beth was like a mother to him after he lost his parents."

Emily's appetite disappeared, "Where are George and Clara?"

"They're at home." Robert's frown deepened. "Are you all right?"

Emily got a grip on her emotions. "I can cope." Her mind turned to more practical matters. "Did you get in touch with Kevin?"

Robert nodded. "I called him earlier this morning. I talked to Larry, too. He's postponed going back to Austin. He's coming out to Mom and Dad's as soon as he ties up some loose ends."

"And Kevin?" Emily asked.

"Kevin is cutting his honeymoon short. He and Stacy will be home tomorrow morning."

Tears filled Emily's eyes. "Only yesterday Aunt Beth said she was not long for this world. I thought she was being melodramatic." The terrible finality of what happened began to sink in. "Get me out of here before I fall apart."

Robert put his arm around her shoulder and led her toward the door. "Where would you like to go?"

"I should be with George and Clara, and so should you. I'll call my office from your car."

Robert ushered Emily toward the parking lot. "Can you leave on such short notice?"

"This is a family emergency. They will understand." After calling her office, Emily settled back and stared out the window at the passing traffic as old memories made her heart ache. She could never remember when Aunt Beth wasn't a part of her life. Often sharp-tongued, sometimes cynical, she was that unfettered relation who showed up at birthday parties with special gifts, the spinster aunt who made holidays special with outings and presents. Despite all her generous gestures, she remained on the periphery of the family unit, distant and somewhat aloof. Had she made these overt demonstrations of thoughtfulness toward others because her own life was bleak and unfulfilled?

Words Aunt Beth spoke to Emily only yesterday, returned to bounce around in her head. *Don't pity me. I made my choice a long time ago, and I never regretted it.*

Robert's voice intruded into her melancholy reflections, "A penny for your thoughts."

Emily turned to stare at his profile. "I was remembering something Aunt Beth told me yesterday. She said she made a choice a long time ago and she never regretted it. I don't know of anyone else who could make such a statement about any decision they ever made."

Without taking his eyes from the road Robert asked, "Do you have regrets, Emily?"

"Doesn't everybody? I'm sure Aunt Beth did, too. She was speaking about a specific choice she made. It concerned her relationship with a man. She told me she was in love with him. Do you know who he was?"

Robert stopped for a red light. "I haven't the faintest idea."

How little Emily really knew about a woman who had always been a part of her life.

"Aunt Beth raised Dad after his parents died." Robert slowed for an intersection. "When Grandpa and Grandma died, she moved in and took over. Some of Grandma's sisters took her to court later, trying to gain custody of Dad. They lost. It soon became apparent that Aunt Beth had a will of iron, some influential friends in high places, and a seemingly endless supply of money."

Emily's curiosity was piqued. "Do your parents know the name of the man Aunt Beth was in love with?"

Robert sped around a slow-moving vehicle. "I'm sure Dad does, and maybe Mom too. I doubt either of them would tell a living soul so long as Aunt Beth was alive."

"I always assumed she was a spinster in every sense of the word." How many of her other assumptions about Aunt Beth were dead wrong?

As the car pulled into the driveway of George and Clara's home, Emily took her cell from her handbag. "I have to make another call."

Robert shrugged. "Go ahead."

She held her phone and waited, hoping Robert would go inside. When it became obvious he intended to stay, Emily asked, "Do you mind? This is private."

Robert didn't budge. "I don't mind, go ahead."

Emily dialed Dennis's office. His secretary answered and told her Reverend Morrison was out. "I'll call back." She dialed the parsonage. The housekeeper answered and explained the twins weren't home. "Thank you." She expected Robert to ask her questions. He didn't.

A smile broke through the scowl on George's face when Emily came through the door. He pulled her into a bear hug.

"Is there anything I can do for you?" Emily asked.

"Just having you here helps." George shook his head. "I'm going to miss my little auntie." Irrelevantly he added, "Debra says she's better off now."

"Where is Debra?" Emily looked around the room.

"She and Mike are making the final funeral arrangements. They should be here before dark."

From behind her, Robert urged, "Go in and see Mama. I'll stay here with Dad."

Emily hurried down the hall. She had traversed this passageway since she was a little girl staying over for the night with Debra. Clara was lying on her bed. Her legs were covered with a patchwork quilt. She smiled when Emily entered the room. "I'm glad you came, although I know it is an imposition."

Emily sat on the bed beside the frail little woman. "It's not an imposition. Aunt Beth was very dear to me, just as you and George are."

"Aunt Beth was good to me, you know," Clara confided. "After George and I married, she was always good to me, even though she didn't really like me in the beginning."

Startled by such a revelation, Emily blurted out, "Aunt Beth didn't approve of you?"

"She thought I was too young and flighty for George. Those were her exact words. 'The girl is too young and flighty for a man like George.'"

"I'm sure she didn't mean it." Emily wanted to find fault with such a blatant affront. She didn't wish to speak ill of one so recently deceased. "Maybe you misunderstood."

"It was difficult to misunderstand Aunt Beth. She always said exactly what she thought. I grew to love her." Clara wiped at a tear. "I understood after a while why she was so protective of George. He was all she had after--." She hesitated.

"After what?" Emily prompted.

Clara sighed. "I don't suppose it matters now. After Morris McCray passed on."

Emily's mouth fell open. "Morris McCray the ex-governor?"

Clara sat on the side of the bed. "He was once a United States Senator, too, and he was very wealthy." She felt around under her bed. "Now where did I put my slippers?" She found her shoes, and slipped her feet into them. "I have to go back to Dad. He needs me."

Emily understood. This was Clara's way of saying the conversation about Aunt Beth's lover was closed. She helped Clara to her feet. "He's in the living room."

As Emily was helping Clara settle on the couch beside George, Larry came through the front door.

He greeted first his grandmother and then his grandfather with a sad smile and a big hug before turning to face his father, "Hi, Dad."

Robert nodded. "I'm glad you are here."

Such formality. They could have been casual acquaintances greeting each other in passing.

Larry came to stand beside Emily. "How are you, Mom?" His anxious gaze searched her face, before he gave her a quick hug.

"I'm all right." Emily dropped into an overstuffed chair.

"Are you sure?" Larry leaned against the wall and put his hands in his pockets. "Dennis says this will be hard for you. I promised him I'd take care of you."

"You talked to Dennis?" Emily was glad he had a father figure to turn to since he and Robert were still on shaky ground. "When?"

"I went by to see him on my way out here. He got the message you left for him. He says to tell you not to worry about Boo. He and the twins will look after him."

"That was kind of him." Thank God she had Dennis to lean on. "Did you lock the house when you left?"

"Yes. Don't worry." Larry sank down on his haunches. "Dennis wants you to call him."

Before Emily could answer, Clara intervened. "You can go to the study. There's more privacy there."

Four pairs of eyes fastened on Emily. Since she could think of no appropriate answer to the silent questions she saw there, she excused herself and slipped down the hall to George's study.

The phone rang only once before Dennis's deep voice sounded in her ear. "Reverend Morrison here." He was, as always, cool, self-assured, and totally in command.

"Dennis?" Emily's tension lessened. "Larry said you wanted me to call you."

"I did. I'm concerned about you." The dulcet tones of his deep voice reached out like a caress. "I know how fond you were of your Aunt Beth."

He understood. "She was very dear to me. I'll miss her."

"I talked with Stacy. She and Kevin are on their way home. I sent someone over to clean their apartment."

Emily smiled. He was someone who was there for her. She had every assurance he would always be. "You think of everything, don't you?"

"I try. Larry says you left your car in the city. I'll be right over."

"Larry's here. He can drive me back to the city." She didn't want Dennis to come here and be hurt by something Robert might say or do.

Dennis was gently persistent. "Perhaps you should have him take you there now."

"I can't leave Clara and George alone until Debra gets here."

"What about you, Emily?" Dennis's anxiety sounded in his voice. "Who's going to look after you? Your ex-in-laws are not capable of looking after themselves?"

His thoughts and concerns were for her. She never had someone, anyone, who put her feelings before their own. How grateful she was for his love and care. "That's not--"

"Please don't tell me it's not necessary. It is. I'll be there shortly."

Emily closed her phone, and sighed.

From behind her, Robert asked, "Is there a problem?"

She hoped not. There was one way to find out. "Dennis is coming out. He should be here within the hour."

"The two of you have become close, haven't you?"

Emily spoke softly. "Please don't make a scene."

Robert shoved his hands in his pockets. "Why should I?"

"I know how you feel about him. He won't stay long. He's taking me to get my car."

Robert took a tentative step in her direction. "You don't know how I feel."

Emily nodded toward a chair. "Why don't you tell me how you feel then?"

Much to her surprise, he obeyed. "I saw you with Dennis at Kevin's wedding, and I knew."

Emily leaned against George's desk. "What did you know?"

Tears stood in Robert's eyes. "I knew you were in love with the Reverend. Contrary to what you think, I love you. That's why I've decided to back off. All I want is your happiness. If that happiness lies with Dennis--" His voice broke on the end of a choking sob.

Did Robert love her? She would never be sure. She was sure she didn't love him. Furthermore, neither of them trusted the other. "You will always have a special place in my heart."

Robert brushed a weary hand through his hair before standing and stepping aside. "When Reverend Morrison arrives, let him in. I promise to behave."

Emily paused in the doorway, waiting, hoping, Robert would give her some assurance that he would keep his word. Like a blow to the head, it hit her. She would never believe what he said again. She walked away slowly.

She sat in the living room with Larry, George, and Clara waiting for Dennis to put in an appearance. She had no idea where Robert might be.

When the doorbell sounded, Larry jumped to his feet. "I'll get it." He opened the door and a pleasant exchange of voices drifted from the foyer into the living room. Larry reentered the room with Dennis following.

Dennis smiled as he greeted George and Clara. "Mr. and Mrs. Franklin, it's good to see you again, even under such distressing circumstances." He shook George's hand and patted Clara's arm. "Is there anything I can do?"

Clara warmed instantly to his charm. "That's very nice of you, Reverend Morrison, but Aunt Beth made her funeral arrangements long ago."

"I am here only to offer spiritual comfort." Dennis dropped a kiss on Emily's cheek. "How are you, my dear?"

Her knight in shining armor was here, rushing in where angels would fear to tread.

Emily smiled at him. "I'm managing."

"Would you like me to take you home?"

"Hello, Reverend Morrison." Robert came from the dining room, walked across the floor with his hand extended. "It was kind of you to come out." He shook Dennis's hand.

Clara looked from Emily to Robert then addressed Dennis. "It would be nice if Emily would stay until Debra arrives."

Without an invitation, or the slightest qualm, Dennis sat on the sofa beside George and put his hat on the table beside the couch. "I'll wait with you. Later we can go for your car."

If he stayed Robert was apt to insult him, or worse. Emily didn't want Dennis hurt because of his concern for her. "Larry can take me to my car. I'm sure you should be getting home to Kim and Amy."

"The housekeeper's staying over. The twins are fine." Dennis was the epitome of gentle kindness. He leaned back and put one arm across the back of the sofa. "Except for being disappointed that you couldn't make it to dinner tonight. They send their love and condolences."

Robert crossed the room and came to stand behind Emily's chair. He laid his hand on her shoulder, a gesture she found blatantly offensive. "You can drive Larry to get Emily's car. She can drive Larry's car home later." He appeared to be congenial. Was he?

Larry looked as anxious as Emily felt. "You wouldn't mind would you, Dennis?" He moved toward the door. "Mom, where are your car keys?"

"In my handbag, it's in the spare bedroom."

Larry volunteered, "I'll bring it to you."

"Take the keys and leave the handbag," Emily called as Larry disappeared down the hall.

Dennis kept his seat. "I don't like leaving you here, Emily."

Emily didn't like staying, but she wanted Dennis out of here before Robert did something that would hurt him, his parents, and Larry. "Please, go with Larry." The heat from Robert's hand burned into her shoulder.

Dennis stood. "Your wish is my command." He retrieved his hat and placed it on his head. "Call me when you get home. If you feel the need for company, I'll come over."

Larry reappeared, swinging the keys to Emily's car around his finger. "We should go. We don't want to get caught in the five o'clock traffic."

As the front door shut behind Dennis and Larry, George stood. "Mama, I think I'll lie down and rest for a spell. Maybe you should do the same."

"That's a good idea." Clara placed both hands on the arms of her chair and pushed herself to a standing position. "You will excuse us, won't you?"

Emily didn't want to be alone with Robert. "Debra and Mike should be here soon. Don't you want to wait for them?"

"You can wake us when they arrive." George followed Clara from the room and closed the door behind him.

Emily drummed her fingers on the arm of her chair. George and Clara had deceived her. They ask her to stay with them until Debra arrived, and then left her alone with Robert. Had he plotted with them? That was the only answer. Why was she surprised?

Robert moved to sit on the couch. "I kept my promise. I didn't make a scene while Dennis was here." His brows drew together in a pensive expression. "You didn't believe I would."

Emily squirmed in her chair. "I wasn't sure."

He flinched as if she had struck him. "I had no idea your distrust of me had eroded away completely."

You had an ulterior motive. Emily drew a long breath. "I'm leaving." She turned toward the bedroom. "I have to fetch my handbag."

Chapter Thirty-Six

The front door opened to admit Debra and Mike. "Where is everybody?" Debra stepped through the entranceway. "Is Dad all right?"

Mike eased the front door shut as he and Debra exchanged bewildered glances.

Emily raced for the bedroom. She emerged seconds later, clutching her handbag with both hands. Veering around Debra, she headed for the front door.

Debra called after her, "Emily, wait." She focused her gaze on Robert. "Where are Mom and Dad?"

Robert inclined his head toward the bedroom. "They're sleeping."

Debra called after Emily, "Don't go."

Emily hurried out the door and down the walkway. Her head was a jumble of confused thoughts. Beneath that confusion ran a hurt too deep to measure. She got into Larry's car and slammed the door. George and Clara lied to her. How could they? Would she have done the same for either of your sons? She backed from the driveway and sped toward home.

She was so lost in her own thoughts that she almost missed the turn into her own driveway. She made a sharp right and pulled to a stop. Larry emerged from the front door. "I didn't expect you so soon."

Emily got out of the car and slammed the door. "I left as soon as Debra and Mike arrived." She offered Larry his car keys.

He dropped them into his pants pocket. "Dennis invited us to dinner. Are you ready to go?"

Dennis would be a welcome sight. "I'm more than ready."

Larry smiled. "I thought you'd jump at the chance to have dinner with the Morrisons." His eyes narrowed. "Did you and Dad have another fight?"

Emily couldn't tell him what happened, and cause more dissension in the family. "Your dad and I were very civil to each other." She laced her hand through his arm. "Let's go."

As always, in the presence of Dennis and his daughters, Emily's spirits lifted. By the time the meal was over and the group retired to the living room, she had pushed her thoughts about Robert and his parents to the back of her mind.

The joy of the evening was overshadowed by the sadness of losing Aunt Beth. Emily needed the comfort of Dennis's counseling. She hinted several times that she would like to be alone with him. When her subtle suggestions failed, she asked point blank, "Larry, would you mind leaving Dennis and me alone for a while?"

Dennis nodded to the twins. "Upstairs, young ladies, Emily has something to discuss in private."

Larry was hesitant. "Mom, if you have a problem, I should know about it."

Emily said, "Go home, Larry. I'll be there soon."

Larry stood. "I have a better idea. Why don't I take Kim and Amy to McDonald's for a soda? I can walk home with you afterward."

Larry was concerned about his mother. That was commendable. It was also unnecessary. She was capable of managing her own life.

The twins, who were uncharacteristically quiet through the evening, begged in unison. Amy's, "May we go, Daddy?" collided with Kim's, "I get to ride in the front seat by Larry."

"Yes. Go. Please. Be back by ten o'clock." He sighed as the sound of the slamming door echoed through the still room. "Alone at last."

Emily moved to the couch and snuggled in Dennis's embrace. "I need to be with you. I need you to hold me."

"You look beat." Dennis kissed her with loving tenderness. "This was a tiring day for you, both physically and emotionally. I know how deeply you cared for Aunt Beth and how attached you are to George and Clara Franklin."

Emily sighed. "George and Clara lied to us. The moment you and Larry were out the front door, they left me alone with Robert."

Dennis held her face with his hands and looked into her eyes. "Do you think they plotted with Robert to do that?"

She laid her head on his shoulder. "Yes. Am I being paranoid?"

Dennis took her hand in his. "Don't judge them too harshly. Robert is their only son."

Emily stared up at him. "They are my family, too, and they betrayed me."

"No." Dennis spoke gently. "They are not your family. As painful as that is, you must accept that."

He was right. "How do I explain this to Kevin and Larry?"

Dennis kissed her temple. "You don't. You can't run interference for them the rest of your life. They will find their own answers."

Emily relaxed. "Interference is the right word. I must let go. They are men now. What would I do without you?"

"I pray you never have to find out," Dennis said then he asked, "How do you think Robert will react when he knows I want to marry you?"

"That's Robert's problem. We have no control over how Robert feels, or what he does."

Dennis nodded. "It's time you put distance between you and Robert and his family."

"All these years I thought they needed me." Emily wiped at a tear.

Dennis spoke softly, "I try never to be judgmental, but this has to be said. For your own well-being you must break the ties that bind you to Robert and his family."

"I've known them all my life." Emily raised her hand in protest and then dropped it. Dennis spoke the truth. Why hadn't she known it before? "Thank you for making me realize what I should have recognized long ago."

Dennis ran his tongue around his lips, a movement Emily found pleasantly sexy. "Emily, darling, they took advantage of you."

"Do you think I've encouraged them?"

He gazed at her with the sweetest smile on his face. "Have you?"

She had, by running to do their bidding each time they called. She stood. "Not intentionally." Doubt like a slithering snake slid into her mind. "They used Aunt Beth's illness to lure me to the hospital. When Robert and I arrived, Aunt Beth was sleeping, or so Clara and George said. They wanted me to be alone with Robert. I fell right into their trap. Why would they do that to me?"

"Robert will go to any lengths to get you back, even enlist the help of his parents." Dennis patted the cushion beside him. "Sit down."

Emily sat, and Dennis once more took her hands in his. "There is a way you can make the break permanent and complete without them feeling you are rejecting them." Dennis watched her with studied concern. "It would entail saying yes to my proposal of marriage."

Something in the tone of his voice made her move back and stare at him. "I don't understand."

"Allow me to explain. I have been called to pastor a church in another state. It's a mega-church with thousands of members."

Emily bit her lip and looked away. "Are you going?"

Dennis dropped her hands. "Yes. Not because it is a huge church with a large congregation, but because I know that is where God wants me."

"You won't change your mind?" Tension tightened in Emily's stomach.

His answer was swift and emphatic. "No. I answered God's call a long time ago. I will go where he sends me. I pray you will come with me as my wife."

There were so many things to consider. "What does Stacy think about you moving out of state?" *What would Kevin and Larry think?*

The muscle along Dennis's square jawline tightened. "I don't know. I haven't discussed the matter with her."

"She's your daughter," Emily reminded him. "Don't you owe her some consideration?"

Dennis's face relaxed into a smile. "No more consideration than she would owe me if she and Kevin decided to move to another state, or another country. My life is separate from hers now."

He was right. How long had she been gazing at the forest and never seeing the trees? "I can imagine what Kevin would say if I interfered in his life." *Yet he constantly interferes in mine.*

He pulled her back into his arms." Will you be sitting with the Franklin family during the funeral services tomorrow?"

"I'll sit in the funeral chapel." She owed Aunt Beth being there to pay her last respects.

As if he had read her mind, Dennis said, "I'll accompany you to the funeral."

"Robert wouldn't like that." The words slipped out before Emily could stop them.

Dennis asked, "Does that mean you don't want me to go?"

She did want him to go, oh so badly. "I'd be pleased to have you go with me."

"It's settled. Tomorrow I would like a yes or no answer to my proposal. I pray it will be yes." He smiled at her and her heart skipped a beat. "Tell me about your Aunt Beth. How old was she? Had she ever been married?"

How easy it was to tell Dennis about Aunt Beth's recently revealed secret lover.

They were still talking when Larry and the twins returned.

Chapter Thirty-Seven

After such a hectic day and trying evening, Emily doubted she would sleep. How wrong she was. She promptly dropped into a sound slumber. Her rest was plagued with disturbing dreams that she couldn't recall when she awoke the next morning.

She dressed in somber black. What lay ahead impacted suddenly. The task of getting through this day was not going to be an easy one.

Larry was dressed and draped over half the couch when Emily entered the living room. "Ready to go, Mom?"

Emily had put off until now telling Larry that she wasn't going with him. "Dennis is taking me to the funeral."

Larry let out a little gasp. "Do you think that's a good idea? You know how Dad feels about Dennis."

Oh yes, she knew. "What counts is how I feel about Dennis."

Larry hesitated before asking, "What about Dad?"

Emily broke her news gently, "You will all be sitting in the secluded family section. I won't."

"Why not?" Larry asked in dismay.

"I'm no longer a part of the Franklin family." She should have had the courage to make this break long before now. "I don't belong with Aunt Beth's family anymore."

Larry's nervous fingers adjusted his tie. "Is this what you and Dad talked about yesterday?"

"The decision as to where I sit is mine."

"Dad put this silly notion in your head." Larry came across the room and glared down at his mother. "Didn't he?"

Emily met his bold gaze. "No, he didn't. The decision was mine." Dennis was right. The sooner she broke all ties with the Franklin family, the better it would be for all concerned.

Larry put both his hands on his mother's shoulders. "You can't run out on your family."

"The Franklins are no longer my family." She had to make him understand. "I was a part of them because I was married to your father. I'm not married to him anymore."

"Kevin and I are your family." Larry dropped onto the couch. "We're your sons."

"And you always will be." This was neither the time nor the place to have this conversation. They were both too emotionally unstrung. "Let's get through the funeral and then we can talk about this."

Larry crossed his legs and stared at his shoes. "You can talk forever and it won't change the facts."

"It may change how you see those facts." Emily laid her hand on her son's arm. "Please try to understand my position."

He shook free of her grasp. "I don't understand anybody's position in this whole stupid mess. I don't understand why Dad left us in the first place, and don't say he didn't leave Kevin and me, too. He did. I don't understand why you didn't try to stop him. I don't understand why now when he wants to come back, you won't let him."

All this time her younger son, her baby, had harbored these bitter, frustrating emotions, holding them deep inside, and she was too absorbed in her own private hell to notice. "Larry, darling, Dad doesn't want to come back to me."

"Yes, he does. Why won't you let him?"

Emily drew her son into her arms and held him as she had when he was a small child. She was tempted to tell him everything was going to be all right. She couldn't. "If it were only that simple."

A sob shook through Larry's body. "I'm sorry, Mom. I shouldn't have said that."

"We are both too emotionally overwrought to talk about this now." Emily brushed Larry's hair back from his forehead. "Go to the funeral and try not to worry. Whatever happens, remember, I love you."

Larry made a visible effort to pull himself together. "I love you, too." He hurried out the front door.

Emily sat on the front porch and waited for Dennis to put in an appearance. The trauma of grief and confusion suspended all other emotions, wrapping her in a cocoon of false serenity. Dennis arrived looking stylish and handsome in a dark, smartly tailored suit. He got out of his van and came to greet her. "Have you been waiting long?"

Emily pulled her mind back from a wasteland of confused thoughts, "I'm so glad to see you."

*****

The foyer of the chapel was crowded. Some of the people Emily recognized. Many of them were strangers. She had been a close acquaintance of Aunt Beth, but she never knew the first thing about Elizabeth Abigail Franklin. Emily signed the guest book and waited for Dennis to do the same.

They found a pew near the back and sat down. Soft somber music floated through the hushed chamber.

Goose bumps appeared on Emily's arms and gamboled across her body.

Dennis put his arm around her shoulder. "Are you cold?"

Emily shivered at his touch. "I'm cold inside."

Dennis took her hand and held onto it.

The service was short and formal, almost ritualistic.

Emily glanced around the crowded sanctuary. Her thoughts skipped like a stone over water to think again, how fortunate she was to have found Dennis. She was thankful for his comforting presence. Her mind drifted backward to pleasanter times and events.

The sound of organ music and soft singing pulled Emily from her reverie. The service was drawing to a close. She whispered to Dennis, "I can't view the body." She wanted to remember Aunt Beth alive and animated, not lying stiff and still on a satin pad in a quilted box.

Dennis accepted her decision without question. He held her arm as they wound their way through the crowd that gathered on the front lawn, and walked toward his van. Once there, he opened the door and helped her inside, then came around and got behind the wheel.

The pallbearers emerged from the building and came down the steps carrying Aunt Beth's earthly remains. The brevity of life with all its struggles struck Emily like a battering ram.

The funeral procession was long, the ride to the cemetery seemingly endless. As they inched along at a snail's pace, Emily stared out the window and tried to sort through the many conflicting emotions that surged through her. Through all the turmoil, one thought emerged. Her relationship with Dennis Morrison was her anchor in a storm of conflict and doubt. She wanted to marry him as soon as possible.

They turned off the highway and drove down a winding thoroughfare. Dennis had scarcely parked his van and set his brake when Kevin opened Emily's door and leaned down. "Grandma wondered what happened to you."

Emily unfastened her seat belt. "Didn't Larry tell her I came with Dennis?"

"He mentioned it." Kevin straightened and stepped aside. "Hurry, the graveside service is about to start."

Emily stepped from the car and leaned against the hood. Even on this somber occasion, was Clara conspiring with Robert? "Tell Grandma I'm here."

Dennis was by Emily's side, peering down at her, concern and anxiety carved into every line of his handsome face. "Run along, Kevin. I'm sure your father and grandparents are waiting for you."

"They're waiting for you, too," Kevin replied. He nodded his head in the direction of the open grave. "Let's go."

Emily wasn't up to explaining to Kevin why she couldn't come with him. "Go on. I'll be along soon."

Dennis intervened. "I don't think your dad would like your mother sitting with the immediate family. Maybe it's better if she and I keep our distance."

Kevin scowled. "Did Dad tell you that?" When no one answered, he demanded again, this time more loudly, "Did he?"

Emily didn't need Kevin and his good intentions, intruding into her life. He had no right. "Your dad and I are divorced."

Kevin grinned. "What's new? Let's go." He took Emily's other arm. "We're missing the grave side service."

Emily fell in step with the two men. Once again, she was taking the line of least resistance.

A canopy covered the open grave with chairs set out for the immediate family. Robert, Clara, George, and Debra occupied the first row. Mike, Larry, Stacy, and Debra's children sat immediately behind them. Every eye turned toward Dennis and Emily as they followed Kevin into the canopied shade and sat down.

Emily's nerves were like electric wires, snapping and sizzling with every movement she made. Afterward, she couldn't recall a word the minister said.

As the last benediction was completed, Emily turned her eyes to stare directly into Robert's accusing gaze. She stared him down.

None of this escaped Dennis's notice. He helped Emily from her chair. "Let's get the formalities over, make a graceful exit, and be gone."

Clara chided, as Emily came to her side. "Where have you been? We missed you." She nodded to Dennis. "It was kind of you to come, Reverend."

George put his arm around Clara's shoulder. "It was thoughtful of you to send flowers, Reverend, and the donation you made to the nursing home in Aunt Beth's memory was greatly appreciated."

Through the next fifteen minutes, Emily spoke to family members and friends, talking and nodding, and smiling occasionally. Her speech must have been lucid and her answers correct, but her mind was blank. It was as if her brain was set on automatic pilot. She gave Robert a wide berth, never looking in his direction and moving when he came too near.

Dennis stayed close to Emily's side. For that she was doubly thankful. Any remark to be made had to be said in his presence and Dennis was a formidable figure, fending off intrusive questions, rebuking unwanted remarks with smooth ease, and in general smoothing the way for eventual escape.

They made their way to the periphery of the circle of mourners. Emily leaned on Dennis's arm. She could hardly believe her good fortune. She escaped without being approached by Robert. She quickened her pace.

From nowhere, Robert appeared to stand directly in front of her. "Are you leaving, Emily?" Grief lined his face. "You didn't offer me your condolences."

"I'm sorry about your aunt's passing." she spoke softly and with compassion.

Dennis intervened. "We must go." His hand tightened around Emily's elbow. "You have my condolences, also, Mr. Franklin. May God comfort you." How like Dennis to offer comfort to a man who showed little respect for him or his position.

"The twins are waiting for us." Emily stepped to one side.

Robert stepped with her. "I'm sorry it had to end this way."

The heels of Emily's sandals dug into the soft earth. "If you didn't want me here you should have told me. One word from you and I would have stayed away."

"That's not what I'm trying to say. You have every right to be here. I'm trying to say good-bye."

Old memories returned to race through Emily's mind with a vengeance. She whispered over the lump in her throat, "I'm sorry too. Good-bye, Robert."

Dennis ran a finger around his cleric's collar. "We should go."

From the periphery of her vision, Emily saw Kevin approaching, taking long steps across the soft ground, his arms swinging at his sides as he hurried forward. "Is everything all right here?" Kevin arrived, panting and out of breath. He laid his hand on his father's shoulder. "Dad, Grandma and Grandpa are waiting for you."

Robert nodded. "I'll be there soon. I have one more thing to say to your mother."

Larry and Stacy caught up to Kevin.

Larry came to stand on the other side of Robert. "Say it, Dad. Grandma and Grandpa are waiting for us."

Robert ran one hand through his hair. "I wish you every happiness, Emily. You deserve it."

Stacy moved to her father's side. "Daddy, are you all right?"

Dennis nodded. "I'm fine." He took Emily's arm and led her around the group assembled in front of her. "Why don't you walk us to our car?" He led Emily away, with Stacy trotting along by his side.

They cut across the cemetery, literally walking on graves in their headlong move to Dennis's car. The three of them were winded by the time they reached the van. Dennis opened her door and helped Emily inside. "Thank you, Stacy. We will be fine now."

Stacy asked, "What got into Mr. Franklin?"

"He's grieving his loss." Dennis opened his door and slipped into the car. "People often react uncharacteristically when they are under stress."

Stacy leaned down and stared into the car. "Loss just about sums it up. I'm glad you and Emily are together."

Dennis started the car's motor. "I'm going home and count my blessings." He pulled the van into gear. "Kevin is waiting for you."

As they drove away, Emily placed her hand on Dennis's leg. She had never dared be so bold before. "I love you, Dennis Morrison."

Dennis smiled briefly in her direction. "I love you, too, Emily, with all my heart." He looked both ways before changing lanes.

Emily turned to study the profile of the man who sat beside her. He was everything any woman could ask for in a husband. How could she have been so blind as not to see that long before she did? "I'm honored that you want me to be your wife."

Dennis kept his eyes on the road. "Would you like to stay at the parsonage tonight?" Her gasp made him hurry to explain. "I thought you might not want to be alone after all the trauma you have been through today."

How dear he was. She couldn't chance someone would find out, put the wrong spin on her stay, and spread gossip among Dennis's congregation. "Don't worry. I'll be fine."

He turned to stare briefly in her direction. "Are you sure?"

Emily once more laid her hand on his leg. He flinched. "I'm positive."

269

"Call me if you need me."

"I will, I promise."

Dennis pulled into her driveway, stopped his car and took her in his arms. His kiss was magical. She returned it with fervor.

He released her. "Good night, my love. I'll walk you to your door."

Chapter Thirty-Eight

Arm in arm they walked toward the porch. Emily was as concerned for Dennis as she was for herself. This afternoon couldn't have been easy for him. She laid her hand on his arm. "Thank you for being there for me this afternoon."

They stepped onto the porch. Dennis put his arms around her. "I will always be there for you."

Amy burst through Emily's front door, waving both hands and shouting. "I thought you'd never get here."

Dennis spoke softly. "Calm down, sweetheart. Where's Kim? What happened?"

Amy collapsed in her father's arms. "We can't find Boo. Kim is out looking for him."

Dennis soothed, "We'll find him. He wouldn't go far."

Emily smoothed Amy's hair. "Maybe someone took him."

Amy wiped at her tears as she pulled herself from her father's embrace. "That's what we thought when we came to take him for his walk and found he was gone. Kim talked to some of the neighbors. Mrs. Callaghan saw him dig under the fence and follow a gang of dogs down the alley toward Main Street."

Emily gave the child a reassuring hug. "Don't worry. We will find him."

Amy gulped. "Ted Hammonds says the Gentry's female dog is in heat again. Sometimes she gets out and all the dogs in the neighborhood follow her around. Do you think that's what Boo did?"

Despite the gravity of the situation, Emily's eyes sparkled with humor. "I wouldn't doubt it."

Dennis put his arm around Amy's shoulders. "Let's go inside."

Larry's car pulled into the driveway and came to a sudden stop. He jumped out, and raced toward the three people standing on the porch. "What happened?"

"Boo is missing," Emily said. "Kim's out looking for him."

Larry asked, "Which direction did she go?"

Amy pointed south. "That way, we think Boo went toward Main Street."

"Make sure your phone is on so we can all check in with you," Larry told his mother. "I'll start looking, too. We will find him. Don't worry."

"Wait," Amy called after Larry. "Which direction are you going?"

Larry pointed as he ran, "North."

"I'll go east." Amy raced down the sidewalk.

Dennis said, "That leaves west. I'll go that direction. Maybe you should stay here and wait, in case Boo decides to come home of his own accord."

Emily sat on the edge of the porch swing and watched Dennis hike off in a westerly direction. If she had been a little more attentive to Boo, he might be home now, instead of running off into the unknown. The similarity between Boo's disappearance and Robert's sudden departure from her life occurred to Emily with sudden, ironic force.

Thirty minutes later, she was pacing the living room floor and chewing her nails. Her cell phone ring sent her scurrying to answer. Maybe someone had found Boo. He was wearing a collar and identifying tags. She almost shouted into the receiver, "Hello!"

The baritone on the other end of the line demanded, "Let me speak to Larry!"

Emily questioned, "Robert?"

"Is Larry there? He doesn't answer his phone."

"Larry isn't home. Boo has disappeared. Everyone's out combing the neighborhood, looking for him." The tears she had held in check for hours gushed from her eyes. She choked between sobs. "Boo never ran away before."

Robert's tone was assuring. "Boo wouldn't run away from you."

"Yes, he would. He has."

"Stop crying," Robert ordered. "I'll be there in five minutes."

"There's no point in you coming over here--" Emily began.

"I'm not two blocks away. I'm calling from the Italian restaurant on Main Street. Larry was supposed to meet me here for dinner." Robert broke the connection.

Emily stared into the phone. With a mixture of anxiety and dread, she went outside to wait for Robert.

She had scarcely set foot on the front porch when he came wheeling into the driveway and stopped behind Larry's car. He hurried up the walk asking as he advanced, "Are you all right? You sounded frantic." Coming onto the porch, he stood near her.

All the confusing events of this long day came crashing down. "I *am* frantic. Boo is gone."

"Tell me what happened."

Emily related the story Amy told her. She ended by asking, "What if he never comes back?"

"He will come back." Robert rammed his hands into his pants' pockets. "Dogs don't disappear into thin air."

Angered by what she perceived to be indifference, Emily glared at him. "Boo is gone." She dropped down on the top step of the porch. "I'm going to miss him." She lowered her head, causing the heavy fall of her hair to swirl around her neck.

In the west, a cloud-covered sun slid toward the far horizon. Robert said, "When it starts getting dark, Boo will head for home. Larry should be back by then, too."

Emily pushed her hair from her face. She should tell Robert of Dennis's proposal. She patted the place on the step beside her. "Sit down. I have something to tell you."

A muscle flicked along the angular line of Robert's jaw. He sat beside her and sighed. "What now?"

"Dennis has asked me to marry him." She waited for his caustic reply.

It never came. "Do you love him?"

She paused and drew a long breath. The man who sat beside her was a stranger. "Yes, I do, and he loves me."

Robert stood and looked down at her. "I am going to find Boo." He hurried down the walk.

Another half-hour passed before Kim returned. Her heavy steps coming up the walk sent Emily rushing to the door. She flung it open. "Did you find Boo?"

"You're home." Kim quickened her pace. "Where is Amy?"

Emily held the door open. "She's out looking for Boo. So are your father and Larry. Robert has joined the search."

Kim came inside and sat on the couch. "Maybe one of them will find him. I walked all the way to Grant Street and Pine Avenue. I found the Gentry's dog and all her friends. All, that is, except Boo."

Emily's heart lurched. "Boo wasn't with the other dogs?"

"No." Kim stretched out on the couch. "I'll rest a minute and then start to look again."

"There's no point in that." Would Boo ever return? "Your dad, Larry, and Robert are all looking for him. They will find him if he's anywhere around."

Mostly because she couldn't bear to be idle, Emily brewed coffee and made sandwiches. "It's past dinner time. Everyone will be starved by the time they return."

With Kim for company, she sat in the living room and waited.

One by one the other searchers drifted back, first Amy, then Robert and last of all, Larry. Each one brought the same sad report, no Boo.

Larry and Robert went for a belated dinner. Even though she was glad to see Robert leave, Emily felt Larry had deserted her.

She set a tray of sandwiches on the coffee table. "Boo has never done anything like this before. I can't imagine where he could be."

"Dad will find him," Kim assured her.

Amy wiped her hand across her brow. "If Boo isn't home by tomorrow, we should put an ad in the newspaper under lost and found."

Emily couldn't deal with this. It came too soon on the heels of losing Aunt Beth so suddenly, not to mention everything else that transpired this long day. "There are soft drinks in the kitchen," she told the twins.

Amy volunteered, "I'll get them.

Kim was on her feet. "I'll help you."

The twins returned with drinks and paper cups. Emily pointed to the table. "Go ahead, girls, eat."

Kim shook her head. "We will wait for Dad."

"I'll phone him again if he isn't here in an hour." Emily was apprehensive.

Forty-five minutes later when Dennis still hadn't put in an appearance, Emily asked, "What could have happened to your dad?"

The twins, who thirty minutes before, decided to have dinner, were curled up on the couch watching TV.

Kim assured her, "Daddy is okay. God will take care of him."

Emily stacked cups on a tray. *Oh, that I could have that kind of faith.*

As she put dishes in the dishwasher, a horn sounded outside. Emily flew to the front door. Maybe someone was returning Boo. She was greeted by Mr. and Mrs. Gentry and their daughter, Jane. They were parked at the curb. Mr. Gentry leaned out his car window. "Sorry, Ms. Franklin, for disturbing you. We're looking for the twins. We saw the Reverend's car parked here. Could I speak to him?"

"The Reverend isn't here, but the twins are. Would you like to come inside?"

From behind her, Kim said, "Is that Jane?" She hurried toward the door. "We forgot this is the night for Christian Youth Council."

Amy stood beside Emily. "Do we have to wait for Daddy to return, or may we go now?"

Mr. Gentry called from the car. "It's all right. Ms. Franklin. The twins always go with Jane to the council meetings."

"We will see you tomorrow," Kim called as the twins hurried down to sidewalk. They climbed into the car and it pulled from the curb and into the street.

"And a good-bye to you." Emily's words died in her throat. *I have been forsaken by everyone, even Boo.*

The sun set; twilight deepened into darkness. Another hour dragged by and still Dennis had not returned, nor was he answering his phone. Emily slumped in the easy chair. Thoughts of Boo and what might have happened to him played through her mind like scenes from a recurring nightmare. She turned on the TV and switched it off again. Had Dennis found Boo in such a state that he was reluctant to return and tell her what he discovered? Or worse yet, maybe he couldn't find Boo at all.

Just when she gave herself over to resigned despair, the front door burst open admitting Dennis carrying in his arms a bloody and battered Boo.

Chapter Thirty-Nine

Emily leaped to her feet. "You found him! Thank God!" She rushed to examine the dog. "How badly is he hurt? Where was he?"

"It's not as bad as it looks. He's been in a fight." Dennis looked almost as blood stained and mud spattered as Boo did. "His injuries are slight. His worst hurt is his wounded pride."

Emily stroked Boo's neck. "He really is a mess."

Boo raised his head and wagged his tail.

Dennis carried the dog toward the kitchen. "His opponent took a piece of his ear as a souvenir. Let's get him cleaned up and put some antiseptic on his wounds."

Emily spread a towel on the kitchen floor. "Should I take him to the vet?"

Dennis laid Boo on the towel. "Later maybe. It's not necessary now. He needs to be cleaned, and fed, and get some much-needed rest."

Emily hurried to retrieve antiseptic cream and swabs from the bathroom. "Is he going to be all right?" She gave Dennis the swabs and cream.

Dennis dried Boo with a towel before cleaning and swabbing his wounded ear. "He's going to be fine, but he will have some battle scars. The nick in his ear is permanent. If he knows to grieve for that, he will be scarred in more ways than one." He gave Boo's matted coat a final swipe. "I suspect his deepest hurt is that he lost his lady love to another dog that was bigger and stronger."

Emily tossed used swabs into a waste can. "A dog in heat is not my idea of a lady."

Dennis smiled up at her. "Nor mine, but Boo wasn't that wise."

Emily couldn't think of an answer to that. She nodded toward the table. "You must be starved. Sit down. We have coffee and sandwiches."

Dennis looked around the room. "Are you alone?"

Emily raised her voice to be heard over the sound of water running in the sink. "The Gentrys came for the twins."

Dennis patted Boo's head before standing. "What about Larry?"

"Larry went out to dinner with Robert." Emily pointed with her measuring spoon. "The bathroom's down the hall if you'd like to wash your hands." She took paper plates from the cabinet. "Where did you find Boo?"

Dennis stopped his advance toward the bathroom. "He was hiding behind an abandoned building over on Maple Street."

Emily gasped. "He went that far? Whatever made you look there?"

With mock gravity, Dennis said, "I asked myself, where would Boo go to lick his wounds? The answer came to me in a flash. The old abandoned warehouse on Maple Street."

He was making light of what Emily considered a noble deed. "Wash your hands and you can eat." She spread mustard on a slice of bread.

Dennis was scarcely out of sight when the doorbell rang. Emily wiped her hands on a paper towel and hurried to answer. Robert stood on the other side of the opening. "I came by on my way home to see if you had any news about Boo."

"Where is Larry?" Emily asked.

"He took off to parts unknown with Gus. May I come in?" Robert looked past Emily and into the house.

"Dennis found Boo." Emily didn't move. "He's here now."

Robert stepped around Emily and came into the room. "Boo or Dennis?"

Emily drew a deep breath. "Both."

"Is Boo all right?"

Robert hadn't come here to ask about Boo and they both knew it. "He's battle-scarred and bloody, but he's going to be okay."

Robert lifted his head and sniffed the air. "Is that coffee I smell?"

"Do you want to come in?" That was a foolish question, since he was already in. "I made a fresh pot."

"I could use a cup of coffee about now." Robert strode into the kitchen. "Could I have a sandwich too?"

"You just had dinner," Emily reminded him.

Dennis leaned against the cabinet with his arms folded across his chest, "Good evening, Mr. Franklin."

Robert pulled out a chair. "Hail the conquering hero. Emily tells me you found Boo."

Dennis glanced toward Emily with a puzzled look on his face. He must wonder why Robert was here. So did she.

Emily set cups on the table as she sought for some polite way to get rid Robert. "A part of Boo's left ear is missing."

Robert sat down. "That's what happens to dogs who insist on pursuing females they have no claim to."

Dennis ignored Robert's caustic comment. He sat at the table and looked past Robert toward Emily. She shrugged and lifted her hands, palms out.

Much to his credit and to Emily's relief, Dennis remained calm and collected. He sipped the coffee Emily sat in front of him, and remained silent.

Emily slapped a top on a hastily made sandwich, and set it before Dennis. "Eat, you must be starved."

Before he could take a second bite, his phone sounded. "Excuse me." Dennis took his telephone from his pocket. "Hello. Yes, this is he."

After a long pause he said, "Yes." On the end of another long silence, he responded, "Yes."

"Another problem?" Emily asked.

Dennis stood and slipped his phone in his pocket. "I'm afraid so. That was Marvin Hudson. His son Jason was arrested for drug possession. Marvin and his wife are very upset. They're coming by my office. They just left the police station. I may be with them for some time."

Any member of Dennis's congregation could call on him at any time, night or day and know that he was there for them. He was a wonderful man and she was a fortunate woman. Dennis stood and backed toward the door. "Good night, Emily." As the door closed behind Dennis, Emily turned to face Robert. "Why are you *really* here?"

He pushed his half-eaten sandwich from him. "I had to see you one last time."

There was no easy way to say what must be said. "It is the last time. I can't see you, or any of your family again."

Robert frowned. "Isn't that being a little selfish? What about our boys?"

Emily stacked dishes and carried them to the sink. She pointed to the door. "Please go."

Robert didn't move. "They will be hurt when they learn about you and the Reverend."

She couldn't believe his hypocrisy. "You swore when you got involved with Susan Barrett that you weren't hurting our sons. They were adults, you said. They would understand, you assured me. Now you're telling me that because I'm in love with Dennis, I am hurting them?" She laid her dishtowel on the cabinet. *Thank you, Mac for helping me see the folly of living my life through others.*

Robert turned pale. "You are mistaking lust for love."

Another thank you, Mac, for showing me the difference between the two. "I can discern between the love and lust. Dennis satisfies me as you never did."

Robert stood and swallowed. "That's hitting below the belt. How much do you think one man can take?" He slammed his fist into his open hand. "How long do you think I can hang around and let you rub salt in my wounds?"

Running beneath the surface of Emily's anger was the knowledge that she had wounded him. With that revelation came regret. "Forgive me."

Robert stood, and pushed his chair under the table. "I will always love you." He spun on his heel and walked from the room. Seconds later she heard the slam of the front door.

Emily went to sit on the couch. A mixture of sadness and relief made her weak. She wished she and Robert could part on semi-friendly terms.

With a grinding of gears and the screech of tires Robert roared out of the drive and sped down Oakdale Avenue toward the city.

Emily was sitting on the sofa staring into space when Larry poked his head through the front door. "Mom, what's happening now?"

"Boo's home." Emily gestured toward the sleeping dog. "He's going to be all right."

"That's good news." Larry hung his baseball cap on the back of a chair. "I'm talking about Dad. When I came home just now, he was backing out of the drive like the devil was chasing him. He took off toward town like he'd been shot out of a cannon."

Emily shook her head. "He's gone, for good this time."

"So, the two of you are fighting again?" Larry moved toward the hall. "I have to get my things and leave." He stopped and asked, "What did you argue about this time?"

"I am going to marry Dennis Morrison." *If he will have me.*

Surprise gave volume to Larry's voice. "What? When? Don't you think you should have talked this over with Kevin and me?" His surprise gave way to indignation. "We are your sons, after all."

"I didn't talk it over with you because it's none of your business. I love you both, but I don't intend to live my life trying to please you and Kevin. I love Dennis."

"Mom," Larry protested, "what if Kevin and I disapprove?"

Emily was a caged bird, suddenly flying free. "That will be your problem."

"Man, Mom, you have changed." Larry disappeared down the hall and returned carrying his suitcase. "Are you going to be all right by yourself? Should I stay?"

Emily shook her head. "Yes, I'm going to be all right and no, you shouldn't stay. I don't need a keeper."

Larry picked up his suitcase and smiled. "Maybe you and Dad should have parted ways long ago. Bye, Mom." He was gone before Emily could reply.

She cleaned the kitchen and swabbed Boo's wounded ear again. Her hands moved deftly through her tasks. Her heart was light. She was like a small boat that found harbor after drifting at sea for a long time.

As she prepared for bed, she relished the thought that her life was hers. With the speed of a thunderbolt, words Aunt Beth said to her the day of Kevin's wedding jolted through Emily's mind. *You can't find happiness until you find yourself.*

A quickening revelation burst across her mind like the shattering of a falling star against a midnight sky. Oddly enough Mac showed her the path to discovering Emily. As crazy as that sounded, it was true. His offer of travel and excitement showed her what she wanted and needed at this point in her life was security. She needed a husband she could depend on and grow old with. Laughter bubbled up inside her and floated from her mouth. How many strait-laced forty-four-year-old women could be thankful for an indecent proposal?

Emily reached for her handbag. She had one more thing to do before this night was over.

Chapter Forty

Ten minutes later Emily hurried up Dennis's walkway, and onto his porch. She made the trip from her house to the parsonage in record time. She shoved her shaking finger into the doorbell and waited.

A female voice called out, "Hang on, I'm coming." Footsteps sounded from inside.

Emily ran her fingers through her wind-blown hair and wished she had taken time to put on makeup.

The door opened and Kim stood on the other side wearing a robe and slippers. She held onto the doorknob. "Emily? What happened? Is Boo dead?"

"No, darling, no." Emily smiled. "Boo is recovering nicely."

Amy appeared to stand beside Kim. "Emily, are you okay?"

She had frightened these children needlessly. "I came to see your dad."

"Come in." Kim opened the door and motioned with one hand. "He's at his office. He should be home soon."

Emily came inside. "May I wait for him?"

In unison, Kim and Amy answered, "Sure." Kim tagged her statement with a question, "Why did you come to see Daddy at this hour of the night? It's almost ten o'clock."

Amy nudged her twin. "Don't ask personal questions. How many times has Daddy told you it's not polite?" She pointed to the couch. "Would you like to sit down?"

Emily sat. "Thank you."

Dennis came through the door looking weary. "Emily. What are you doing here? Has Boo taken a turn for the worse?"

"Boo's okay, I need to talk to you."

Dennis came to sit beside her. His arm wrapped around her shoulder. Without looking their way, he said to the twins. "Go to bed, girls."

Amy turned toward the stairs.

Kim hung back. "We want to hear what Emily came to tell you."

Dennis stared into Emily's eyes. "Go. Now."

The twins climbed the stairs, Amy hurriedly, Kim reluctantly.

As Kim's footsteps died away, Emily's words tumbled over each other in their haste to be said. "I found Emily, the real Emily. She hid from me for so many years. The newly discovered Emily wants to marry you. She wants to go where you go, and live where you live. She doesn't care if you chose to abide at the ends of the earth." *This time, I won't make the mistake of neglecting the man I love.*

Dennis hugged her close to him. "How many times have I longed to hear those words? I don't know how you found that elusive Emily, but I'm glad you did."

She rested in his arms, safe and secure. "We should tell our children."

Dennis dropped his arms. "Will it matter to you if they object?"

Emily looked into the depths of his questioning eyes. "Not in the least. What about you?"

"All three of my children will be elated, but it wouldn't matter to me one whit if they objected."

"I love you, Dennis, with a mature love reserved for those who have weathered the storms of change and heartache."

He pulled her into a smothering embrace before holding her from him. "Our wedding must be soon. I am due in my new pulpit in two months."

She laid her head on his chest and listened to the steady beating of his heart. "We don't need an elaborate wedding. A simple ceremony will be enough."

Dennis kissed her deeply, passionately, before lifting his head. "I would like my bishop to perform the ceremony. He is also a dear friend."

Emily readily agreed. She stood. "I must go now. Before I do, I have to tell you one more thing. You are my hero."

He protested, but not strenuously, "Emily, please."

"You are. You found Boo."

"It was a matter of being in the right place at the right time."

"No. It wasn't. You found him because you refused to give up." She smiled down at him. "Just as you refused to give up on me."

He caught her hand and pressed it to his lips. "Until tomorrow, my love."

THE END

Epilogue

Emily stood by the row of windows that opened onto a broad expanse of front yard, staring out at a sparkling winter wonderland. Icicles hung like crystal chandeliers from the branches of the huge old oak trees. Soft flakes of snow fell from a leaden sky and piled in drifts along the fence row. The weather might be cold and dismal outside, but inside all was warmth and happiness

Two weeks after Emily paid Dennis that unexpected night call, they were married in the church's chapel. Bishop Hogan, Dennis's good friend, performed the ceremony. There were no guests in attendance, other than their children. Kevin and Larry were not only accepting, they were pleased. Stacy was overjoyed. She kissed Emily's cheek. "Thank you, for making Dad's life complete again."

The twins were ecstatic. Kim summed up the situation by saying, "We now have a mother, two big brothers, and a dog."

Two weeks later, Emily sold her home, packed all her belongings and with Boo in tow, moved into the parsonage. Once again, she was dealing with adjustment to change. This time the adjustment was smooth and relaxed.

Each day she fell a little more in love with Dennis. His innate goodness and his love for his family and his church were rare and welcome discoveries. He was also the consummate lover, sweet but passionate, tender, yet fiercely adoring.

Two weeks before he was to preach his first sermon, Dennis flew north to their new home.

Emily stayed behind with the twins and Boo, to oversee the movers and tie up all loose ends.

One week after Dennis departed, Emily, the twins, and Boo said wrenching good-byes to Kevin, Stacy, and Larry, and flew to be with Dennis.

The moment the plane touched ground, Emily hurried the twins through disembarking procedures. After what seemed hours, they passed the last barrier. Emily ran into the waiting embrace of her husband. She had found herself, and she was home.

The end

DISCUSSION QUESTIONS

1. Discuss how Emily's divorce changed her life, immediately and over time.

2. Do you think the divorce changed Robert? If so, how.

3. What role did Boo play in the story.

4. Discuss the advice Aunt Beth gave Emily. "You will never find happiness until you find yourself."

5. Do you agree with Emily's decision to marry Dennis?

6. Did Aunt Beth give Emily good advice? Do you agree with it? Only part of it?

7. Why do you think Emily chose not to go back to Robert?

8. Why did Emily refuse Mac's proposal?

9. Faced with this choice, which man would you have chosen? Why?

10. Why do you think Emily chose to commit to spending the rest of her life with Dennis?

11. Do you think Emily would have made the same choice if she had been ten or twenty years younger?

About the Authors

Billie Houston and her daughter Carlene Havel write Christian romance novels. Both are graduates of the University of Texas at San Antonio. Discovering Emily is their first collaborative effort, although both have previously worked with a co-author on other books.

Billie's venture into Christian romance began when her husband of many years fell victim to Alzheimer's. She writes romantic tales about relationships, stories that explore the problems and pleasures of living a Christian life. The plots revolve around ordinary people caught in extraordinary circumstances and faced with difficult decisions.

Carlene Havel has lived all over the world, courtesy of the Air Force. In 2005, she became a believer in Jesus Christ as the Savior of the world. Along with everything else that changed, she developed a passion for writing. Her stories tell of faith, hope, and love.

The royalties from this book help support an orphanage in Mexico.

BOOKS BY BILLIE HOUSTON

Asking for a Miracle

Honey in the Rock

John Jacob Worthington Jones

Sparrow on a Housetop

Summertime in my Heart

The Potter's Wheel

The Road to Jericho

BOOKS BY CARLENE HAVEL

A Hero's Homecoming

Baxter Road Miracle

Evidence Not Seen

Here Today Gone Tomorrow

Parisian Surprise

A Sharecropper Christmas

Texas Runaway Bride

The Twice-Shy Heart

BOOKS BY SHARON FAUCHEUX AND CARLENE HAVEL

Daughter of the King

Song of the Shepherd Woman

The Scarlet Cord

Please help the authors and prospective readers by posting your honest review of <u>Discovering Emily</u>. Your opinion matters!